The Sound of
DISTANT THUNDER

An Appalachian Novel
by
JACK R. PYLE

The Sound of
DISTANT THUNDER

An Appalachian Novel
by

JACK R. PYLE

Cover Concept by Crispin Tovar
Cover Design by Morris Publishing
Page Design by Crispin Tovar

Published by:

AAcorn Books
P. O. Box 647
Micaville, NC 28755

ISBN: 0-9663666-2-X

Library of Congress Card Number: 98-73972

Printed in the United States by:

Morris Publishing
1212 E. Highway 30
Kearney, NE 68847
800-650-7888

This book is dedicated to
Dot Jackson
and
to all those other people who love
the mountains of
Western North Carolina
as I do.

ACKNOWLEDGMENTS

To the mountain folks whose roots grow deep
in Appalachia and who have helped me in
writing this book, even if they are unaware of their contribution,
I would like to thank:

"Duck" Boone
Gary Carden
Henry L. Gilley
Sheril McKinney
Mildred Pitman
Charlotte Ross
Jo Woody

and also

Stephen Kirk
Norman Wintermute

and

Yancey County Sheriff Kermit Banks and his staff
for answers to a variety of questions

A GATHERING

There is an echo in the land,
Like wheels of an ancient caravan.
The chill you have is live and real,
All you have to do is feel the currents in the air—
Everywhere.

Don't plow these pregnant thoughts asunder:
How close is the sound of distant thunder?
How near is the danger of flashing light?
How real is peace, how near a fight?

The gathering storm seems far away—
For another time, another day;
and yet
Charged atoms abound, all around you,
Filling the air that now surrounds you.
So, ask yourself—and do not blunder—
How close the wrath of distant thunder?

Violet B. Mundy
Point Pleasant
October 29, 1900

Chapter 1

sarah pendley

I watched Mama as the foreman read from the piece of paper in front of him. It was another hung jury, just like the other time. She knew there wouldn't be another trial. The quick flash of hatred for Buck Price that showed in Mama's eyes was real, but it was gone so fast I couldn't swear I'd seen it.

We all knew the truth of it. It would be hard to convict a Price, even in Madison County, and impossible in our own. One way or another, the Prices were kin to most of the folks within fifty miles.

Damn the Prices, damn them to hell, all of them, but damn Buck Price to the hottest fires, way down in the lower reaches, down where there ain't no more flames, just white hot cinders.

That's the kind of wild, dream-like, vicious thoughts I had every time I stopped the work I was doing, even for a minute, and yet I knew my damnations, however good they made me feel at the time, would not bring justice.

But I wanted to do something. I truly wanted to think of something I could do that would make him pay. Buck killed my sister.

My own shame in laying-up with Buck Price came out in court, and now the whole town knows all about it. They know how I slipped off to Granny's old cabin to meet him. We never had a date, not a real one, but there was more than a few of the other kind. I ain't excusing myself. Once we done it the first time, I'd be there whenever he told me to.

And in the courtroom, in front of my kin and everyone for who knows how many miles around, I had to tell about carrying-on with him, and how mean he got one day when I didn't just roll over when he told me to.

Back then, Buck wasn't doing right by me, keeping me hid like he did. I wanted to talk it out; I wanted to make him take me into town and treat me like someone he was courting instead of a fat girl from up in the holler who'd do anything he asked her to.

But in that courtroom, when I had to testify, I did what the sheriff said. I told them what they asked, every question, but I didn't look at Mama the whole time I was sitting there being dishonored in front of the whole world.

Them lawyers picked and picked at everything I said, digging at me, heaping on the shame, but I kept back some of it, some that they didn't ask a pointed question about. I kept back the part that left me feeling naked: the names he called me, the way he slapped me and backhanded me.

When I tried to fight back that last time, he picked up a log chain and he slung it around hard as he could, and it near-missed hitting my head, but I could hear the sound of it as it brushed my hair. Yes, it's true, I know more than came out in court. And I know he killed Bekka. I know that much for sure.

And I also know it's true, what Mama said last night. She was afraid that today the jury'd come back hung again, like it done the other time.

"There won't be another trial, Sarah. If he skids by this time, he'll walk out of there a free man," she said, "and if he does, then there ain't no justice."

Mama poked at the burning log in the fireplace and put another one on top. It's spring, but there's a chill to the night air. As the flames leaped up she said, "No, maybe there is. Maybe there's an older kind of justice."

That day, when the second trial was over, when I touched Mama's arm there in the courtroom, she turned toward me. That earlier flash of pure hate toward Buck was gone, but I knew the thoughts of an older justice still lingered.

2

She didn't say much. Mama had almost stopped talking to anybody and especially to me. She had changed a lot, ever since they found my sister Bekka's broken and bleeding body up the holler in Granny's cabin

It was Buck Price that killed her, but not till he ruined that pretty face. Bekka was dead, but Mama couldn't find a way to accept it.

Maybe I think too much. Maybe my mind stays filled with things that never were and will never be. Maybe I should just admit that I'll never be as pretty as Mama or my sister Bekka. I look more like my Daddy's folks. I never was as pretty as Bekka, even as a baby. I'm fat, like the Pendleys.

Change what you can change and live with what you can't. That's what they say. I can't quite do that. I think too much. I always have.

Maybe I should tell Mama all of it. Maybe it would help my own shame if I did, but Bekka's death, more than a year ago, is still too fresh in all of our minds. Mama ain't said nothing to me about what I done, not a word. She's been too worked up over Bekka, but one day it has to be my time to try to explain my own sin.

Someday she has to know that I couldn't help going up there whenever he asked me to.

When I try to be honest, I know I was as much in rut as he was, but knowing it in your head and having it spread all over three counties ain't the same, and it don't excuse it none.

Yes, Lord, I've thought about telling Mama every bit of that last day with Buck up at Grannys cabin, I've rolled it around in my head, but somehow I can't; I just can't bring myself to do it. Not right now, anyways. If Mama knew all of it—if she knew all I know about how straight-out mean Buck can be—she'd want to know why I didn't warn Bekka.

I have to think about that, too. Why didn't I?

Now, after the two trials, there ain't nobody who don't know what I done with Buck Price. Everybody knows. It came out in court. I had to tell it. The sheriff said I had to.

Yes, I knew Bekka made goo-goo eyes at Buck, but I didn't believe it was more than that. Well, maybe I did—maybe I did think it could've been something more, because back then I was jealous of anyone who even looked at Buck; maybe I might have thought Bekka was more than flirting this time.

I don't even know what I think now or what I thought back then, not for sure, because I have to admit I'm still jealous, even though it's over between me and Buck.

After that day when he truly tried to hurt me, I never met Buck up there at Granny's no more.

But jealousy can make you blind. Maybe I wanted him to move in on Bekka, to scare the hell out of her; maybe I wanted someone to punch some sense into her seventeen-year-old bubblehead.

Mama could accept what Bekka did, how she dressed, how she acted, but I just wasn't ever allowed to be wild, not that I could have been like my sister if I tried.

And if I told Mama everything, all the scare of it—all about how Buck just went more than crazy for a spell—what good would it do? It wouldn't bring Bekka back, and that's what it would take to wipe away the sorrow I could see on her face.

Mama didn't say much, but I knew. Her life, everything about her, ever since Bekka died, reminded me of an eventide gathering in winter, with shadows that blur the edges, and with smoke that seems to hug the earth the way it does just before a storm.

None of that was like Mama. Before it happened, she always seemed like she just couldn't hide the laughter that always seemed to be there or the smile that was just waiting to shine through. But that was before.

Now, it's different. When she looks at you, the dark blue barrier just blocks you out, just shunts you aside. There in the courtroom for a split second, had I seen behind that veil?

Had I, in that quick time, seen the fire that would be there if the only two people left in the world were Mama and Buck Price? He's bigger and stronger, but she'd kill him, sure. No question of that.

Or were these my own feelings? The feelings I hadn't the courage to carry out? Were they my dreams of what I'd like to do to Buck? And yet, aside from knowing he killed Bekka, I have to tell you, I'm afraid of Buck Price.

After that second trial was over, after we all realized it had come to an end, the air in that courtroom was still hot and choked with the fear that came from both sides, from both families, every day of the trial.

That fear, along with a cold clutch in my stomach, clung to the walls of the courtroom, to the ceiling with its cobwebs and cracks, and to the paneled section behind the judge's bench. It was a fear that filled my head and my lungs, just as it filled every corner of the old building, because I knew it was not over. The trial was over, but the rest of it was not.

As we sat there in court, my fingers must have been too tight on Mama's arm. She pushed my hand away and her gaze went back to his lawyer's table up at the front of the courtroom. Buck's folks were hugging him and crying, and I guess I can't blame them for that, but they must have known, just as I did, that he was as guilty as homemade sin. They raised that boy. They had to know about the mean part of him. That ain't something you can keep buried in a family.

They knew. But they hugged him and kissed him and wiped away tears like they thought he'd been saved from something he didn't do.

Mama just sat there staring at the people up front. I thought we should get out of that courtroom. Folks were beginning to look our way. They always do at a time like that.

I took her hand and said, "Mama, hadn't we better go?"

She pulled her hand loose. The glare she gave me stripped me of all kinship. I was a stranger. The look was accusing.

Didn't I know her daughter, her baby, had been near-raped, beaten and then killed? Didn't I know what it must have been like to crawl all the way across that cabin floor, trailing blood and gasping for breath, trying to get to the old dinner bell to call for help?

Yes, I knew.

I knew in a way Mama could not. I knew the kind of man he was. I had seen that blind rage. I had seen the golden-haired boy at the front of the courtroom when he was a monster, a wild man with spit running out of his mouth and down his chin; I knew him when he couldn't even make words come out. As he lunged at me, he could only make noises, like grunts and groans or muffled screams.

Yes, Mama, I know about Bekka, because I knew Buck when he had no mind to reason with and no wish other than to crush everything in his way.

I knew all this because I'd once been where my sister must have been

I got away because I landed one lucky blow with a piece of firewood, and because even a fat mountain girl can be strong and sure-footed. I could run, and I did.

Mama didn't have to accuse me. I knew. My own guilt had dug a strong toehold in my head.

I didn't tell anyone about Buck at the time it happened, because you don't tell when you've been a fool. You make up good stories for where you've been or how you got the black and blue marks, but when your sister is found beaten and dead at the place where your trysts had always been, you know — you know in the way the guilty always know — and you also know it could have been you.

I said I didn't tell anyone about that last day with Buck up at Granny's cabin. That's not altogether true. I didn't tell Mama, and I didn't tell my brothers. I was afraid of what they might do. But, after Bekka's death, I did tell most of it to the sheriff. After they found Bekka up there in the

6

cove, I told Wilfred Huskins. I told him about it, no matter how it shamed me in front of him.

Wilfred is a friend of my brother John. He's knowed me all my life I guess. He could see I was holding back, so he kept at it, careful with what he said and gentle with what he asked. Wilfred seemed to know how hard it was for me to say what he got me to say.

It was easier for me to tell him all the things I did when he made me understand it would be Buck's defense. Buck would say that he'd met me up there, lots of times. Wilfred said it would all come out in court. He said Buck's lawyers would bring it out. But I held back some of it—I held back the pain I felt, my own personal shame.

There was sign that Buck had been up there at the cabin, plenty of it Wilfred said, and if Buck told his lawyers he'd been up there with me, they'd say all that sign was from when he met me there, so that none of it tied him in with Bekka or the murder.

Wilfred wanted all the details, and I told him as much as I could ever tell any man, including some of my own deep guilt. He was always nice to me, and when our talk was over he thanked me. He said it might help him to build a case, but I guess it didn't help enough. Another hung jury, the second. I plain knew they wouldn't try Buck again.

Mama didn't know how much I knew about that old log chain either. She didn't know Buck had swung it at me. He missed, but the sound of it still stays in my brain. I remember the chain, because the same one, covered with blood, was there in the cabin when they found Bekka. She was dead by then, but she must have lived for a spell, because she managed to drag herself as far as the door. The blood, pooled in places on that old puncheon floor, told how hard it had to have been for her.

In the courtroom, after Mama pulled her arm away and gave me that cold look, I was forgotten. Her eyes were on Buck.

The flash of hatred was gone. Not a sign of it showed. At that moment she seemed unable to move, unable to even blink. Mama watched Buck Price almost as though she didn't see him, but I knew she did. She knew it was another mistrial; he was going to go free. The thought that he could walk out that door sapped Mama's spirits. However blind justice may be, Mama knew who killed my sister and so did I.

Everyone knew who killed Bekka, the whole county knew, but proving it, like Sheriff Huskins said, was another matter. I know for sure it was Buck. He'd hit me a time or two before when things didn't suit him, but he always apologized. One time he was so sorry he even cried.

Then there was that last time, the time I'd seen the really wild and crazy side of him, when he had no control. One time like that was enough for me. I stayed clear of Buck Price from then on. But Bekka didn't.

When that second trial was finally at an end, the courtroom turned stony silent. The meaning of what had happened was slow in coming. It was over and done. Buck was about to walk away a free man. You could hear the babble grow. Then the noise and confusion dampened, and Buck started to walk in our direction. With his arm around his mother, with that Asheville lawyer and the whole Price clan bunched up behind him, he started up the center aisle of the courtroom.

Mama was on her feet. She was across in front of my knees so fast I hadn't been able to move. As Buck reached the end of the row of seats we were in, Mama was at the last one waiting for him.

He had been laughing and talking as he walked toward the courtroom door, but then he glanced up that slanted aisle into my mama's face. Buck always seemed like such a big man, a man who would know no fear if only because of his size, but I knew then that wasn't true. I saw fear. Buck Price didn't have that sunburned, outdoor color to his skin then. He was afraid— afraid of what she might do—and so was I.

On the far side of the room, the sheriff had suddenly come alive too, and he was heading toward what was sure to be real trouble.

Only then did I remember the gun we had at home. It was an old service revolver, but that old gun was kept in good repair by my brother John. Until then, I never gave it a thought. Did she have that gun with her? Was this a time when Mama might do something foolish?

I don't know how I got to her side. I saw no gun. I thought, thank you, God. From the corner of my eye I saw the sheriff.

Buck's arm was no longer on his mother's shoulder. It was limp at his side. There was a moment that seemed to hang in space, a moment when all eyes were on the two of them, a time when their eyes were on each other.

Then, maybe because the sheriff was there, almost as though the moment with my mother had not occurred, Buck Price moved forward and the crowd behind him followed.

The sheriff laid his hand on Mama's arm. "Mrs. Pendley," he said, "please—"

Mama's voice was without the warmth she always showed my oldest brother's good friend. "Don't try to lecture me, Wilfred." That's all she said.

wilfred huskins

I've been in office about two years now. I know what it says on my office door: "Wilfred Huskins, Sheriff, Asa Gray County."

Right now, as I watch the Prices go one way and the Pendleys another, it's the first time I ever wondered if I might be too young to be sheriff. Oh, I won the office fair and square, and I've done the job better than the corrupt guy before me, but I sure as hell don't think justice had been done this time, and I wondered how much of it was my fault. I've taken every course I could get at our two-year college and at UNC-A, but I couldn't help thinking that this whole ordeal had been the blind leading the blind.

My deputy, Russ Silver, stood there with me on the back steps of the courthouse. He's an older man, the only one I kept on after I was elected sheriff. Russ is honest and he's been a real help to a greenhorn sheriff. We watched the two families move toward their cars. The Prices loaded into a Bronco and an older Plymouth Caravan parked beside it. The Pendleys, mother and daughter, were still at the edge of the parking lot. I didn't see the boys.

Ora Lee Pendley seemed to be holding back, or maybe her energy had all drained away with her disappointment in the courtroom. She had always been a strong woman. She didn't look it today. I knew how I'd feel in her place. I knew she wanted to kill Buck with her bare hands, and although I'm working the other side of the law now, in her place I know I'd have had the same feelings.

I knew I'd have to keep an eye on Mrs. Pendley. I didn't know what she might do, and I don't think she knew either. But right now, I had to see that nothing happened until they got out of the parking lot and away from the courthouse.

Buck Price hadn't turned or looked back until just before he got in the car, the driver's side, but now he did. I knew he would. He looked back. It was one of those furtive glances, almost from under his eyebrows, the kind of glance that doesn't really have a name, at least, not that I'm aware of. Oh, I know that kind of hidden look. I've seen it with a lot of the mountain people I've known all my life. You drive down the road. They never glance up as you go by, but once you pass, they slide in that hidden glance that takes in the whole scene.

Sure, I know the look—hell, I've done it a million times myself. I still do. It's a look that doesn't acknowledge the other person, but it still keeps you aware of their presence.

"That got sticky for a minute, Wilfred, back there in the courthouse," Russ said. "I didn't know what Ora Lee was going to do."

"Neither did I. It scared the bejesus out of me."

"Well, don't think it's over, buddy."

"I know," I said, "God knows I know."

Russ shifted that damned match stick he always has in his mouth. "I don't know what the Pendley boys are going to think of this, but Ora Lee—"

"Yeah, I saw it, " I said. "You're right about Mrs. Pendley, and I know you're right about the boys, too. They won't like this second hung jury one damned bit. Luke is the most hotheaded. Sometimes I think he's on something. I need to talk to her and to Luke, though God knows how I'll go about it. I wish to hell Edd Price would move his family back to Baltimore."

"No chance. He's from here. Born here. All their kin lives here, both sides."

"I know. The pigeons have come home to roost."

It was a familiar story. A mountain man may move away to find work, as Edd Price had done years ago, but they come back; they always come back. The mountain man may stay away for a day, a year, or for twenty, but when he can find a way, he always tries to come home; he tries to find the place he dreamed about all the time he worked in the mills or whatever his job was. He always dreams of coming back to the place that perhaps never was, but it's that memory, or that perception, that always draws him back to the ridges and coves of his past. That's what had happened to Edd Price. And that's how we got young Clarence "Buck" Price back in the county to make us a murder.

"We could ask the courts to try him again," Russ said.

"No chance, not without new evidence. You know that. Unless someone comes forward, someone who knows something we don't, there's no chance to reopen this case. Face up to it, Russ, it just won't happen."

Russ didn't answer because there is no answer.

And then the Prices were gone, gone out the back way of the courthouse parking lot. I watched as the two Pendley ladies got into their little white car. They headed out of the lot toward Main Street. I was glad to see it wasn't the direction the Prices had taken.

It had been a bad day. I was as tired as if I'd spent these last long hours plowing new ground.

"Take me back to the office, Russ."

We headed toward the patrol car, but the thought wouldn't go away: If you know deep down in your gut that you would kill Buck if Bekka had been your kid—or your sister—can you expect less from the Pendleys?

I knew the answer.

Chapter 2

luke pendley

"Now, Luke," Mama said to me, "get them crazy ideas out of your head right now. Justice just didn't happen, but it ain't up to us to try to put it right."

I let her rant on with all that stuff about the Bible and vengeance. I didn't know what I was going to do or how I was going to do it, but that big son of a bitch with his shoulder-length hair was going to pay. I know that much.

The funny part of it is that Bekka was a good girl. She looked flashy, she dressed too damned tarty for her own good, she had a smart mouth, and she came on to every male in three counties, but all the guys knew it was just in fun. When they were out there on the prowl, they didn't waste time with Bekka. They all knew about Bekka. Maybe it was Mama's morals or maybe her own, but she was determined to wait for the right guy, the one she was going to marry.

How Buck Price got her to come up to Granny's cabin is an unanswered question, but it sure as hell wasn't for the same reason that I use the cabin. When a girl agrees to meet you up there, way up the end of the holler where no one is likely to be, it gets you pretty excited, because you know why you're going. So how did he get her to come up there?

Even if Bekka agreed to meet Buck at the cabin—and I just can't think she did—he had no right to try to force her to do it and then kill her because she wouldn't—or did he even try to rape her? Maybe only killing was on his mind.

Whichever way, what a bastard. Two hundred pounds of

muscle, topped with that long, pony-tailed, hair. You never saw him in town that he wasn't looking at his own reflection in a storefront window.

Mama's voice brought me back from my thoughts. "Now say it, Lukey, say you won't do anything dumb."

I hated for her to call me Lukey, but she always did when she thought she had to coax me. That kind of sweet, baby talk made her sound stupid and Mama ain't a stupid woman.

"OK, Mama," I said, "OK. Anything you say."

"That was too easy, Lukey; that just rolled off your tongue. I want you to promise me. Really promise me."

"OK, Mama. I promise."

"You're my baby, Lukey; you're all I have—"

"Mama, you're being crazy. You've got Sarah, and Matt and John."

"But you're the baby now, Lukey."

More of the sniveling, more of almost silly talk, more of everything Mama wasn't. Hell, my mother is a woman who was widowed at thirty-one with five kids under 13. She didn't carry on back then like she's doing now.

After Papa died, she got a job at the thread mill, she taught us all how to do our share around the house and she made a family. I was only seven then, but I had my jobs to do, just like the others. I don't know this woman I've seen every single day since Bekka went away.

That's the way she always says it. "Since Bekka went away." Hell's bells, Mama, face it. Bekka didn't go away. She was hit on, and then because she wouldn't, he beat her damn near to death. Then he got scared and killed her. Bekka didn't go away.

"I'm waiting for your promise, Lukey, a real promise; I'm waiting for your bonded word."

So I said it, I said what I had to say. "I won't do anything stupid, Mama, I promise."

She was crying when she left. She cried a lot since Bekka's

funeral. I promised her I wouldn't do anything stupid. I'll keep that promise. I don't know just exactly what I'm going to do, but whatever it is, once I get a plan worked out, I know it won't be stupid.

It may be Christian to turn the other cheek like Mama says, but my ideas are more basic: an eye for an eye, a tooth for a tooth...

wilfred huskins

We've only got 18 people on staff in the sheriff's office, and that includes me and those on the inside as well. There's not a lot we can do about keeping our eyes on some special person, but in the case of Ora Lee Pendley, I talked to Russ and some of the other guys, and we decided that we'd fix a little schedule so we could make the exception in her case. That's what we're paid for, to maintain the peace.

There's another side of it though. When you're sheriff in a small county where you know damn near everybody by their first name, you know the skeletons in their closets, too. I knew that two of Mrs. Pendley's folks—Ora Lee Hall she was before she married Zeb—had done time for killing. They just didn't wait for the law; they did for themselves, in the same way they cleared the land and grubbed a living.

All the guys on patrol know where Mrs. Pendley works and when her shift ends. We'd just make it our business to mosey around nearby until we know she's safely home. That poor woman has been close to the end of her tether ever since Bekka Pendley was killed. She'll come back, she'll be right as rain again, but until she does, we don't want her to do anything that could only make this whole mess worse than it already is.

I know my job is to serve all the people in the county equally, and maybe I have bent a little because John Pendley is one of my coon-hunting buddies, but I sure don't want to see his mother do something we'd all regret—not if any one of us here in the department could do something to prevent it.

"Sheriff, it's Edd Price on two."

This was one of the times I regretted that I'd given up smoking. When you don't want to take a call and you know you have to, somehow it's easier if you light up first. They say old habits die slow, and they're right. Maybe that's the way it is with me and Marylou, but that's another story. I had a last swallow of my cold coffee and then I picked up the phone.

"What can I do for you, Edd?"

"You can get them damned monkeys off my back, that's what you can do." He took a deep breath. I could hear the air rush into his gullet. "You can do that, Wilfred, you can put a stop to it, or I'll shoot one of them, and I don't give a damn which one. They're near driving Essie crazy."

"Now, Edd, slow down, slow down. What is this? What's the story? What's this all about?"

He told me how the cars slowly cruise by his house at all hours of the night. Sometimes two or three times in an hour and sometimes nothing for hours on end. He said it was bad when they came by, but sometimes the waiting for them to start again was worse. He said it had him on edge and it had put Essie to bed with exhaustion.

"Who are they, Edd? Do you recognize any of the cars?"

"I don't know, sheriff. It's those damned cars with black windows. I can't see who it is, even when I turn on the floodlights."

"Can you get a license number?"

"Look, sheriff, that's your job. Do it, or I tell you now, I'll put a stop to it myself."

There was nothing gentle about the way Edd Price banged that receiver down. I silently cursed Buck Price and cursed the day Edd and Essie moved back here and brought their boy with them.

For days now, I'd been putting off talking to Luke and Ora Lee Pendley because I wasn't sure where to start. Now I knew I couldn't ignore it any longer. The pot was boiling and the lid was beginning to chatter with the amount of steam building under it.

Luke is a mechanic at the Ford place just outside town. I figured I'd rather talk to him there than at home. I didn't want to add to the problems his mother already had.

The employees park at the rear of the building. I parked the patrol car there, too. I couldn't help noticing that there were several cars in the lot with what Edd Price called "black windows." I pulled in beside one of them, the one I was pretty sure belonged to Luke.

I went directly into the shop through the employee's door, and I walked over to the bay where Luke worked.

He glanced up to where I stood. There was no greeting, just the cold look the Pendleys can give you when they want you to back off.

"What time's your lunch, Luke?"

"Brought my lunch."

"Well, eat it or leave it, but today I'm springing. Lunch is on me."

"I'm greasy."

"Shuck off the coveralls, Luke. Won't take a minute."

"If you've got something to say, Wilfred, say it."

"They're paying you to work here, Luke. You're on Robert's payroll. I won't use his time. You can talk to me over lunch or I'll come by your house. You decide." I waited. He didn't like being pushed. "Of course, if you haven't had your coffee break, we can go out back, but one way or another, we need to have a talk."

He came out of the pit. "I'll change."

Not a word was said by either of us until we got a booth at the Chinese place and ordered. "OK, Wilfred, what is it?"

"Someone's stalking the Price house, Luke. Know anything about it?"

"Stalking? Ain't that some kind of an uptown word, Wilfred? You trying to talk like a sheriff?"

"OK, Luke. You've answered the question. You know about the cars that drive by there at all hours. So, let me say it short and sweet, and then let's enjoy our lunch. Stop it, boy. Stop it now. If you don't, somebody's going to get arrested or going to get hurt. If I don't get it stopped, Edd Price is going to start shooting."

"I ain't afraid of him."

"Doesn't your mother have enough on her now, Luke? Think about it."

The subject wasn't mentioned again, but the stalking stopped, as I knew it would.

And yet the uneasy feeling I had that day is still with me. The whole county is still in shock over Bekka Pendley's murder and it's not getting any better. If Edd Price doesn't get that boy of his out of this town, something is going to happen. Luke doesn't know what he's going to do about his sister's death—not yet—but he will. I feel sure the stalking Edd complained about was only a diversion, something to do while Luke Pendley pondered on a safe way to get Buck. I had to remember, some of that Hall blood runs in Luke's veins, too.

As I get older, as I get farther and farther away from the Shakespeare Mrs. Geouge pressed on us in high school, the more I remember it. And, here it is again. The phrase runs around in my brain: "We have scotched the snake, not killed it."

sarah pendley

I ain't her daughter for nothing. I know how she thinks. If Mama had known exactly what she was going to do, she'd have gone to it like a martin to its gourd. But she didn't know—still doesn't know—and that's what puts time on our side.

On that sunny spring day when she came home from work, I had the windows wide open to let the smell of the fresh-plowed garden in.

As Mama pushed open the screen door she said, "It's early,

Sarah. Soon as I change, I'm going to walk up to the woods, just to get the cobwebs out of my mind. That mill was a crazy place today."

I was fixing supper, but I watched her as she walked down the back steps and out through the gate. At first I didn't know what caught my eye, and then I knew there was something odd about the way she held her arms and the way she walked. I put supper on hold. As soon as she was out of sight, I shut off the burners and set out behind her.

You know where we live, up at the very end of the cove. Years ago, my great-granddaddy owned all of this land, from ridge to ridge, all the way down to the state road, but he'd chop off a piece here and a piece there for one or the other of his kids to get a start on, and he sold some, so now the only thing we have left is the hundred and fifty acres that runs up to the ridge behind the house.

There weren't many new leaves on the trees, but I managed to stay out of sight until Mama disappeared up the path. Out behind our house there's what's left of the wagon road that goes up to Granny's cabin. It's still wide enough you can drive on it—they drove up there to bring Bekka's body out—but, over the years, Mama wouldn't let the boys drive cars up there because it rutted the road too bad. Back when they used the road, back when Papa was still alive, every spring we'd have a bad wash. She just put a stop to it. It's a wide and real pretty path now, now that the woods are trying to move back in along the sides.

I stayed hidden by the brush at the sides of the road but the cover wasn't much. The late spring held back all but a few new leaves. I was careful that she didn't see me. By the time I caught up with her, Mama had already begun the job she had come up in the woods to do.

There's that place out near the spring where the big rock juts out of the hillside for fifty feet or more. That's where Mama was when I first saw her. She was busy setting up a kind of row, chunks of bark with a little stick behind each chunk to give it support.

It began to make sense to me when she walked back a good piece and picked up my brother Matt's rifle she had leaned against a stump. She'd made a row of bark targets. I didn't have to think it through; I knew why Mama was trying to learn to shoot. I could only hope that she'd never master it.

That part looked good, too. Maybe she couldn't kill Buck with Matt's rifle. Her first shot was ten feet wide of the mark, and the second and the third. She was having trouble with the scope. She tried to shoot with and without her glasses, but the chunks of bark were as safe as if they were in God's pocket. Mama just didn't like that scope. She turned the gun on its side. I guess she was trying to think of a way to take the scope off.

When it was clear to her that undoing the scope was more than she could handle, she went back to the target practice with more determination. And she got better. She still missed with every shot, but she was getting closer, she was beginning to get the hang of using that scope.

I knew it was bad. I didn't like the idea of Mama ever getting good with that gun. It meant trouble—trouble for all of us— but as I watched her, I could see what one of her problems was. She was jerking the gun with every shot.

Matt let me shoot his rifle a time or two, and I remember him saying, "You don't pull the trigger, Sarah; you squeeze it, squeeze it real easy. Just get the target in your sights and then squeeze the trigger."

After twenty or more frustrating minutes, Mama picked up the rifle and headed for Granny's cabin.

Even after what happened to Bekka, Mama wouldn't hear of tearing the cabin down. "The past is our heritage," she said. "No amount of tearing down will bring Bekka back. The old Pendley homestead stays."

As I watched, Mama came out of the cabin door. She looked

around for a long minute, scanning every bit of the open field. She even looked in my direction, but she didn't see me. Then she set out for the house.

Without the gun.

Chapter 3

wilfred huskins

"Has she come back home, Wilfred?"

"No, buddy, she hasn't."

Russ Silver is the only one I've told about Marylou. Oh, sure, they all know she's gone to her mother's, but most folks think it's just for a visit. Her mother hasn't been well. They know that. From time to time, Marylou has gone over to Sylva for a week or two, but this time it's different.

To be honest, the problem was simmering there, way down at the bottom of the pan, before the Pendley girl got killed, and then I guess it just came to a full boil.

I know I spent a lot of time away from home after we brought Bekka Pendley's body out of the holler, but I couldn't let the rancor between the Prices and the Pendleys get out of hand or we'd have had real trouble here in the county. Neither family is good at backing off, especially the Prices. That jut-out chin that their granddaddy had in his day is still there. He's gone, but the Price chin is still right there, on everyone of them. The quieter they get, the more the chin juts out, and the more the chin juts out the more dangerous the situation gets. The worse it looked for Buck after we found Bekka, the more you could see the chisel-chin of Edd Price—and Buck's brothers for that matter.

"When you going to go over there and bring her back?"

"You don't go over and bring Marylou back, Russ. She has a mind of her own."

From the day I first met her, Marylou's been independent.

It's one of the things I've always liked. She's a strange mix of intelligence, independence and shyness. But, yes, like I told Russ, she sure did have a mind of her own. I guess I wouldn't love her so much if she didn't, but this time maybe it's gone a little beyond independence. Whatever it is, I won't be going over and bringing her back.

And then I said out loud the fear that had been unspoken back there in the back of my brain: "When Marylou is ready — if she ever is — she'll come back, but I won't be bringing her back."

"Well, if she was my old lady, I'd go over there."

"I've been to Sylva, Russ. Her mother said she wasn't there. Emily Carlyle didn't even ask me in. We just stood there at the door and talked, like I was the insurance man or something."

"You think Marylou was in there?"

"I don't know. I honestly don't."

We don't have any kids, Marylou and I. We've been married for five years. Maybe that's one of the problems. Not that we tried one way or the other. It's just that we didn't have any. Maybe all women want kids. Hell, I don't know.

I just don't know what it was that caused this last rift or when it started, not for sure. She didn't say anything — I don't remember anything.

Maybe she was bored. Maybe she wanted a job. Maybe she wanted to go back to teaching. She had her teaching certificate when I met her, but she only spent one year in the classroom before we married. It might be my fault. I didn't want her to work.

"You only went over there once? You ain't been back? That won't do it, buddy. Not when a woman's mad at you."

"No, Russ, I went back a time or two, but I just drove by the house. I wasn't ready for standing on the porch again."

"You being hardheaded, Wilfred?"

I got another cup of coffee and sat down over by the radiator. Our office is in the old courthouse. That building creaks, it

23

groans, it has its own kind of musty smell, it has hairline cracks in the plaster, and, yes, it has radiators—the kind you don't see much anymore.

Rachel stuck her head in the door. "For you, sheriff. Line one. The Pendley girl."

Sarah Pendley told me about her mother and the target practice up near the old Pendley cabin, up at Granny's house.

"She left the rifle there the first day, and she's been up there twice more that I'm sure of. It scares me, Wilfred. She wasn't much good at first, missed the bark by a mile, but she's getting better at it."

"I thank you for calling, Sarah," I said. "I'll have a talk with her."

I spoke as calmly as I could, but I wasn't calm inside. I didn't like what I heard. A rifle and a scope? Trouble was the only thing that could mean. The pressure was on me now. I didn't know how to go about talking to Ora Lee Pendley, but I had to find a way. I couldn't put off going to see her any longer. What made it more urgent was the last words Sarah said, "...she's getting better at it."

john pendley

"Get that mud out of here, John Pendley," Sarah said. "I just scrubbed that floor. Go around to the front, but take them muddy boots off and leave them on the porch. Don't you go trackin' that filth in."

My sister Sarah had taken over the house after she graduated from high school. She wasn't trained to do anything, and God knows little enough of school rubbed off on her. In a kind of funny way, she just fell into being a mother to all of us. She kept a clean house and she put good food on the table, but she didn't really want to work out. Sarah's a little on the heavy side, maybe that's what's made her so bashful. Anyway, I know that working out somewhere—anywhere—would be hard for her. All of us knew it. We never pushed her.

Sarah ought to be married, that's what she ought to be. She'd make a fine wife. She's a good cook, good housekeeper. She didn't date much in high school. I remember all the tears when no one asked her to the prom, but what could we do? Sarah looked like too much woman for those thin-looking, shiny-faced school boys.

That big Phillips boy dated her once, Harley Phillips. He was the only one tall enough to look right with her on the dance floor—if they danced at all—but that didn't work out either. I know he tried to date her a time or two, but she just looked past him. She's too damned shame-faced for her own good.

Now Bekka—there wasn't a shy bone in Bekka's body. Two sisters, and nothing alike. I can't say I understand either of them.

I guess, in the total of it, only about two guys ever had enough courage to try to date Sarah, so that's why the town couldn't believe the things she told on the witness stand about what she was up there doing with Buck Price. I can't believe it. I heard it. I know she swore to it, but I still can't believe it. None of it, not one word, was like the Sarah I know.

Hell, man, she just didn't date—ever. She never had a real boy friend, and yet we heard out of her own mouth how she had been laying-up with that worthless son of a bitch. None of us, not one of us, knew it or even thought about it. She told it there on the witness stand; she swore to it. I know it happened; I just can't believe it.

We're her family. If we didn't know, who would? We all knew the quiet girl who was afraid of taking a job, an outside job, even somewhere in town. We knew the steady girl who preferred to stay home and cook for us.

Maybe we should have made her go out and work for her own good. It might have made a difference. If we had, maybe this wouldn't have happened. But that's spilt milk, ain't it?

However it happened and whoever's fault it is, since high school all of us, including Mama, just let things go on in a way that would be easy on Sarah, so that's how she became the girl who wouldn't let me walk across her fresh-mopped floor.

As I was told to do by my sister Sarah, I went through the front door, boots in hand, and I went on up to my room to change. Logging ain't the cleanest job in the world, not on a rainy day, and if I sat down in the family room, she'd have been on my case sure.

After I showered, I was plain tired. I stretched out on the bed and turned my country station down low, thinking I might just nap till supper. But napping wasn't there either. My little sister Bekka was on my mind, and of course that made me think of Buck.

Like everybody else, I know he killed her. One part of my mind wants to arrange an accident for Buck; another part wants to kill him slow and make him know who's doing it and why—wants to make him suffer in the same way Bekka did—but common sense has to be reckoned with, too.

Where would it end if we did that, any one of us? If a Pendley killed a Price, would another Price kill another Pendley? I know the answer.

I wish I could say the idea of killing Buck is clear out of my mind, but it ain't. I ought to do it; I'm the oldest and the steadiest. It's just that other things get in the way, just crowd what needs to be done to settle the score off to the side.

There are bigger worries in my head right now. There's Luke. He's hotheaded and he smokes a little grass. His room is next to mine. Sometimes I can even smell it. And I know he's thinking about what ought to be done to Buck, too.

I've heard the rumblings around town. I've even heard some of the things he's said to some of his skin-head buddies and it worries me. It really worries me. Not that he might kill the Price boy—that would be deserved—but that he might be dumb enough to get caught, or that it would start something none of us might not be able to stop.

No, just the fact that Luke might kill Buck Price ain't the

whole reason my brother stays on my mind. It's that he can't do nothing right with his hot temper, and when you add the pot smoking...

Well, you see what I mean. It worries me because I know he's too damned dumb to do it right.

wilfred huskins

Ora Lee Pendley's shift was over at three. I gave her time to get home from work, take a shower, put on her clean clothes, and then I pulled the patrol car into the Pendley drive. I figured on being there before she took off for target practice. She was in a rocker on the front porch, taking advantage of a real nice spring evening.

"I came by to take you to supper, Mrs. Pendley."

"What was that, Wilfred?"

I was off to a bad start, but when you have your foot in your mouth sideways, even if you know it, it looks even worse to back-tread, so I went on. "I say, I thought we might go out to eat somewhere." I was on mushy ground, that was plain to see, but I went on. "Marylou is still over at her Mama's in Sylva, and I could use some company."

"Well, if that ain't the dumbest thing I ever heard you say, Wilfred, then it's got to be close to it. Go to supper with you? Now, how would that look? It'd be the talk of the town in two hours. 'There was Ora Lee, in that police car with Wilfred,' they'd say. 'Now, what do you make of that?'"

She took in another big gulp of air and went right on, "They'd make a lot of it, I can tell you, and they'd think I was dangerous or something. Enough people already look at me like I might sprout horns and gore that Price boy to death, and if they saw me in that police car out there, that would cap the stack, wouldn't it?"

"OK, Mrs. Pendley. It was a bad idea. But the truth is, I need to talk to you, private, and I never thought of how riding with me would look."

When I said, "...talk to you, private," her rocking stopped. She gave me that look. It was almost as though I were an outsider, not someone who had been here in the mountains all my life.

"You can talk to me right here." It was terse.

"No, ma'am, I'd rather not. Sarah might interrupt, and John ought to be home soon. No, I want it to be just the two of us." She just stared at me, so I finally went on. "Why can't we walk up the trail back there, back towards Granny's cabin. There won't be anyone back there."

I'd blundered again. I saw it in her face. The lines around her mouth, the expression in her eyes, were set in stone. Then she spoke.

"You'll talk here or not at all, Wilfred." She stopped to let that soak into my brain. "What call have you got to question me anyway? And that's what you're here for, ain't it?"

There was no good answer to that. It was a question almost like, "Have you stopped beating your wife?" Knowing she was on safe ground, she went on. "I've knowed you since you was born, but if you push in where you're not wanted, Wilfred, I'll cut you dead—now, and every time I see you. I know you're friends to the kids, but watch that mouth. You hear me?"

This was not the way a sheriff is supposed to handle an interview. I'd lost control. I had to get it back. I had to stop looking like a chastened schoolboy, or the whole problem with Ora Lee Pendley was going to grow worse, and, if it did, I'd have no way to keep tabs on her or the gun.

"Mrs. Pendley, I know about the target practice."

I had the ball again, maybe for the first time since I drove up. I knew she heard every word I said. She continued rocking, but her fingers gripped the arms of the chair so tight they turned white.

Then, that was it. It was all over. She got up, walked to the door and went inside. She closed that front door behind her even though the day was more than pleasant.

The click of the latch said a lot. I heard it. I wasn't absolutely sure what all her abrupt departure meant, but I had the strong feeling that I'd stepped in a leg-breaking pothole. The sound of that latch click wasn't good.

Chapter 4

harley phillips

How long can you watch someone you love hurtin' without doing something about it? I don't give a damn about the crazy time Sarah had when she laid-up with Buck, there in that old cabin under Pendley Knob. I can forgive that. Sure I'd like it better if it'd never happened, but it did, and it's done, and there ain't nothing we can do about it.

When I first heard about her and Buck, with all the sniggerin' going on in town, it tore into me like a knife into a hog's belly, but after a while my good sense come back.

You got to understand that I love Sarah and I have ever since we were in first grade. She didn't know it then, and I reckon she don't know it now. I ain't so good at talking to her, but I'd better learn to get good at it, or she'll just stay up there at her Mama's, and one day she'll wither and dry on the vine and so will I.

I know she's a help to her mama, but Ora Lee Pendley would do just fine there by herself if it wasn't for them three boys freeloading on her. Well, that's not really right, is it? They must pay something, so they ain't freeloading exactly, but they do have a house, a housekeeper and a chore girl and it sure as hell don't cost them much.

If I could talk her into it, if I could take Sarah away from there, they'd get by. Them boys might even have to hire someone to come in and do Sarah's work, but they got the money; they can afford it. Luke don't pay a dime, so I hear; Matt spends his check running down to Myrtle Beach or some such place;

and John, God knows he's got ninety-five cents of the first dollar he ever made. They can hire someone and still come out ahead. It won't hurt'em none.

Forget about Buck Price, I want to marry Sarah,whatever she's done, just like I've always wanted to do. Somehow, I'm just going to have to find a way to tell her how I feel and make her know it. But now—now that there's been so much bad talk— it won't be easy.

I'd like to kill Buck Price and all his kin, but I guess I'm to blame, too, for all our troubles. If I'd only worked up my courage before he come back to town with his folks, I wouldn't have all the mess I've got now.

It ain't going to be easy, I know that. I know how people around here are and how they think, and Sarah is just as steeped in it as I am. When I ask her to go somewhere with me, first thing that'll come in her head is bound to be "...what's he got in his mind?" Sure it will, and that's what everybody else is going to think, too; they'll believe that I think she's loose and that's why I'm asking her out.

That's not what I think. Oh, sure, that thought passed through my mind a couple of times. It's just a natural thought here in the mountains where we live, but I'm not as dumb as I look. I know Sarah—knowed her all my life—and she's just not that kind, I tell you.

I know how it happened. Buck, he come back to town with all that hair and that big smile, and she was easy prey—she was ready to find a man of her own, and I was too damned dumb to see it. My uncle from Charlotte—Ossie, daddy's brother— used to say, "You ain't too swift, Harley," and he's right I guess. At least he's right about the way I let Sarah almost slip away from me.

So I'm going to call her up and see if she'll go for a ride with me. Maybe we can drive out somewhere, out away from the town and all the gossip, and maybe I can make her see that I don't think about her the way she probably figures I do.

You know, if I can only get her to be around me for a time, long enough to really get to know me, even if it's just for a ride, or a movie, or going over to Asheville to find a good place to eat, she'll know I ain't like that. If I can get her to be around me for a time, she'll see I ain't thinking no thoughts about how easy she is. I know she'll see it, because I ain't.

Now and then, you have to stop and think about yourself, you've got to go back to the bedrock of your life. I've prayed about this, God knows I have, and one of the things I keep remembering is something that my own Granny said to me: "Great is Truth," she said, "and mighty above all things."

My Granny often spoke the words of the Bible, though sometimes I don't think she knew for sure what they meant. But that's what she said. She said, "Great is Truth, and mighty above all things."

I hope so, Granny. I've got to make Sarah know I don't see her as no fallen woman; she's got to know that I see only the girl I loved since she wore cotton school dresses and shiny patent leather shoes.

In my heart I know that I've got to walk over to that phone right now and call her. However much I'm afraid of what she might say to me, I've got to go over there and do it.

The dialin' part of it wasn't easy, every number of it, but when I got it done without hanging up, on the third ring, she was there.

"Hello?" It was like a question; it was like who's calling at this time of day when I don't want to talk—not to nobody?

I'd come this far. I wasn't turning back, so I said, "Sarah, this is Harley." There was a quiet on the other end of the phone, nothing but her breathing. "It's Harley, Sarah. Harley Phillips."

"Oh, Harley Phillips." There wasn't the first warm sound in those words. "Well, Harley, what in the world do you want? Why are you calling?"

I could almost see the frown on her face, and I knew what she was thinking, but I'd messed up long enough; I'd messed up all those years by not speaking my mind. I couldn't help thinking how I might have been at least partly responsible for what happened with Buck. It was way past time for me to act like a man, so I said, "I want to come out and pick you up, Sarah. I'd like to go somewhere where we can talk."

There was no reply. In that silent minute, I realized how what I'd said might have sounded to her. Take her for a ride? Out somewhere where we could talk? I sure hadn't thought it through. My words were the wrong words, and I knew it. They sounded like I wanted to get her off in the woods somewhere. That wasn't what I meant at all.

It was a long time before she said anything, long enough that I thought she might be about to hang up on me, and then she said, "I think not, Harley. Don't call me again. I've got work to do." And then she hung up.

The click I heard on the line was as final as Judgment Day, and maybe that's what she meant it to be, but I had gone too far now. I'd blundered bad. I'd made her think exactly what I didn't want her to think, and the more it festered in her mind, the worse it was going to be. I had to make her listen to me, right now.

I got in my car and drove out to Pendley Holler.

luke pendley

Jim Bob Williams has a little house of his own on the back of his daddy's land, there at the foot of the Bald. Jim Bob ain't his name. His name is Horace, but he hated it so much when he was little that everyone started calling him Jim Bob and it just kinda stuck.

Anyway, I was over there in the house with Jim Bob and we got to talking about the only thing we ever talk about any more, other than girls and smoking a little dope. I didn't like the way the talk was going either. Everybody likes Jim Bob. He's a good old boy, but he don't always think straight.

He said, "Got it all figured out, Luke. Too many people are

33

watching you, so someone else has got to get that Buck bastard. I reckon I'm the best one for it. I ain't got no reason to kill him, so no one would even question me, and if it looked like an accident — and I could do that — that'd be the end of it."

About one thing he was right: They were watching me like hawks looking for a field mouse. At first it was just Mama who watched everything I did, and then Wilfred Huskins got on my case. Wilfred's changed since he got to be sheriff a year or two ago. He's been off to school a couple of times and now he thinks he's doin' more than playing at being sheriff. Wilfred's OK, but he's beginning to bug me.

But it's not just Wilfred and Mama. The damned situation is getting worse all the time and the crowd gets bigger. John keeps an eye on me, and even Sarah wants to know where I'm going and who I'm going to be with. Matt's not so bad, but I know he's like the rest. They all think I'm about to explode or something. It's just not true. I'm smart enough to do it the right way. But let me tell you this: I'm beginning to get shit full of it. Your family ought to be with you, not against you, especially with something like this.

One thing you can bet on though, I'm going to get Buck, but I sure as hell don't need Jim Bob's blundering to screw it up for me. He's a great little guy, but he ain't got enough sense to do it.

They're right about one thing though, all of them; they know I ain't forgot my sister Bekka. Bekka was special to me, so I'm going to get Buck when he least expects it, but I don't plan on doing anything dumb enough to land me in jail. That's not in my plan at all.

But Jim Bob, now that's another problem. He's a good friend, been a friend all my life, but Jim Bob, he just plain needed another washer when they screwed his head on. I had to get this Buck idea out of his mind, but with old Jim Bob, you handle it real gentle so he don't fly off like he sometimes does. I hope he don't ever do it, but Jim Bob could hurt someone bad some day.

While I tried to think of some way to turn his thoughts in another direction, Jim Bob started laying the whole thing out to me.

"I've watched Buck Price, watched him a lot. He goes out to his Granny Ballew's most every Sunday afternoon."

I knew Buck was kin to the Ballews. Around here we say Blue, like the color blue, but it ain't spelled that way. Miss Grant, she tried to say it the other way back years ago when we were all in school, and that oldest Ballew girl said, "Teacher, our name is Blue, just like the sky. Ain't no call to try to fancy it up none," so Miss Grant, she was from Mooresville, she just started saying it like we do.

I guess my mind had kinda drifted away there, thinking about Miss Grant and what pretty legs she had, and the next thing I knew I heard Jim Bob saying, "...I could just ease up to the side of old Buck, right there at the curve just below the top of the knob—ain't no guard rail there—cut in on him and he'd be off the road in no time. A fall like that'd kill him sure, even if the car didn't catch on fire, and it probably would."

I didn't think it was idle talk with Jim Bob, not from the first, but I had no idea he had it all worked out in his head.

And then he started all over again, almost the same words, like he was trying to get his plan all set in his mind, so he could follow it without thinking. "I'd just wait there at the top of the knob," he said, almost to himself, "on that old loggin' road, and when he comes by, well, I'll just ease out behind him and by the time he gets to that real bad place where the road narrows—I'll have him pretty scared and he's going to speed up some, and then all I got to do is slip up beside him and cut him to the edge. And that's it, Luke. That'll do it."

You don't just say no to Jim Bob. You have to lead him real easy-like to where you want him to go. It ain't so much because he's a big guy that makes you want to go careful. Hell, he ain't but about 145 pounds, but old Jim Bob's as strong as an ox, and when he loses it, he gets a kind of power that's like a raging flood stream. You just have to stand back till his rage eases off. If you don't, you can get hurt real bad.

"It's a good plan, Jim Bob," I said. "But, you know something, buddy, it might be too quick for the son of a bitch. You know, off the road he goes and in thirty seconds he's dead."

"Yeah, Luke. He's dead. That's what he deserves."

"But what I'm saying, Jim Bob, it might be too easy for him. He gave Bekka one hell of a lot of pain. You was up there at the cabin, you saw what it was like. He wasn't easy on Bekka, and I say we just can't be easy on him."

Right then, the good part of it was that I had his attention and he wasn't riled.

"Good point," he said, "good point, good point, good point," and as he spoke his voice grew softer. I was sure I had him calmed down.

Jim Bob slowly rolled a joint. He was calm. It was better than I'd hoped. It was like he had lost all interest in the idea. He scrubbed a wooden match across the floor, lit up and took a deep drag, and then he said, "You got a better plan, Luke?"

He didn't look right at me, but he was watching just the same. And then he said it again, "You got a better plan?"

"No, Jim Bob, I don't. I ain't got it all worked out yet, but I'm working on it. When they get off my case a little, I'll be ready with it, and I mean to make him suffer, I mean to make him live long enough to know what it was like for Bekka."

I went on like that, telling him what I wanted to do to Buck, and he let me talk, just watching me, not saying a word and when I got to the end of it, he said, "That ain't much more than what you said the day Buck walked out of that courthouse a free man, Luke. And what's happened? Nothing, that's what."

I knew then Jim Bob was not as calm as he looked on the outside. In his head, his plan was still alive. In his head, he'd pictured Buck's car going off the side of the road up there below Mace's Knob, and if somebody didn't do something to stand up for Bekka, and do it soon, he was going to do it. I could see that much, fixed right there in his eyes. Jim Bob meant to stand up for Bekka.

"I'm going to do it, Jim Bob, I'll get him, I promise you. Just you wait and see."

"Tell you what, Luke. If you ain't done it in two weeks, then you just stand back, boy. Jim Bob will take care of it. You hear me? Two weeks."

Chapter 5

wilfred huskins

I don't know whether I'd even consider running for sheriff for another term. When things are skimming along in the county, when it's only an occasional drunk or a fight; when it's only wrecks and traffic and speeding; when it's just a patch of pot to go dig up or a pusher at the high school to arrest, then being sheriff is not a hard job, and the pay's not all that bad, either.

But that's not the way things are here in Asa Gray County. Along with the day-to-day problems, we have a murder, a really grisly murder, one that everyone in the county can't resist talking about. The shock is beginning to wear off but the horror of it hasn't. Two trials have kept it alive.

To a man, they all have an opinion. And even if some of them are happy with the way those two trials turned out—because Buck is some kind of kin—all of them, whichever side they're on, harbor the idea that I screwed up the detail some way. I can almost hear them say, "Wilfred is just too young, too inexperienced, too slight for the job."

No, they don't say it to me, but I'm not blind. I know these people, I grew up with them; I'm one of them. Sometimes I think some of the old-timers haven't quite forgiven me for going off to school at State, and then staying gone a year or two after that. But I'm not an outsider. In the end, I'm like the rest of them. They ought to be able to see that. I couldn't shake the mountains out of my brain, so I came back.

I might even be able to cope with all the havoc this murder has made in my life, but when you add the rest of it, it's just not worth it. Hell, I've lost my wife over it. Well, maybe that's not the whole story with Marylou, but the job didn't add anything to the harmony at home.

And when you complicate being sheriff with the fact that the murder involved two families that are both well known, and where the feelings on both sides are racing along faster than a woods fire in March, then you begin to wonder if it would be worth any kind of money to run again.

No point in wallowing in my misery. I've got about two years to go. I've never given a job less than a hundred percent, and I'll give this one all I've got, too, even if I end up with the also-rans in the history of the sheriffs of Asa Gray County. I've had time to think of that illustrious list. God knows we've had a few that wouldn't win any prizes even though, by hook or crook, they managed to stay in office for years.

That last idea, that hook or crook idea, at least makes me smile, even though I'm about ready to go out to do a part of my job that I'd prefer to avoid. My Granny Ledford used to use that expression, "...by hook or crook." She'd say, "he'll buy that horse. By hook or crook, I tell you, so you can lay money on it, he'll end up with that horse."

The crook part of it seemed to fit in with what she was saying, but the hook part made no sense at all.

When I was a kid here in the county, to hook something used to mean you'd steal something. You could "hook" a ride on the back of a wagon, with your feet up on the axle and your hands hanging on for dear life to the back of the floor boards, and you'd go jolting along, out of sight, happy with the fact that you were doing something wicked—you were stealing a ride from someone who didn't even know you were there. Or you could "hook" an apple from the basket in front of Westall's store, but could that really be an answer? That was just everyday slang, but is that what was meant? Did she mean stealing? Was that it? I doubt it.

Most of Granny's sayings went right back into antiquity. If

Jack R. Pyle

you asked her about any one of them, she'd say, "Lord, child, my own Granny used that expression years ago when I was just coming up. I don't know where it got started, I declare I don't."

But for me, this is now and now is important. The time for thinking about what Granny Ledford used to say was over. I had to forget the expression "hook or crook," and all the others she used. It was way past time to get on with the job at hand. I knew the longer you put off doing something you don't want to do, the worse it's sure to get, and I had already put off going to see Matt Pendley too long.

That rifle with the scope was his. It was his gun and his mother. If Ora Lee used Matt's gun on Buck, we'd have another tragedy. And the worst of it was, it could happen. Sarah said her mother was getting better at her target practice.

I have to admit it, Ora Lee Pendley is just one more place I might have been remiss as sheriff, but I had tried to talk to her. I know I should have done it a lot sooner.

Be that as it may, I'm back to the beginning: This is now, and you can only start from now. I had to see Matt Pendley and make him aware of what was going on with his mother. It was Matt's gun so it was his responsibility to take care of it.

Like it or not—and I didn't—it was time to take another of the Pendley boys to lunch. I called him at the post office, and we went to the back booth in Hardee's.

He hadn't even taken a bite out of his roast beef when Matt said, "OK, Wilfred, what is it?"

"I thought we'd eat first."

"I can eat and listen."

So I told him about his mama sneaking the gun out of the house, setting up her targets, and then hiding the gun in the old cabin so she could go back for practice. I told him she'd not been much of a danger at first, but now she was better at it. None of it seemed to bother him, except for one thing.

"How'd you know about all this, Wilfred? You ain't got our house under a watch, have you?"

40

I'd done it again. Only a real dummy would open his mouth and screw up the detail as many times as I have with the Pendleys. I screwed it up with Ora Lee a day or two ago. Now she won't even talk to me, and if I told Matt the truth about the target practice and how I found out about it, Sarah would be put in a bad light with her brother.

People around here like to keep family things inside the family, so what I'd already said called for a lie, a straight-out lie, because of Sarah.

Too late, but it was clear to me, I'd boxed myself in good. If I told Matt how I knew, Sarah would be in for trouble at home with all of them. I tried to skirt the truth.

"I've seen your mama's target practice with my own eyes, Matt." And that was true. I had parked my Jeep up there on the knob and followed the old logging road down. I guess I watched her for five minutes or more, and while she wasn't going to win a turkey shoot, she didn't miss all the time.

"You say you saw it yourself?"

"Yes, Matt, I did."

"And you saw her sneak the gun out of the house—that's what you said. You said she snuck the gun out and then kept it in the cabin."

I hate to lie, I always have, but the time had come when it was either tell a lie or cause Sarah more grief than she deserved. And, if I'm bone honest with myself, I have to admit that there's another reason that a lie is absolutely necessary. If I told on Sarah, it would seal off my only source of information from inside the Pendley house.

Since the trial, I tried a couple times to talk to John Pendley. I got nothing from him but a granite face, one that seems to be made from the same rock as our hills. When you crowd a mountain man or woman, you don't get much in the way of a reply. The features take on a set expression. It's as though you hadn't spoken; if you persist, it's as though you aren't there. John is one of my good friends, but, with family, there's a line you just don't cross.

I'd waited too long to make a reply. Matt leaned forward, staring straight into my eyes. "You gettin' ready to lie to me, Wilfred?"

"Don't need to lie, Matt. I have nothing to lie about."

"Then you admit you had our house under a watch?"

"No, Matt. There's been no surveillance—"

"Knock it off, Wilfred. Luke told me you tried to play sheriff with him, too." I could hear the sarcasm. "We know you, Wilfred. Use big words on the tourists."

That's the kind of mistake I kept making with the Pendleys. I'd known them all my life; I'd been friends with all the boys, especially with John, and now using my own big mouth and my little bit of education I was breaking up a friendship that goes clear back to school days. I started to backpedal. "There's been no watch on your house, Matt. Get that out of your head."

He kept those clear gray eyes boring into mine. He was looking for a lie, and he was dangerously close to finding one. Mountain people have always had some kind of a deep, inborn resentment of the law. Maybe they brought it with them from Scotland or Ireland, but it's there. They seem to think it drains some of the marrow from their spines or the freedom from their bones.

I'm one of them, all my folks come from around here, and at the same time I'm not one of them—not anymore. I'm the law. Maybe that's another reason I don't even want to think about running again.

"You sure? We ain't been under a watch?"

"I swear to you, Matt."

"But you know Mama snuck that gun out of the house?"

Now was the time for the lie, but somehow now—now that his big anger was only that we might have been watching their house— it was easier to do.

"I guess that's just my way of figuring out what she must have done, Matt. Pure guesswork. It just seems logical. She wouldn't be waving that rifle as she walked out. You're not but about 500 yards from the Baileys, maybe a little less. When the trees are bare, they can see your back yard. You know that."

It satisfied him. Some of the anger had drained out of his face. He leaned back a little in the booth, took a look at his watch and said, "I'd better be getting back to work."

I stopped him. "Matt, you'll go to the cabin and get the gun?"

"Yes."

"And if there are other guns in the house, put them in some safe place, will you?"

"Yes."

He slid out of the booth, picked up his jacket and went back to his job at the post office.

I finally got to my sandwich and Coke. He wasn't as mad at me as his mother was, but there was nothing buddy-buddy about his scowl. I'd somehow passed over a barrier. I was no longer an old friend to Matt; I was a lawman.

sarah pendley

"Sarah, I need to talk to you," Mama said.

I knew it was coming, I just didn't know when. Ever since Wilfred came out here and spoke to Mama on the porch, things have gone from bad to worse between me and Mama, so I knew it was coming.

Wilfred wasn't here talking to her all that long that day, but when Mama came in, she went straight up to her room, and she wouldn't eat no supper, so I knew he must have mentioned the shooting she was doing up at Granny's.

"Make us both a cup of coffee. Sarah. I want to get this all over before John comes home. This isn't the way I meant to spend my day off, but you don't always get your druthers, do you?"

I didn't say anything. I didn't know what all Wilfred said, so I decided to just let it come out the way she wanted it to. I've done that most of my life anyway. I never was one for pushing my way on someone else, and I found that it's just plain easier if you let those folks who are in such an all-fired hurry do it their way.

When I put the coffee down and handed her the cream, Mama said, "I don't suppose you know anything about how Wilfred knew I'd been shooting Matt's rifle up at Granny's?" She waited. "No need to answer now, young lady, your guilt is clear enough."

I put some sugar in my cup—that's all I use. I don't like cream in my coffee, and then I stirred it, just to keep from saying anything. Mama didn't seem to notice.

"I want to tell you something, Sarah, something you may have forgotten. This here old house is mine. It don't belong to your brothers and it don't belong to you, leastaways not as long as I'm living."

She looked at me so directly I knew I had to say something, so I said, "I know, Mama, I know."

"Well, if you know it, you have to know the rules around here are mine, and the first one is, whatever goes on here, stays here. I think you know what I'm getting at, Sarah. Do you want me to repeat that one?"

Mama's voice was low, but I knew she meant every word. "No, Mama, you don't need to."

"You're welcome here, Sarah, as long as you want to stay, but I won't put up with no gossip about what goes on in this house, do you understand that? Whatever goes on here, and I don't care how bad it is or how much you disagree with it, it stays here. Not a word of it will run up and down this holler. Whatever is our business, whatever goes on behind these walls, it don't get talked around. Is that clear?"

"If you want me to leave, Mama, I will, as soon as I can find a place. I'll get a job. I can make out."

"I didn't say that, now, did I?"

"No, Mama, you didn't say it right out, but—"

"Move out, if you don't think you can keep your mouth shut."

The words cut. She meant them to. She'd spent most of two days avoiding me, so I knew she planned to make her words hurt. She wanted me to remember.

I know, and I knew when I called the sheriff, it's Rule One in the Pendley house, and I guess it is in most houses in this county. Private business—family business—don't get talked around. We're big for how things look. No, we don't put on airs, but we do want everyone to know we're decent people, and you just can't do that if some of the things that go on in some of the houses turns into gossip.

There was plenty of talk, all over three counties. The gossip about me was bad enough, but, more than that, everyone knew how Mama felt about Buck, and knowing that she was a Hall, they expected her to do something about it. The Halls don't take nothing from nobody. You can't blame people for talking. We all knew that Mama might just try to make up for what happened to Bekka.

"There's enough whispering already, you know that, Sarah. You've heard it. Just what kind of a story could they make out of what I was doing up there with Matt's gun? It would burn up the telephone lines from here to Barnardsville. I don't ever want to hear that again, young lady, and if I do, I'll know exactly where it came from."

"You won't hear it, Mama."

"I'd better not," she said. She moved her half empty cup to one side of the table, pushed her chair back and went upstairs to her room again.

It was over. We had talked. She had said what she had to say. And it was plain enough, she was still mad at me. I hated that. Mama can hold a grudge for a long time.

If I could—if I even thought I could—I'd pack up and leave right now. But going to Asheville to find a job, living in one room somewhere, with no family, no friends, not even a car— the thought of it made my stomach tighten into a cold, tight cramp.

Then more of the "ifs" started coming, just as they had since Bekka was found up there. My mind was always churning out the "ifs": If only I had not laid-up with Buck, and I accept my blame for that; if only I had told Bekka, when I saw her flirting with him, about how he could just go crazy without reason; if only I'd told her he used dope; if only she had sense enough to listen to me; if only Buck had not killed Bekka; if only I had been a little more encouraging to Harley...

If, if, if.

Chapter 6

harley phillips

One of them spring soakers we have here in the mountains just kind of slipped up on us, coming up from out of Texas, and the weather man says it just stalled out. Whatever it did, it's been here for two days. It's got the ground plumb soggy. If this keeps up, we're going to have some real bad problems. The creek out there in front of my house is right at flood stage, and that little old bridge I built last year over to my boxwoods is washed out. Been out since yesterday, late.

I'm not working this morning, and I figure John Pendley ain't either. I can't do much with the shrubbery in this kind of weather, and if I can't, I guessed maybe John would be home, too. Oh, he can log in the rain, but I just don't think he'd be out there in the mud on a day like this. He'd be bogged down half the time.

I've been meaning to talk to John, but I've been puttin' it off and puttin' it off, but if we both have a wasted day, why not now?

I just picked up the phone and give it a try. Sarah answered. I was afraid it might be Sarah, and it was.

When she heard my voice she said, "Now, Harley Phillips, don't pester me. I still don't want to talk to you or go for a ride, and that's all there is to it."

It was an echo of what she said when I wasted my time driving over there to talk to her a week or so ago. It was my first real try to get her to talk to me, and it didn't work. She plain shut me out; she wouldn't listen.

The preacher says a soft answer turneth away wrath, so I tried it. "It's nice to hear your voice, Sarah, even when it has an edge on it, but I wasn't calling you this time. I need to talk to John. Is he there?"

She said, "Oh, I'm sorry, Harley." It almost sounded like she was, too, but maybe I read too much into the change in her voice. "I'll get John for you. I'm not even sure he's up. He ain't had breakfast."

I heard her calling him and after a time he got to the phone. "Hello," and that had an edge to it, too. All the Pendleys were testy this morning. I guess I didn't speak fast enough, so he said, "Harley, are you there? What the hell do you want?" Without waiting for an answer, he said, "I ain't even had breakfast yet."

"Well, forget breakfast," I said. "Come on down to Hardee's and I'll buy you a sausage and egg biscuit. I've got something I've been puttin' off talking to you about, and it just might be a good deal for you and for me." And then I used the magic word on John. I said, "You ain't the kind of guy who'll walk away from making a dollar and neither am I. I've got an idea that could be a winner for both of us."

He grumbled, but I knew he'd meet me.

"Put on some pants, John. I'll see you there."

I was there five minutes before John Pendley arrived, and it give me time to think over what I needed to say to convince him. I'd pushed the idea around in my brain for a long time, and I'd have talked to him long before this, but Bekka's death put it on hold.

When he slid into the booth he said, "This better be something special, Harley. Damned good morning to sleep, and all I get is interruptions."

"It's a good deal, John, you'll see." And then I told him about how my tree and shrubbery business had used up all the land my papaw left me, and all the land my dad still had, so I needed more space if my business ever was to grow any bigger.

"And what's that got to do with me?"

"You own land, John. I looked it up in the county records."

He squinted when he looked at me over the rim of his coffee cup.

"Oh, I wasn't checking on you," I said. "What you do is your own damned business, but that piece down at the mouth of Pendley Holler looks real good to me for dogwoods, so I checked to see who owned it. I wanted to work out a deal—to buy it, lease it, or work it on some kind of a percentage basis. I found out you owned that land, John."

"Yes, I do."

"And that forty-acre piece next to it, too. That piece is yours. It's a little harder to get to but not if you come in there by the fence. You own that land, all except for the house and that little half-acre strip there by the road and along the creek where old Mrs. Styles lives."

"I'll be damned."

"I wasn't buttin' into your business, honest I wasn't, but my eyes just fell onto that other piece—it's on the same page in the courthouse."

"I'll be damned," he says again.

"You pay taxes on that land, John, and it ain't giving you back a dime. I know mountain land, if it ain't being used, it ain't taxed for much, but every dime of tax money is down the drain and tax money seems to count up real fast."

"The land ain't for sale, Harley."

"I didn't figure it was."

"You figured right."

"If I could put trees on it, it'd be farm land. It would cut the tax base way down, but I'd have to have twenty acres or more. I wouldn't want to fool with anything less, anyway."

He was still a little wary, but he was interested. Money is a magic word with John Pendley. If the tax base got cut, it would save him money. You could see the thought of a tax cut darting around in his brain.

"How'd you know this, about the tax base?"

"I asked, down at the tax office, that's how."

Then he said, "I'll be damned" one more time, but this time it had a different sound. I was sure I had his attention.

"If you don't believe me about the taxes, check into it yourself. It's a fact."

"And you think me and you could work out something?" He looked me right in the eye. "I won't sell the land, you know. It's going to stay in my name and that's that."

"No problem, John, no problem at all. I'm not looking to buy more land. First of all, I ain't got the money for it, and second, I've got a shrubbery business to tend to. Hell, man, that takes all my time. But in this case, you own the land lock, stock and barrel. We'll keep it that way. I just want to use it. And if I use it—put it in shrubs and trees—if it's farmed—your taxes come down. Then after we net it all out, the costs and all, we can split the profits from what we bag up and sell. You'll be saving money on one hand and making it on the other, and you won't have to do a damned bit of work to do it. It's like I always hear on TV about the new tax bills in Congress: 'It's a win-win situation.'"

"You just about had me convinced, Harley, until you got to that, win-win horseshit. By the time them win-win things get down to where my taxes start, it's always a lose-lose deal."

We both laughed because that's about the way I'd experienced the win-win malarkey out of Washington, but the good part of it was that I had him. He was ready to go for the deal.

"Say the word, John, whenever you want to go by the lawyer's office and get it drawn up legal, you just say the word."

"My lawyer or yours?"

"Either one. It's a straightforward deal. We'll go to anybody you say, and I'll pay my half."

John ordered two more sausage biscuits and another coffee, and then he said, "I'll go make a call. Maybe we can get it done today." When he come back he said, "We're in luck. We can go by and get the paperwork started at eleven if that's OK with you."

I nodded. He sat down and started wolfing down the second breakfast. Doing business made John hungry.

"There's one other thing," I said, "nothing to do with business." He stopped in mid-bite. The Pendleys are a wary bunch and John was probably the worst of the lot, at least those that are still living. "Now, don't go into orbit," I said. "I just want your advice, and your help, if you're willing to give it to me."

"I'm listening."

I never have been good at talking about things that deep-down matter to me. When I get to even so much as thinking about my own private thoughts, I can get red in the face, but talking about them—putting words to them—is a very real pain right at the pit of my stomach. I can't talk to Sarah the way I'd like to, that's why I'm really to blame for what she did with Buck.

John Pendley sat there looking at me, not an expression on his face. Right then I wished I'd never said a word to him. It was dumb. My words sounded pretty stupid the moment I got them out of my mouth. What did I think I was doing? I wasn't able to talk to Sarah, and now, even worse, I was trying to talk to her brother, and I just didn't know where to start.

John waited. Finally he said, "Is there some kind of catch to this deal, Harley?"

"No, John, no. This ain't about business. It's more personal. It's about Sarah."

"Sarah?"

There was no backing up now, so I blundered on. "I'm in love with your sister, John. I guess I have been forever. At least, I don't know when I wasn't."

"So don't tell me." John was embarrassed, too, and it made it easier for me.

"She won't see me, John; she won't talk to me; she won't go for a ride with me."

"There ain't nothing I can do about that, Harley. Maybe she just plain don't like you."

"She likes me, I know she does."

"I don't get it, Harley. What do you want me to do?"

"Put in a word for me. You're her big brother, closest thing to a daddy she's had for a long while. She'd listen to you."

"No."

"She's shame-faced, John, I know she is, thinking about all the talk around town, especially after the last trial, but I ain't never had nothing but good thoughts about Sarah. If I can't ever be nothing else, I'd like to be her friend. I'd like to take her for a ride on a Sunday afternoon, or to the ball games, or to church. I just want to be near her, John. I want to see her smile again, I want to hear her laugh and have her touch me, even if it's only in friendship."

"There's nothing I can do."

"You could put in a word for me."

He took a long look. It was pretty clear I'd embarrassed myself for nothing. I remembered all I said, every word, and it was pretty dumb sounding. But at least he didn't laugh at me.

And then, with no expression on his face, John said, "We might be able to work us out a deal on the farming, Harley, but there's nothing I'll do about talking to Sarah. Nothing."

john pendley

After me and Harley Phillips met with Jethro Poteat down at the law office, I came on back to the house. Yes, Jethro's my lawyer, not his. I was just more comfortable using Jethro. I was sure my interests would come before Harley's, though I wasn't trying to cheat him or nothing. In the end, Harley and me, we settled on a deal that I think is fair on both sides.

As happy as I was when I walked through the door, that's how glum Sarah looked. It was hard to believe how woebegone she was, especially with the kitchen filled with the good smell of fresh-made yeast bread.

"Why don't you cut a piece of that hot bread for your brother, Sarah? Pour us both a cup of coffee and tell me why you look like the end of the world is coming."

"Thought you ate at Hardee's."

"I did. That was then; this is now."

She cut a big piece of the bread, the whole rounded top of it, and spread it with homemade butter. Nobody's supposed to be able to sell butter house-to-house anymore, but we buy it from the Weathermans down on Petersons Creek. We figure what we do up here in the holler is no business of the government's anyway. Nothing like fresh churned butter on warm bread.

She sat down across the kitchen table from me with her cup of coffee, but her mind wasn't on me or the coffee. She just stared out the window and the far-away look was about as sad as any I've ever seen, even at a funeral.

"Now, Sarah, nothing can be that bad."

"I'm going to be moving out, John, before long. When I find a place, I want you to help me."

I told her I would, of course, and I will help her move if it comes to that, but not having Sarah here to do everything she does for all of us is going to make this old house crumble into nothing. How else do you say it? She's the life of the house, the soul of it. She has hot meals for all of us, whenever we get in; she keeps the place clean and does the laundry; I plow it for her every spring, but it's Sarah who puts in the garden and does the canning. It's Mama's house, but Sarah makes this old two-story farm house into a real home. I don't know what I'd do without Sarah, and I don't know what the rest of them would do, either. Mama can't do it; she works, same as we do.

"When are you thinking about moving, Sarah? And why? I don't even know why you're talking like this?"

Then she told me about Mama and Matt's rifle, and about Wilfred coming out and getting Mama's dander up. Damn that Wilfred! Why didn't he talk to me first. Maybe I could have

53

done something. I don't know what, but maybe—I might have thought of something.

As far as Sarah was concerned, I just kept talking. I had to get her out of this black funk she was in. "And Mama's mad at you for talking to Wilfred. Is that all? You didn't put her shooting lessons in the *Gray Democrat and Gazette*. Don't worry, Sarah, Mama will get over it."

"Maybe she will; maybe I won't."

"You both will. It ain't that big a deal."

"She asked me to move. She's never asked you to move, has she, John?"

"Did she actually say that?"

"Not in those words, but it was plain enough."

"It was wrong, what you did, Sarah. You know that. What goes on here, stays here. That's the way we are. Whatever it is, we can work it out. Like Papa used to say, we don't wash our drawers in public."

"You'd rather she shot Buck? Is that what you're saying?"

"Someone should."

"Mama wouldn't make it in jail, John. That woman is a Hall, all the way, but I just know she'd die in jail."

"Some of the Halls have made it, in and out of jail."

"Don't argue, John. I did what I had to do. There was no other way. I had to talk to Wilfred. Mama was just acting too queer. She was about to do something. I could see it coming, something none of us could back up from. I tried to stop her, that's all I did, and I'd do it again if I had to."

Was it as bad as she thought? Did Mama really tell her to get out? That was hard to believe. Or were Sarah's feelings just hurt? Was there anything I could do?

But Sarah wasn't through talking. The good part, though, was that she didn't look so downcast. Maybe the anger she had toward Mama lifted her spirits. But whatever it was, the whole feel of the kitchen was better than it was when I came in.

"I only did what I thought was right for all of us, John.

But Mama had to get on her high horse about it. She spoke to me in a way she has no right to do. She didn't care about my feelings, and now she treats me like I'm not here no more, so I know I have to move; I have to find a job and a place to stay."

Now understand, I had no intention of talking to Sarah about Harley, but to see her ready to leave and scared as hell at the very thought of it, somehow I just said what I hadn't meant to say at all.

"Have you ever thought of getting married, Sarah, getting married and settling down right here where you belong?"

"What in the world are you talking about? Who would I marry—why would I even consider it?"

I don't know why I said what I did about getting married. I do know that the very thought of Sarah leaving, with of all of us trying to make-do there in the house without her, was something I didn't want to even think about. Maybe I was just trying to slow her down until Mama was able to patch things up with her, or she was able to patch things up with Mama. And maybe, in the back of my mind, having Harley come over to court Sarah, as shy as he was and as slow as he'd be, would add to the time before she did actually leave us to work our lives out for ourselves. My mind was chewing on my own worries so much I hardly heard her questions, but I heard the next one.

"What's this all about, John? What kind of talk was going on when you met Harley for breakfast?"

I looked away, but at that moment she was just as furious with me as she had been with Mama a few minutes earlier.

"What kind of talk was it, John? Gossip is one thing, and there's been more than enough of that, but the last thing in the world I expected was for one of my own brothers to add to my humiliation."

I didn't know what to say. She was madder at me than she'd ever been before.

"I know Harley is trying to hang around," she said, "but you don't think I'd let him when I know what he's got on his mind. And, you, John, you of all people. I didn't think you'd be a part of such a thing."

"Now, Sarah, Harley's a good man—"

"And I'd be lucky to get a good man after the kind of reputation I have now—"

"Stop it, Sarah. Stop it. It's nothing like that—"

"Let me tell you what to do, Big Brother John: Mind your own business. I'm not a piece of baggage to be pushed around. I'm a human being—maybe I'm a little flawed—but I still have human feelings and I don't need pity. Not from you and not from Harley. Just do me one favor, John: Butt out. Butt all the way out."

Chapter 7

luke pendley

I guess Dylan Hoilman is the best friend Jim Bob ever had, so, since I needed help with trying to control crazy Jim Bob, Dylan was the guy I had to see.

I realize now there wasn't much talk between us after we left his mama's house and started that long valley drive in the direction of Mount Mitchell. He didn't bug me about it, he didn't even grunt, but after about twenty miles with no talk at all, when we started going up the hill there at Busick, he finally spoke.

"Let me tell you why you came by to pick me up, Luke." I didn't say a word, so he went on. "You're worried about Jim Bob, ain't you? He says you're getting chicken. Are you? You can tell old Dylan."

Maybe I was. Killing a man ain't your everyday chore, and it did bother me some if I stopped to think about the nuts and bolts of it, but killing Buck Price is no problem at all to me when I think about what he done to Bekka.

Even so, private thoughts are private. Until I needed help, there's no reason to do a lot of talking. All of the real worry about me doing a killing, breaking a Commandment, has been waddling around in my head, but none of it is going to get said right out to Dylan — not ever.

"No, I ain't chicken," I said, "but I ain't a damned fool, either. We all know what's got to be done, all the gang, and I'm the one that's got to do it, but it's got to be done right."

"Right? And what does that mean, Luke?

57

"It means doing it right, that's what. It means making him suffer like he made Bekka suffer. It means making him know who's doing it to him and why."

"And you're the man to do it."

"Sure I am. I'm her brother."

"But you ain't doing nothing, that's the point. It's not just Jim Bob. We've all noticed. We've talked about it. We can see it, Luke. You're stalling. Maybe you're yellow. Jim Bob just said out loud what we've all been thinking."

That was it.

I kept having the feeling that something wasn't quite the same with the guys, but I figured a part of the problem might be just in my own head, because I knew how helpless I felt with everybody's eyes on me, waiting for me to do something — or trying to keep me from it.

No part of the mess in my mind is easy. I can't even think about how to get even with Buck, not with all the shit I've been under. God knows I think Buck should get his, in spades. Killing him would be easy, if that's all there was to it, but killing him and getting away with it, like he done, ain't all that easy. I'd do it in a second if I thought I could get a hung jury a couple times like Buck did, but that ain't a given.

"Look," I said, "I know you fellers are going to help me, and I know you'll do whatever I ask when the time comes, but don't push me. You can push me right into a mistake, and I'll end up in jail. Wilfred watches me like a hawk, and so does John, and Mama, and Sarah. You know that."

"It's been a long time since Bekka got killed, Luke."

"But there was reason to wait then. The law had him. It was in the courts."

"It ain't there now, Luke."

Dylan was right about that. It's way past time for me to make a move, but the truth is that I don't know what to do or how to do it. How do I get him off in the woods somewhere without anyone knowing about it? And when I do, what do I do to him that would be bad enough—bad enough to make him feel the pain he done to Bekka, but not bad enough to get him out of his misery—not too soon, anyway.

"You got a suggestion, Dylan? It ain't as easy as you think. How'd you get him to go somewhere—how'd I do it, that's my problem. That's where it's at."

"Maybe you can't, Luke, but one of us can. One of us could smoke a little pot with him—not me or you, of course, and not Jim Bob. He already knows how we feel about him, but one of the guys could do it, and with a little extra bait, the extra draw of some angel dust, it could be done. I can get the crystal. I've got a source. We'll tell Buck it's in a stash somewhere. He could be suckered right out into the woods, or a house, or some-place out of town."

"It might work," I said.

"Sure it will. Buck is bad about angel dust. He's a nut about that dust from what I hear."

"Do you have any?"

"No, but I can get it."

"Let me think about it. I've got to think it through. Where can I take him? It's got to be out where he won't be heard when I start working on him. Granny's cabin would be just right, and fitting, too. A fitting place. Right where he killed Bekka. Poetic justice."

"Knock off the poetic shit, Luke. Come up with a plan that won't fail. That's what's called for. There's going to be more than you involved in this. Remember that. We've all got our skins to worry about, and we can't afford to fart around."

"Give me a day or two. I'll work it out."

"Put on your thinking cap, good buddy. Time is running out. Jim Bob loved Bekka, and he's going to get Buck. He's going to do it, Luke, if you don't. You know he will, and I know it. Ain't no stoppin' Jim Bob. He done told me that, and he means it.

And I knew what Dylan said was true. When Jim Bob gets

Jack R. Pyle

something on that single-track mind, it stays there. I had to move. My stalling days, my putting off taking care of Buck, was about used up.

Whether the whole town was watching me or whether it was all in my head, my time had just about run out.

Like Dylan said, "Ain't no stoppin' Jim Bob."

wilfred huskins

This damned little office I have here in the courthouse can get as confining as a chicken coop, especially when things just aren't going right. This was one of those days. The building has been around since 1910, and it might have been big enough back then, but now it's crowded as a cathouse on payday, even with the annex we have next door. Looks like the county could afford to rent a place for the sheriff's office, but every time it comes up at Council, there's a hassle over whose property to rent, so nothing gets done.

Russ came in with two cups of coffee. "What's eating at you, Wilfred? You've been moping since you got in this morning."

"Nothing, I reckon," I said. There was no point in telling him about sleeping in a cold bed, getting up to a cold house and then going out for every damned meal, Hardee's or somewhere. That's no kind of life.

"The feud seems to have quietened down," Russ said. "I don't hear nothing from the Pendleys or the Prices. Maybe it will all just slowly die without any kind of bloodshed. I didn't like it there for a while. Too many hotheads. But now I don't hear nothing from either side."

"Is that a good sign or a bad sign, Russ?"

"Good, I'd say. When there's a rumble, I usually hear it. Ain't heard nothing."

Neither had I, and that's what scared me. When the teapot rattles the lid a little bit, that lid is less likely to blow off, but when there's a fire under the teapot and everything gets quiet,

60

you better think about doing something to move the pot or put out the fire. That's the way I saw it.

Finally, I said, "Maybe it's too quiet, Russ."

He took a sip of his sluggish-looking coffee. That man can ruin a perfectly good cup of coffee in short order. He made it half milk and three-quarters sugar. It's a wonder he has any teeth at all, and he has few enough.

"Too quiet." He said it almost to himself. He put his coffee cup on the corner of my desk, stood up and said, "I guess I'll be moseying along, Wilfred. Talk to you later."

I'd given Russ something to think about, something that had nibbled at the edges of my brain for a day or two now. Just passing the thought along made it a little easier somehow, but even so, not having answers was beginning to close in on me. The worry of it made me unable to stand the fustiness and the smells of the cubicle I was assigned in the courthouse.

I had to get out of there. The longer I stayed, the worse I felt. Maybe Russ would find out what was going on. I knew something was. I had no proof, of course. I just knew it. Deep in my bones, I knew it.

I drove towards Tennessee, not for any reason, but mostly because the car was pointed in that direction. There was no sign of the light frost that had been all over everything out my way earlier in the morning. Even the chill that had been in the air was gone.

My spirits should have been lifted by the way the sun was warming the earth, and by the signs of spring that were everywhere around me. The sarviceberries were in full bloom all over the hillsides and the dogwoods were getting close to full, but none of that wiped away the feeling I had that something, somehow, just wasn't quite right.

My hope was that Russ could find out what was going on. It was clear to me that I couldn't. Recently, I had been all but cut off from the Pendleys. Sarah simply hung up when I called, Luke was polite to the point of intimidation, Matt was indifferent, even my buddy John seemed distant, and I didn't have the nerve to call Ora Lee Pendley.

It was quiet, the whole town, the county, but I knew the fire was under the teapot.

I was parked on a turnoff right up there by the State line, when the radio got my attention. It was Russ.

"Meet me back at the office." That's all he said.

Chapter 8

sarah pendley

Dark, gray, rainy days are not for people who have already dug themselves deep into the black hole. It seemed like I'd heard the rain most of the night, so when dawn finally came, I got up and came to the kitchen. As far as Mama was concerned, I might as well have stayed in bed.

She couldn't have missed the smell of the coffee as she breezed through on the way to her car to go to work. I started to speak, but all she said was, "No time. I'll grab a biscuit at Hardee's Drive-Thru."

But it was more than the day and the rain and the gloom. It was a deep feeling I couldn't put words to. I had to talk to Mama. The situation at our house was growing worse each day.

We're not huggy-huggy, kissy-kissy people and never have been, but we've always loved each other, I'm sure of that. Our kind of closeness is not what I've seen at some of my friends' houses, but it's real all the same, even when it's never said out loud.

So far as I can remember, it's always been that way, but when Papa died, I know we drew closer together. We had to. Mama said we had to make a life for ourselves. She said she had to find work, so we'd all have to pitch in. I was only nine then, but the cooking became my job. I was always in the kitchen, so I already knew how to make easy things; and Mama, even when she was tired from the thread mill, was never too tired to show me how. I learned real fast.

Mama cooked when she was at home, but I was there in the

kitchen, helping, learning, finding out how to make gravy with no lumps. Sunday dinner in those early days after Papa died was lesson time for me, a time when I got better at doing what was my allotted share. And the garden was mine, too. The boys got it ready, but I tended it, and I did all the canning for the coming winter.

But since they brought Bekka's body out of the holler there's been a difference in the kitchen. That difference is everywhere in the house, but I feel it especially in the kitchen.

If I think back on it, it must have started when Mama first found out about me and Buck. Mama knows, I know she does, that I didn't tell Bekka how bad-tempered I knew Buck can be.

Bad tempered? Why do I try to fool myself? Even my thoughts won't let me harbor an outright lie. It's more than bad temper with Buck, and I know that full well.

Back then, I knew he doped a little, I knew that from the very first time, but sometimes when he did it, he seemed OK, and sometimes he was a danger to himself and everyone around him.

Like I say, I saw the bad part twice, but only once when he was gone plumb crazy, when he could have killed me as easily as he killed Bekka. I knew about that side of Buck. I'd seen it firsthand, but even when Bekka started flirting with Buck, I didn't tell her, I didn't warn her. I could have, but I didn't. I'm not sure why. I don't want to think of why.

Now I wish I had, oh, how I wish I had; I wish I had told her the whole thing, whatever she might have thought of me for laying-up with Buck every chance I got. Bekka would never have approved. She believed in waiting. But I didn't say a word to her, and it's too late for wishing. Wishes are worthless. Wishes get washed away easily, just like my wishes today are gone with the cold rain I see soaking my garden this morning. I could almost see my wishes sinking into the earth or washing down the pane in front of me.

Yes, there was a difference, a kind of parting, between me

and Mama from the day when she first knew some of the truth about me and Buck. At first I hardly realized anything was wrong, but now I know it was there. I know something was different in the same way a faint smell clings to the hairs in your nose—a nuisance that you can't quite find the source of, or know for sure what it is, but you know it's there.

There's nothing colder than a cold spring rain. The kitchen is warm enough with all the cooking going on, and I have a big, loose sweatshirt on over my blouse, but I can still feel the chill.

The kind of gray day that's outside the windows right now makes me doubly sure that, whatever it is—whatever name you could put to it—the feeling between me and Mama is worse now. Is it because Buck is back out roaming the streets again? I don't know, I just don't know.

However bright my kitchen lights are, however good the smells from the oven and from the simmering pot of pinto beans, the gray from outside—the pall that hangs over the mountains, and the mist that continues to fall—just seems to seep in around the sash, or through the glass, so that it dims the lights inside, and chills the air, and makes me want to cry.

Right then, I got jolted back into this day and my own life. I heard the sound of boots on the porch, and before I could recover, John came through the door with water dripping from his wet clothes and from the brim of his hat.

"Stand right there 'til I get you a towel."

"Don't mess up my kitchen." He was mimicking me.

I ignored that. I could see he needed more than a towel. "Why don't you go up and shuck those clothes. You're wet through."

When he came back in dry clothes and with his damp hair plastered down, I poured him a mug of the coffee that Mama had no use for. Then I poured one for myself.

"Wherever have you been, John? With weather like this, I thought you were still in the bed. It's not a day for logging."

"You're right, but it's still a day for working, especially when you've got work to do. I've been up since before dawn. Been having trouble with that knuckle boom loader. That grapple ain't holding like it ought to, so I tore it down this morning. I couldn't see nothing wrong, but I fixed at it and put it back together again. I'll give it a try. It's work I've been putting off. Might have to replace a hydraulic cylinder. I'd like to avoid that expense."

"Had breakfast?"

When he shook his head, I got out a couple of eggs and the liver mush. As I cooked I said, "Oh, I'm glad to see you, John, even wet and hungry and worrying about spending your money. I've been having the blue funks all morning. The rain, I guess. Mama rushed out, without even a cup of coffee. She's up to something, that's for sure, but I don't know what it is. She don't come home regular from work. It ain't like Mama. Says she's shopping in Asheville."

"Maybe she is."

"In a pig's eye."

"That's over, Sarah. She ain't playing Annie Oakley no more. Matt hid the gun. Right now, for the first time I can remember, there ain't a gun in the house. Ain't much like a Pendley house with no guns."

"I tell you it's not over. She's acting queer. She's doing something."

"You ain't talked to no one. You ain't called Wilfred, have you?"

"No. I messed up once. All of you were on me for that."

"Mama will get over it, Sarah. Give her time."

"She ain't getting over it; it's getting worse. Sometimes I think she hates me, and I know she blames me for Bekka."

"Now, that ain't true, Sarah. We all know it was Buck. She'll be all right once he's gone."

"He's leaving?"

"Well, one way or another, he is. It's all so damned quiet

right now that you have to know the damned lid's going to blow."

"Have you heard something, John?"

"It's more what I've not heard. When you hear a lot of talk, there ain't much action. The talk has quietened down. I tell you, Sarah, I worry about Luke. Sometimes I swear that boy ain't got good sense. I just hope it ain't Luke."

"Or Mama."

wilfred huskins

Russ was already in the office when I walked in. I had a longer drive. Not only did he have that sugar-thick cup of syrupy coffee in front of him, but he had already smoked three unauthorized cigarettes in our "smoke-free" courthouse. I could see the butts in a jar lid. It's hard to discourage Russ from smoking. He seems bent on meeting his Savior in his own way.

"What's the deal, Russ? What's in the wind?"

"Damned if I know for sure, but something's up, something big is in the making and it's going to be this weekend. What the big city boys call my 'usually reliable sources' just seem to have dried up, but when you've been a cop for as long as I have, you begin to feel it when trouble starts pressing in on you."

"You didn't call me down here just to tell me that. You could have done that on the radio."

Russ smudged out the cigarette he had cupped in his hand. He could see that the smell of it was beginning to annoy me. Just to show me he wasn't being bossed around, he took out another one, but he put it behind his ear. He did that sometimes.

"You're taking your time in telling me," I said. "Let's get on with it."

"That's the hell of it, Wilfred. There ain't much I can put in words. I thought if I just chewed the rag with you for a while, just put words to the stupid feelings I have, maybe you could tell me what it is that's bothering me, and maybe the two of us could figure out what to do about it."

"OK, Russ. I'll get a cup of coffee, and you just begin chewing and I'll listen. We both know it's too damned quiet right now."

When I got back from the coffee urn, Russ was reared back in my swivel chair, with his feet up on my desk and his hands over his eyes. Yes, that battered old chair is technically mine, because I'm the sheriff, but everybody uses it when I'm not in. The girls in the office like to eat lunch in here when I'm gone, because it's quieter than out there in the pool, but that's OK. Any way we get the job done is OK with me.

In Russ' case, it was even less of a problem to me, because Russ always had his shoes polished and free of mud. He was downright fussy about his feet. The rest of his uniform might have stood a cleaning, his shirt front may have had a gravy stain, but his shoes were things of beauty, always polished to a high sheen, and always clean even on the soles. In the patrol car, he keeps a cloth just for his shoes. He's a strange guy.

I sipped my coffee. It was too hot to drink, and I don't use cream. After a while he started to rub his eyes with his fingers and he began to talk.

"Now what would Dylan Hoilman want with angel dust? I know the boy smokes pot, that whole gang does, but that's been it—at least up to now. There's something out there now that just don't compute."

Russ sat loose in my leaned-back swivel chair, with his eyes shut, and the chewed match stick moving slowly from side to side. He was relaxed, drowsy-sounding and talking to himself rather than to me.

"And why do they all clam up when I mention Jim Bob's name? He ain't a bad boy, never has been. Oh, I know they all hang out over there at his dad's place, in that house he lives in, but long as that's all it is, we ain't got no real call to hassle any of them boys, leastaways that's how I see it."

He took his feet off my desk, leaned forward and took a dusty-looking handkerchief from his pocket. As he gave those gleaming shoes another rub, he kept on talking. "And what about Luke Pendley? What is it about Luke? Everyone seems to go quiet on that name, too. I don't like it when someone tries to steer me off in another direction, and that's the feeling I get all over town whenever I mention both those names."

"And why do you think whatever it is, is going to happen this weekend, Russ? Why now?"

"I overheard a remark, that's why. I don't know what it means, but someone's getting itchy—I heard that from the Gunther kid. No, I wasn't supposed to hear it, but I did. I heard another part of the conversation, too. Someone said, 'and the two weeks ain't even up yet.' Now I don't know what that means, but somehow those two tie together."

"How do you know? Why did you even pay attention?"

"Because there's something going on. You know that, Wilfred, same as I do. Something ain't going to wait."

"Yeah," I said, "sounds that way."

"And unless you can figure out whatever it is I've missed, there ain't a damned thing we can do about it."

Chapter 9

wilfred huskins

Russ left the office when a call came in about an accident out on the river road. Someone missed a curve and went off into the water. There weren't any details, but the river is shallow in most places this far up towards the headwaters. It didn't sound like something that needed me, so I stayed to ponder what was cooking that all of us could feel and almost smell and yet not quite identify.

With Russ gone, I got to sit in my own chair, and I might have put my feet up on the desk so I could think better, but my shoes weren't as polished as his, so I kept them out of sight.What I'd like to do is arrest Buck and bring him in and park him in jail, but you just can't do that without cause. Buck gave us no cause. The next best possibility was to get him out of town, at least until this newest thing, whatever it was, blew over.

Edd and Essie Price live in the old Westall house out on Oak Street. They still own the farm out there on the other side of the mountain from the Pendleys, two hundred acres or so, up there in the next cove. Their land goes right to the top of the ridge and abuts what's left of the Pendley land, but the old Price homeplace has been allowed to run down over the years and when they came back to town, Esssie just wouldn't live there. Edd says he's going to fix up the old house, but he never has.

The Westall house dates back to the 1800s. It's the only house left in town with a turret room sticking up beyond the second floor. There were others on our quiet streets, but they were not a part of the heirs' spendable inheritance, so the younger generations tended to abandoned those old houses to mold and rot and fall apart. In the end, all the other grand houses of the era had to be razed.

That's the way it is when you live in a town that can't come up with jobs for all the kids that get bred there. The young people leave, and absence brings a total lack of care. In a few generations that kind of neglect changes the character of the town as it has with ours.

There was always a great deal of care given to the Westall place because all of Westalls stayed in the area. They would build a little grocery store here and an insurance office there, and all of them—whichever one inherited that old house from the other—managed to keep it up. One of the Westalls, Ollie, still owns the house. Edd just leases it until he can fix up the old home place, but I have the feeling that Ollie has a long-term renter.

The house is back from the street. Edd could see the patrol car when it came up the drive, and I could see him standing there on the porch waiting for me. He didn't look too pleased to see me.

"A good day to you, Edd," I said, and I was answered with a scowl. Edd Price has a permanently pinched face and squinty eyes. He looks like he has never had a really complete bowel movement, and maybe that's his problem.

"You going to ask me in?"

"We can sit here on the porch, Wilfred. Essie's layin' down, and I don't think she saw you pull in here in that patrol car, at least I hope she didn't. She worries about what the neighbors will think."

As we walked over to Essie's white wicker porch furniture, he said, "Why don't you drive a regular car, boy? That damned thing out there draws all kinds of attention."

It was my turn to ignore him. He heaved his bulk into the oversized chair with oversized roses on the cushions, and said, "What brings you here? This ain't a social call."

"Well, Edd, in a way it is," I said. "I've come to ask a favor of you. Something for the good of the town."

"I've given to every damned drive you can think of, even the Volunteer Fire Department, and I know they get tax money. What is it this time?"

"It's not a drive, Edd, and it's not money this time. I simply want to ask for a favor, but, yes, it is, like I said, for the good of the town." His scowl deepened and he lowered his head. He was the picture of a bull ready to charge, so I really expected to be gored.

Recently I seemed to have had a knack for saying the wrong thing, for making myself a barrier every time I tried to make my job a little easier. He waited.

"There's something going on in town, Edd. I'm not going to try to sugarcoat it, there's been a lot of half-hidden threats since the last trial, and some damned fool might just act on one of those impulses."

"Nothing new there, Wilfred. My boy got off scot-free, and that's that. Some people may carry a grudge, but that ain't no reason for me and my family to back up one damned bit. You may be afraid of rumors and cowardly threats that are never in the open, but we ain't. I ain't, and Buck ain't."

"I never thought you were a coward, Edd, not you and not your boy, but we've had enough trouble—the whole county has—and we sure as hell don't need any more of it. I know this whole ruckus will all die down in time, but with Buck here, it just keeps the wound raw."

"Buck belongs right here. The Prices have been here since before there was a town, or a road. No one has more right."

"That's true, but that's not what I'm saying. What I'm saying is just a temporary thing. If Buck could go stay with some of your kin or you could take him to Myrtle Beach for the summer—anything to let the whole thing cool off. That's all I'm asking."

"You're asking too damned much. Ain't ever been a Price

who was a coward. We ain't running, and that's how it would look."

"Buck might get hurt."

"That better not happen." He was deep-down quiet when he said that, and his pig-sized, black eyes never left my face. And then he said, "You know what I mean, don't you, Wilfred?"

"I know what you mean, Edd, but if something happened to Buck, more killing wouldn't bring him back."

He knew I was right. I saw that flicker of worry cross his face, so I pressed the point. "There's not a boy alive who wouldn't like to spend the whole summer at the beach, Edd. Rent a place for him. There are girls all over the place down there in Myrtle. He'd jump at the chance to go."

It was a while before he said anything, but then I heard it, one word. It was quiet but it was firm: "No."

"Why don't you let him alone, Sheriff? You heard what the man said. Back off." It was Buck, the golden boy. How long had he been behind us on the porch? How much of this had he heard?

There was a sly and triumphant grin on Edd's face. He looked like the poker player who had taken a quick peek and found a wild card in the hole. "Don't ask me, Wilfred," Edd said. "If you want Buck out of town, ask Buck."

You had to wonder how Edd could ever have been the sire of the tall and handsome guy who stood there with a sure-footed stance, but I couldn't admire the arrogance that I saw written on those almost-classic features.

"Let me tell you, Sheriff," Buck said, "without you having to ask. If ever I decide to leave this broken-down hick town, it will be on my terms. For now, though, you can depend on it: I'm here to stay."

luke pendley
I never knew what it was to feel like an outsider until this past week. I can tell you, I don't like it, but there's no question

about it, it's happening to me. When I come up to a group—a group of my own friends—the same kind of change falls over them as when one of them damned summer tourists tries to butt in. We don't have that many tourists around here. I mean, it's not like up around Boone or in Maggie Valley, but to my way of thinking, we have too many.

Anymore, around my own friends, in a strange way—an almost unnoticeable way—I'm an outsider. The conversation shifts. That's the way it is every day now, and I'm not sure when it first began. Maybe a little of it has been there since Buck's last trial, but it's strong now.

People here in the county expected me to take care of Buck in short order. I'm considered rash by some—that's what they called me in high school, willful and rash—but I'm not as dumb as they think I am. I'm going to get Buck; I just have to do it my own way.

I would've done it long before now, but you can't do much with every eye in town on you every minute of the day. The fault's not all mine, but the guys I hang with—especially them—they just don't seem to understand that they ain't making it a damned bit easier, either.

Here it is, Saturday night, and there ain't nothing going on—or if there is, I don't know about it. I spoke with four of the guys today, and the talk just seemed to peter away. No one was doing a damned thing—if you can believe that. No plans. Nothing.

I come home after work and eat me some supper and now I'm going to drive into town and see if they're cruising Main Street. I'll bet they are. I'll bet they just cut me out, though they sure as hell don't have a reason. I ain't done nothing—or maybe that is the reason. It has upset some I know, but I just won't do a dumb thing, even with pressure from them.

So I drive on into town and the streets are pretty quiet. Oh, there's some cruising, but not many from my bunch. Maybe it's just a dead Saturday, a nothing day.

I drive on out to Jim Bob's house. Nothing there either. Just two cars: Jim Bob's and Dylan's. You don't knock at Jim Bob's; you just go on in. Inside it's quiet, too. It's just the two of them, drinking wine and smoking. Only had one light on and it was no more than a forty watt bulb.

I spoke and they kind of grunted an answer. It's the treatment, still going on.

"Where's everybody?"

At first there was no answer, and then Dylan said, "There's the Bluegrass Jamboree the other side of Marshall. Maybe they're there."

"All of them?"

"I don't know, Luke. I just don't know." The feeling that I wasn't wanted was clear enough.

Jim Bob hadn't said a word. He just sucked on that smoke he had hid behind his fingers and looked intently at nothing somewhere across the room.

"OK, guys. What is it?"

It took a while. No one moved. They didn't even take a drag. They weren't ready for me, didn't want me there, and, for my part, I damned sure wasn't ready for what I was getting.

Jim Bob went first. "Got your plans worked out, Luke? Dylan's checking around, but he says you ain't even talked to him about getting that dust or nothing, not one time."

He didn't look at me when he spoke; he just kept his half-closed eyes on that faraway place. I didn't answer. Hell, what can you say? They knew my hands had been tied.

Then Jim Bob goes, "A week's gone by, Luke. I done told you what I was going to do. I give you some time. Looks to me like you ain't done a damned thing."

There was another of those never-ending silences, then Jim Bob poured some wine, took a deep drag on his smoke, and after what seemed like forever, he said, "Buck's struttin' all over town, Luke. You must have seen him. Lordin' it over all of us, and now he's started dating the Brewer girl from over near Celo. What you waitin' for, Luke? Another killing? Waitin' for another girl to die?"

I can feel the anger coming up from my chest. I can taste my stomach churning. It'd be better to keep my mouth shut. I know he's goading me, but sometimes you can't keep quiet.

"You bastards," I said. "You want blood. You don't give a damn about how high I'll hang, just as long as Buck gets it. You're bastards, both of you."

"Better watch your mouth, Luke," Dylan said. "I don't want to hit you."

"You'd be afraid to try it."

"There's two of us. Don't you forget it."

He's right about that. When you hit one of those two, you hit both. Jim Bob and Dylan ain't much for fighting, but when it's forced on them, rules don't get in the way. They'll fight, kick, bite—whatever it takes—and it can get pretty rough. I've seen it. They both get on a kind of fighting high, and then look out.

It got quiet again in that dim room. If I've ever been lonely in my life, it was now. You don't expect treatment like this from your friends. I just stood there. I didn't know what to do or what to say.

There was more of the silence. They let it sink in.

Finally Dylan said, "Why don't you go home, boy. When you work out your plan, come back. If we can help, we will, but don't give us no more shit. Either do it, or back down."

What else could I do? I just turned around and walked out to my car and drove home. Could I have a fool-proof plan for getting Buck Pendley in another week? And if I didn't, would that crazy Jim Bob give his plan a try?

I took off my clothes and got into the bed, but I couldn't sleep.

Chapter 10

wilfred huskins

Nothing happened on Saturday night. I'm glad we didn't alert the rest of the force. We'd have felt pretty silly, but because we both had the same hunch about trouble, Russ and I stayed close to the office in the courthouse. We had supper at the Mountaineer Cafe, and we let the slow hours tick away.

Well after midnight it dawned on both of us that our vigil was a complete waste of time. Even the cruising on Main Street was lighter than usual and there were no fights or near fights. It was a bummer.

"I almost forgot," Russ said, "Marvelle told me to ask you to come to dinner tomorrow after church. Can you do it? Without Marylou there, being home on a Sunday must get a little lonely."

"I'll survive, Russ. The charity is appreciated but not needed."

"Now, don't get steamed up, Wilfred. I didn't mean that the way it sounded, and neither did Marvelle. She asked about Marylou. I told her Marylou was still at her mother's, so she wants you to come for Sunday dinner. That's it. That's all there is to it."

I apologized. I'd been too sharp with my reply to a nice guy who didn't deserve it, but it is lonely in that house and I know it's beginning to get to me.

As I always seem to do, I put off things that must be done. I'd been doing this with my marriage, same as I had with my job, and no one knew it better than I. Russ had given me the gentle needle a couple of times, but I just couldn't bring myself to face facts. Either the marriage was on or it was off. I might as well know, and then I might as well move on from there.

Right then I made up my mind. I'd contact Marylou on Monday, even if I had to do it by letter.

With all our waiting for something that never happened, Saturday had turned into a day that seemed like it would never end. Sunday morning was more of the same. I'd swear I'd heard the sermon that morning a dozen different times before. I was glad to get out of the church.

I was at Russ and Marvelle's house at one, the appointed hour, and the only good thing about the day so far was the smells from that kitchen.

Marvelle is not much of a housekeeper, at least not by Marylou's standards, but she's a cook to rival any in the mountains. The pot roast was everything the smells told me it would be, and there was a salad with green onions, radishes and lettuce from Marvelle's garden. Too early for good mountain tomatoes. She had to use the store-bought kind and they were tough and woody like they always are. Shipped-in tomatoes are one of the major things that makes me hate winter. When they are packaged and wrapped in cellophane, the only thing they have is color.

Later, we had fresh, spring, rhubarb pie and coffee out on the porch. Once Marvelle did a quick clean-up in the kitchen, she joined us and the day slowed back down to a creep. Nobody had much to say. Even the air there on the porch seemed to press in on us. The afternoon was like the morning had been, as slow and tedious as yesterday was, while we waited for something that never happened. You could hear the big old grandfather clock in the hallway, and it seemed to hesitate with each tick. Then it happened.

I swear Russ Silver's telephone would rouse a hibernating bear. I know he keeps it loud on purpose, but when it rang on that dead Sunday afternoon, it almost brought me to my feet.

He answered it, and I heard Russ say, "We'll be there. Yeah, know where it is. We'll be there." I looked at my watch. Ten after five.

Russ was on his way to the patrol car without waiting for me. "Come on, Wilfred. Been an accident. Sounds like a bad one."

On the way, he told me what he knew. It wasn't much. There'd been a one-car accident over on the unpaved county road just below Mace's Knob. Car must have missed the turn. Call came in from a farmer who lived down below. He had heard the noise, and from his house he could see where the hillside had been torn up when the car came crashing down.

luke pendley

I was still in the bed that Sunday afternoon when the call came.

I hadn't slept the night before. I didn't know how much I depended on the guys I hang with until they just sort of moved away from me, like I was some kind of a leper out of the Bible. And the damnedest part is, I didn't know it was happening. Worse yet, I didn't know what to do about it, and I didn't know what to do about Buck. I don't know when I ever felt so down. Not only was my head messed up, but my stomach was sour from the bitter thoughts of the mire I was in.

My dreams, if you could call them that, were like trying to find your way through a laurel thicket. I'd wake up in a near panic because I'd squeezed my way deep into a tangle of meshed branches and twisted roots as I tried to fight my way through. Every direction brought me to a place where I couldn't push forward no more and there was damned little room to edge backwards.

They say an animal can get through any hole big enough for his head, but that ain't true with a man in a laurel hell. Many a dead one has found that out. You can even see the light on the other side, just a few feet away, but them intertwined laurel

Jack R. Pyle

branches and roots, once you get deep into them, begin to squeeze in on you. They're alive. They're like man-eating evergreen monsters intent on holding you until all that's left is bones.

I wasn't doing much more than tossing and fighting with the sheets when I first heard the damned wake-up-the-dead sound of my pager. You know I'm a volunteer fire fighter, but you might not know I'm a First Responder. We're sometimes closer to the site of an accident, so we get there and do what we can until the EMS guys arrive with the ambulance.

Some folks think I'm a no-good bum, a worthless pot smoker, but I'm trained for this emergency work, and I took my training seriously. I'm as good as you'll be lucky enough to get if you should ever need it.

Even half awake, that pager brought me to life with a location and the barest of details. When I heard the words "below Mace's Knob" and "car down the side of the hill," my heart sank. Could that damned fool Jim Bob had pushed his schedule ahead? Had he gone out there and forced Buck off the road, like he said he would. I bolted into my Levis and I was out of there on my way to old man Obediah Hensley's farm. That's where the 911 call came from.

There ain't many times I regretted being a First Responder. To tell you the truth, most of the time when I flipped on my red light and raced to an accident scene, I got a kind of high. And, no, this one wouldn't be the first time for us to have to hack our way into a wreck, but this time I knew what I'd find. There ain't no kind of training that can prepare you for that.

There were two of our guys there when I got there, and two more just behind me. We unloaded our gear and got on the way.

From the other side of the Hensley pasture, we started cutting a path through the vines and second growth. I had a small chain saw, and my working buddy, Ken, had a machete for the lighter stuff.

We moved in quickly. Fifteen years ago, this land had been farmed. It used to be in corn, they tell me, right up to the rock-face the car plunged over. The stuff we cut through looked worse than it was. Nothing was really big, just troublesome. In twenty minutes we were at the wreck.

The car was totaled. You could see where it had turned end over end, banging rocks and trees as it came down. The roof was crushed in and you could smell gasoline, although there was no fire.

My first shock was when I realized it was not Buck's pickup. Wrong color. It was an older car, a rusty-looking blue-gray. Even then it didn't dawn on me; the color of the car, its age, nothing about it registered until I drew closer and looked in the broken window.

The head was off to a crazy angle, the light brown hair matted in blood, and the face—I still can't believe it—I'll never forget the face.

wilfred huskins

By the time Russ and I got to the Hensley farm, two other deputies were on hand, along with the EMS guys. The First Responders from the Fire Department were already ahead of us, all the way across the pasture and beginning to cut their way through the woods to get to the wreck.

We tore down some of the fence so we could take the ambulance over closer to where we knew the wreck had to be. Hensley didn't like what we did to the pasture, but when a life is in danger, you don't say much. We caught up with the First Responders before they got to the wreck, so we were all in a clutch when we found it. It was a tangled mess of crushed metal. Not much chance anyone was alive.

I saw Luke Pendley stagger back, and I saw Ken Proffitt support him a little, and lead him back to the side of the clearing. Poor Luke. Whoever it was, Luke Pendley knew him. Tears were streaming down his face and his blue eyes couldn't seem to blink.

I pushed on up to the front. Then I knew what had Luke in such a state. The dead boy—and I was sure he was dead even before the EMS guy nodded—was Jim Bob Williams.

Russ took hold of my arm. "Nothing we can do down here, Wilfred. Let's go up there, up to Mace's Knob, and take a look," he said. "Let's see if we can piece together what caused this."

As we walked the area up there on the road just under the Knob, it was plain to see what had happened. As you crest the hill, the road takes a pitch downward, then it levels off before a sharp turn back to the left.

On the wrong side of the road, the left side, you could see where Jim Bob—that had to be the assumption—had gone off the road-bond surface for a short distance. Then you could see where he brought the car back onto the road. The two wheels on the left of the car had made a clear trail of the path of the vehicle, traced in mud, there on the darker surface.

"What in the hell was he doing over on this side?" Russ virtually trotted along as he followed the mud tracks along the road to where the car had gone over. "And, look here, Wilfred, look at this. Too much speed. The car didn't topple over. It shot over. Look. It's hard to tell where it happened. Ain't no edges broken away here at all."

You could see where the car had gone over plainly enough, but it wasn't because the edge of the road had broken off. As Russ said, the car hadn't slowly toppled over.

"Was Jim Bob trying to pass someone? Looks like it," I said, "but, why? This never has been much more than a one-lane road. It's not a place to speed under any conditions. He's a local boy, Russ. He knows this road."

Russ walked back to where Jim Bob had driven his car off the surface on the left, along the muddy ditch on the mountain-side of the county road. "You can get a pretty good tire print along here, Wilfred, but I'll lay you big odds they're going to match the tires on that wreck down there."

Like Russ, I had the feeling that Jim Bob was trying to pass someone, but why? This isn't a road for passing—or for horsing around. Jim Bob had to know that. Why would he try to pass someone, and just before a bad curve?

When we got back to the bottom of the mountain, the crowd of gawkers had expanded considerably. Word had spread. It had been radioed back to town, and I guess every scanner in twenty miles had heard it. Russ steered through the crowd with the blue lights on, found a place to park, and then I went in to see old man Hensley.

"Obediah," I said, "now think back on this carefully and try to remember. It might be important. After you heard the crash, and looked out there and saw where the wreck tore up the brush coming down the mountain, did anyone come down this road from up at Mace's Knob?"

He thought for a few seconds. "I'd say, no. Maudy called 911, and I've been right here since then. Ain't no one come down the hill. Ain't much traffic ever on that road, Sheriff. Out here, when a car passes, it's worth looking up to see who it is." He laughed at his own joke.

"You're sure?"

"Well, almost sure." Obediah still wears bib overalls, and he tugged at the two sides of the top of the bib as he thought. "Maybe I couldn't swear on it, Sheriff, but I'd have to say, no. First car that got here, either direction, was them fire department boys, and they came in the other way."

"If you remember a car coming down, Obediah, or a truck, call me, will you? You may recall something after this army of people finally get out of your yard."

"Yes, sir, Sheriff, I sure will. I'll call, but I'm pretty clear on it right now."

"Has the Medical Examiner been here, Obediah?"

"Been here and gone, Sheriff. He went back with the ambulance."

"Which one was it?"

"The new one. That Dr. Hill."

The new one? I had to smile at that. Dr. Hill has been here at least eighteen years. But he was from California, so that made the barrier even larger.

We don't have a coroner here in the county. We use a rotating system of medical examiners in cases like this. I just didn't have any idea of which one it might be.

"Let's swing by the EMS office, Russ. I'd like to see Doc Hill if he's still there, and then, whether I want to or not, you better drive me over to the Williams place. I know they've heard about Jim Bob. Bad news travels fast. But, it's something I need to do."

It had bugged me when we were up there at the Knob, and it still hung there in the back of my head. Was there someone else up there at the same time as Jim Bob? There just had to be. Jim Bob must have been trying to pass someone or he would never have been over in that left ditch, even on that narrow road.

But who? And why?

Chapter 11

edd price

It was late on Sunday, almost supper time. We were on the porch, Essie and me, waiting for Buck to come home from his Granny's, from over in the Cane Community. It was way past time for him, but he wasn't here yet, and I was more than a little worried. I know a lot of people would like to really hurt Buck. It ain't fair. He had his trial.

Now, I ain't saying this 'cause he's mine, but you can't find a better boy than Buck, praise the Lord. It's not every young feller who'll visit his Granny every Sunday, rain or shine. I've seen him go over there in some mighty bad weather since we moved back here from Baltimore, and he went just to be sure she had plenty of dry wood in the house.

My brother Arly lives there with her, but he ain't worth a tinker's dam. He's OK when he ain't drinking, but that ain't often. Arly's the drunk in the family, but don't you tell that to Mama. She ain't much for size, but she's all spunk.

Now, understand, I ain't saying Buck's perfect. Like his Granny, he can fly off the handle without much of a reason, but he ain't a killer like some say. I know my boy. These days, you got to have a big dollop of spunk to get along in this old world. I'm glad Buck's got it, and I think he got it from his Granny.

Me and Essie, we're peart now, but time is catching up with us. Buck's our youngest. We didn't expect him—but we didn't really plan the other two either—but Buck didn't come along until Essie was forty-five, maybe a little more than that. She called him a gift from heaven, but there have been times when

I wasn't all too sure which direction he did come from. But don't get me wrong. Buck's high-spirited, but he's a good boy.

On that afternoon, when the springtime shadows started stretching out a little too long, I really started to worry about Buck. He was always home for Sunday night supper. Sunday was Buck's day with his folks, praise the Lord. Church in the morning, home with us for a quick dinner and then he was off to Granny's. Supper was always with us, with his Mama and Papa. Now you can't call that anything but a good boy, can you?

I'll admit it right off, it worried me when it got late and there was no sign of Buck. Then the phone rang. No lie, it sent a chill down my spine. It was my oldest son. He asked if Buck was here. I said, "He ought to be, Harold, but he ain't here yet."

He told me he had his scanner on that he heard there was an accident over at the Hensley farm, down there below Mace's Knob. He didn't have no details, but he said a car had pitched off the road. Lord, I tell you, I felt the strength just drain out of my body.

I don't know if I even made a sound, but I must've done something. Then I heard Harold say, "Now, Papa, don't go off crazy on me. Call over there. Obediah Hensley's some kind of kin to Mama. He'll tell you what happened, but don't drive over there like a crazy man, or two or three more might get hurt."

I don't know how I looked up that number and got it dialed, and then I had to sit there with the redial button, trying to get through. I just couldn't do it. It was busy all the time, so I got in my car and drove over there, but I didn't drive wild.

There were people everywhere, and when I got out of my car, I heard what had happened in short order. It was that crazy Jim Bob Williams, and he was dead. Maybe you ain't supposed to be glad to hear news like that, but, the good Lord forgive me, I was. It wasn't my boy. It wasn't Buck, like I feared.

By that time, more and more people were still driving in, clogging the road and parked every-which-way. Nosy gawkers most of them. My car was so hemmed in I had the devil's own time getting out. It must have taken me more than an hour to drive out there and finally get back on the highway.

When I pulled in the drive, Essie walked out to the car. In the state I was in, that scared me too, Essie walking out to meet me.

"Buck home yet?"

It was a relief when she told me he was, "But, Edd, he must be sick or something. He looks bad. He wouldn't talk to me. He's gone up to his room. You'd better go up."

I knocked but he didn't much more than grunt, so I went in. I can tell you he did look bad: face white and eyes fixed on the ceiling.

"You sick, son?" He didn't answer.

I tried to get him to talk a couple more times, about what time he left Mama's and like that, but he just didn't answer, so I stopped being soft with him.

I knew he always come back from Mama's on that road where the Williams boy had been killed. It's the quickest way from the Cane Community back to town. We all come that way because it was miles closer than going out to the Asheville Highway and around the other side of the mountain. He didn't say a word, just kept staring up at the light fixture.

If he wasn't sick, he was either scared or guilty. I had to know what he'd done. I just had to know. I know that there was bad blood between Buck and the crowd that Jim Bob Williams hung out with, all growing out of the Pendley girl's death, so I asked it, straight out.

"Did you force Jim Bob off that road, Buck? Is that it?"

You could see the color come back to his face, and that blue vein in his neck stood out. He was mad as hell and at me, that was plain to see, but I'd rather see him in a rage than white-faced and cowering in a corner. The Prices don't care much for a man who don't stand up like a man. In that second, I tell you, it was no more than I got the question out of my mouth, than Buck become a Price again.

"How damned dumb can you—"

"Buck." I said it firm. I didn't want him to say something he'd regret.

He stared me right in the eye and I stared back. I didn't back down none and neither did he.

Finally he said, "You want to try it the other way around?"

I knew he had more to say and I wanted him to do it in his own way. It's best if you don't try to rush Buck.

"He tried to kill me, Papa. I saw him in the mirror, coming up on me from behind, too fast, way too fast, so I got over as far as I could, and when he was alongside me, I saw who it was, and I knew what Jim Bob meant to do. That silly grin of his told me plain as if he'd spoke. They'd sent him to do it.

"But, Papa, I've never been so calm in my life. I just eased on the brake and let him shoot on by, and I watched him go over the edge. I watched him go over, Papa, and I heard the crashing as he hit rocks and trees and then the final crash and, after that, no sound at all."

As he talked, the iron came back to his spine. He sat up, put his feet squarely on the floor and I could see my boy again, the way I expected him to be. He was a Price. He was back in control.

"I knew what I had to do, Papa. I didn't even have to think about it. I damned sure couldn't be connected with that accident, or all hell would break loose. I drove on down the hill to that little side road. You know the one, to that drive that turns off to the Vance Cemetery. I pulled in there, turned around and headed back toward Granny's. But I was afraid to go out to the Asheville Highway. Too many people know me along that road, and I didn't want to go by Dillingham's store, so I took that old road toward Ivy Gap, and I worked my way on up toward Burgins Creek, and then I got on the highway back to town."

"And you think no one saw you?"

"I'm sure of it. Didn't meet a car on the mountain going down, and that Ivy Gap road is right there, before you get to the first house."

Buck was right. If he got tied in with Jim Bob's death in any way, the talk would outrun the facts.

"And that's why you're late?"

"That's it. I was fine until I came in the drive and parked my car. Then, Papa, I lost it. I just turned cold and sweat popped out all over me, and when I got out of the car, I got sick all over the garage floor."

Right then, it was clear to me what I had to do. Wilfred might come to ask some questions. Most folks knew Buck was always over there on a Sunday afternoon. I had to get it all slicked over and I had to do it soon. I didn't want Essie to know anything about this. She talks too much. But I knew we could handle it, Buck and me.

"I'll go clean up the garage, Buck. You just get up and wash your face and comb your hair, and then come on down to supper. You don't need to eat much. I'll tell Essie you ate something over at Mama's that must have been in her refrigerator too long. Essie always says that Mama does that, keep things too long. That's what I'll say, and she won't ask no questions. You just tell her you want a little soup, and let it go at that."

I knew we could handle it. No one knows Buck was up there on Mace's Knob when that crazy Jim Bob went off the road, and no one needs to know.

sarah pendley

I heard about Jim Bob before Luke got back. Poor Luke. He'd be among the first to get there. It worried me. I knew how much he loved Jim Bob—almost as much as he loved

Bekka. Them boys had been friends since before either one learned their ABCs.

It was a fact I had to consider. Luke already knew about Jim Bob. He had to. I heard the sound of his pager; I saw him drive out. I knew he was there with the other volunteers, and now I also knew where and why he went. The pager was about Jim Bob. Jim Bob was dead. I'd already had two phone calls about the accident, and then I figured out how to turn on Matt's scanner, so I knew all of it even before Luke came in the back door.

If I hadn't known it was Jim Bob when he walked in, I might have thought Mama had been in an accident. Luke looked just like he looked when they found Bekka up at the cabin. His body still moved, but the life in it was gone. When I tried to get him to eat something, or to have a cup of coffee, he glared at me. I really wasn't ready for how bad it tore Luke up, but they had grown up together. I should have known.

The Williams family lived here in Pendley Holler, just down below the church till his papa heired that old farm they live on now. That was back about ten year ago.

When I tried again to get Luke to eat or drink some coffee, the look he gave me said more than all the words he had avoided using since Bekka was killed.

You might not really know what scorn is until you see it up close. I'd seen a little of it since people in that courtroom heard about me and Buck, but it was nothing like the look I got from my own brother. He said it all without saying a word. The look said whore, slut, betrayer; the look said why wasn't it you instead of Bekka? And then he went upstairs.

I did what I always do when I'm upset. I started to cook. I started with a coconut cake. Later on, I'd ask John to take it over to the Williams' farm. There'd be family coming. They'd need food. Tomorrow I'll make a pot of soup and a casserole. The cake, with what the other neighbors bring, would be enough for now.

I kept thinking of the look Luke gave me. All my life, I never could understand why anybody might want to kill themselves.

With Bekka, Jim Bob and the scorn from my baby brother, I understand it now, like I never thought I would.

harley phillips

You never know how the news of a death is going to hit you until it does. I knew Jim Bob. I don't think there's a soul who lives in the county who don't know Jim Bob. He wasn't crazy, but he didn't have all the dirt packed around his roots either.

He's been running with the wrong crowd lately, but before that, when folks hereabouts got to know the little boy who had walked every road, every lane, every cow path in the county, he was the area's favorite kid. A kind of pet. And the funny thing is, no one seemed to resent it, not even the guys his age.

Jim Bob had a way—I guess you'd call it innocence—that made everyone his friend. On a warm summer's day, he was the kind of boy the farm women for miles around would call in from the dusty road for a piece of cornbread and buttermilk, or sweet milk and cookies or a cold glass of spring water.

Jim Bob Williams liked the outdoors in every kind of weather, and he liked the people and the animals he met along the way. He liked to walk to nowhere and back, he liked to roam the hills, and he liked to talk to people. If you were digging shrubs—and that's my business, trees and shrubs—he'd stop and help you; if you had a flat tire along side the road, he'd help you fix it, too, or if you were cutting wood for winter, he was ready to spell you while you rested.

I swear I think Jim Bob could melt stone with his smile. Those big blue eyes and pale brown hair left you as vulnerable as he was, and you just don't see that kind of selflessness anymore.

When I heard about what had happened out there below Mace's Knob, it just pulled something out of my gut that I knew would never grow back. It's not a nice world we live in. Whoever first said "dog eat dog" had it right. There's too much of the "what's in it for me" all around us, and I mean right here in Asa Gray County. No, we don't want to admit it, but that don't make it any less true. In a lifetime, you ain't likely to know a Jim Bob Williams, and if you do, count yourself lucky.

It tore me up when I heard about that boy. I was working on my books, a job I don't much like, and I just put my pencil on the desk and went to lie down, hoping that bad feeling would go away.

It didn't, but like we all do, our bad side overpowers our good side. Before I knew what had happened, I was thinking, not of Jim Bob or his folks, but of myself. I'm ashamed to say it, but it's true, I plain drifted away from thoughts about Jim Bob. My mind was taken up with me, with Harley Phillips, and how this death—Jim Bob's death—out there at the Hensley place, would only add to my problems.

Sarah was already heaping the guilt of Bekka's murder on herself. Everyone might not see it, but I could. Maybe she didn't say it out loud, but I saw it back when she was testifying there in the courtroom. I tell you, I could plain see beyond the shame of telling about the times she met Buck out there at the old Pendley cabin. I could see the guilt mounting in her mind, just as plain as day.

You can see it now—today—in the way she's treating me. She won't even give me a chance to talk to her.

And now with Jim Bob dead, it's sure to be worse. I know that sooner or later she's going to wonder about what Jim Bob was doing up there on Mace's Knob.

I'd heard in town how he talked about what ought to happen to Buck, what he'd do if he was Luke. That was just barbershop talk, just rumors. But I'd heard him make some pretty crazy statements myself, so it's not all rumor. That boy wanted something done to Buck.

And, when you stop to really think on it, it all ties in. We knew—we all knew—that Buck went over to the Cane Community every Sunday to see his granny, and that he came back over that knob. So you have to know that Jim Bob knew it, too.

And if you give it just a little thought, you know that Jim Bob had no real business over there, on this Sunday or any other day—not that I knew of—so you have to ask yourself: What was he doing up there today, and how did he get himself killed on a road that we all know well, every crook and turn of it. There isn't a man among us who hasn't hunted over that way and used that road a thousand times.

Jim Bob knew that road, and he wasn't known to drive reckless or burn rubber, so why the speed before that curve? The thought stayed in my head: Why was he there?

If this tied in with Bekka's death, and I felt in my bones it did, what would it do to Sarah? Before long she'd ask herself the same questions. And if she did, would she have two departed souls on her conscience now? And if so, where did that leave me?

I hated myself for thinking it, but once I realized Jim Bob was gone from these mountains forever, my only thought was for myself.

How would all this affect me?

I had to admit to myself, the dog-eat-dog, what's-in-it-for-me attitude was there. I tried to shame it away, but it wouldn't go. It was there.

Chapter 12

wilfred huskins

I was in the courthouse early on the day of Jim Bob's funeral and so was Russ. We had just enough people in the office to keep it open and the telephones answered. You don't expect much activity when there's a funeral in the county as large as Jim Bob's was sure to be.

"You've made all the assignments, Russ?"

"Sure have. It looks like a morgue in here right now, but the guys will be out there at the church from nine on. This funeral is likely to be bigger than old Miz Peterson's. It ain't due to start until ten, but it's going to be push, cuss and shove at that church, even with the new addition to the parking lot. Don't worry, Wilfred, our guys will be there early."

Russ was right. Ida Belle Peterson's funeral was more than any of us ever wanted to see again. She was kin to everyone, one way or another, and that got complicated sometimes by the amount of double-first cousins they had in that clan.

The fact that Mrs. Peterson was just a shade past one hundred and two years old made her someone everyone in the county knew, someone they could remember for all of their lives. The church couldn't hold that many people. They poured out all over the front lawn and sides of the churchyard and beyond, back all the way out to where the monuments started.

There would be a crowd there today for sure, even though the funeral is mid-week, so our streets and highways won't fare much better this time.

Jim Bob died on Sunday. The funeral was on Wednesday,

just long enough for kin to get there from the State of Washington, and from Texas, Florida and South Carolina.

"You think this one will be that big?" I don't know why I said such a stupid thing. I had the same feeling. I knew most folks would be there. Jim Bob wasn't related to as many as Mrs. Peterson, but there was a special place for him in everybody's mind and in their hearts, too. Maybe it was because he always seemed to be a little outside the edges of reality, or maybe it was because everyone somehow or other felt Jim Bob needed their special protection—the kind of protection that only they could possibly give him.

Whatever the reason, this was going to be a big funeral and a huge problem in the county because a good many of the early summer people were already here, driving as though they owned the roads.

Around here, folks put great stock in the size of a person's funeral. There are people who actually count the cars, and that number becomes needlework talk for the next five or six weeks. Size is an important thing. It's a measure of respect, but it goes beyond size. There's all the talk about who was there and, sometimes more important, who was not. There's always a lot of talk about the flowers, about who sent which spray and the size of it. Another topic is exactly what was worn and by whom. Funerals in Asa Gray County are solemn occasions but they also have a social significance.

Russ brought me back to reality. "What's on your mind, Wilfred? What's bothering you?"

"Nothing. Just thinking about large funerals."

"I've got to know you pretty well, son. We spend a lot of time together. It's more than the size of this funeral. Hell, man, we can handle that part of it. Someone may scrape a few Florida fenders, but it'll all be over by noon. We'll keep 'em in line. It's not that, is it?"

"It's nothing, Russ. Just—just the tragedy of this whole damned thing, I guess."

"OK. You don't want to talk about it. Fine with me."

Good old Russ. He'd never been anything but a cop of one kind or another. He'd been a town cop, he'd served with several different sheriffs, and even in service, he was with the military police. He didn't simply hear things or see things, he felt them in the air.

I didn't know I showed my concern, but he was right as usual. I wasn't worried about the cars on the road or the congestion. The traffic problem might be bigger today, but it was routine. And, yes, there was something hovering in the back of my mind, and it had been there since the day the two of us walked the accident scene.

"I can't help wondering who was on that road with Jim Bob," I said. "There had to be somebody or he wouldn't have been off the road on the left like he was. So you have to ask, who was on that strip of road?"

"I thought so. I thought it was either Jim Bob bothering you or something to do with Marylou."

I said nothing. It was easier on me that way. Sure, Marylou nagged at my mind, too. I'd planned on trying to get together with her early in the week; I planned on trying to get her to come home, or on finding out for sure that she never intended to come back, but Jim Bob's accident just shunted my own life aside—or at least that's what I told myself.

Russ had the good sense to drop the Marylou angle. I was grateful to him for that. He said, "We both know Buck was up there; we all know where he goes every Sunday afternoon. So, yes, he was there, either before the accident or after it—"

"Or at the time of it." I finished the sentence.

"One of us has got to go over there to his daddy's, Wilfred. One of us has to go talk to Buck."

It's my worst habit, as sheriff, and maybe in my life, too: I put things off. The less I want to do something, the more I put it off.

"I know it," I finally said. "I'll go there tomorrow."

sarah Pendley

Mama went with me to Jim Bob's funeral. My brothers were in the car, too, but they have a way of just disappearing when you get to something like that, but Mama was there, right beside me, through it all.

She came in my room while I was dressing. "You're not going to wear that, are you Sarah?"

I didn't say the words I thought. Things were bad enough between us. As she spoke, I was slipping the dress over my head. Of course I planned to wear it.

"What's wrong with it?"

"It's a little too fancy, that's what," she said. "You bought it in your trying-to-keep-up-with-Bekka days. Wear the blue one."

Yes, there was a time when I tried to dress with a little more of Bekka's splash, but I didn't need to be told about it. It was Mama's way of reminding me that I had always been jealous of my sister. She didn't want me to forget that.

I guess I'm still a child to Mama, and I let her get away with it—maybe we all do.

"The blue one's old and out of style, Mama."

"It's Jim Bob's funeral, Sarah, not a style show."

She rubbed in a little more salt. Mama can do that. She can lay it on you. She can do it so that if you fight back, she becomes the injured party. "Why, Sarah, Sarah. What are you thinking?" she would say. "I never said anything like that."

I'd had a lot of her double-edged remarks since Bekka was killed, and now she was at it again, this time with Jim Bob, like I might have had something to do with that death, too. It was clear to me: I had to get out of her house, just as soon as I could make it look right. I couldn't—no wouldn't—take much more of this. That's all I got from her anymore. It was either being politely ignored or being the butt of her digs.

I put on the blue dress.

harley phillips

I made it my business to be in the church long before the Pendleys arrived. I know their mother, so I was sure they'd be there early. One of the Edge boys, one who had been on the football team with me, was an usher. I found out from him that a place was being reserved for the Pendleys, so I knew where to sit so I could see Sarah without being too bold about it.

The parking lot was full, but people were still milling around when the Pendley's car got there, although the church itself was already more than half full. I saw Sarah coming down the aisle behind Terry Edge, with her mother and Luke. I'd watched them earlier in the parking lot as they all got out of the car. By the time they found seats, John and Matt had drifted off in some other direction.

I'm worried about Sarah. She's losing weight. That dress hangs loose on her frame. She might be happy about that; I'm not. I know from little things her brother John said to me that she's having trouble with her mother, and I know how hard it is for her to come to any kind of a public meeting after the things she testified to in open court, but if God can forgive, why can't we?

As far as I'm concerned, that part of her life is past, something to be forgotten.

Sarah just sat there in the pew, and somehow she looked hunkered down, like she was hiding, but when she first come in the church, she tried to look at the people there, she tried to move past her worry. When they turned away or when their eyes drifted from her face, I could see her shrink into the dark blue dress, trying to fade out of their sight.

I had to keep telling myself that all these folks gathered here called themselves Christians, but just looking at them and their coldness toward Sarah, trying to convince myself of their Christian understanding was a losing battle in my mind. Christians would have extended a hand. Didn't they remember Jesus and Mary Magdalene? Have they all lived such spotless lives that they could dare make judgment of anyone else? I know better.

Sarah was burdened. I know the scandal with Buck was the biggest burden, and the fact that she considered herself too fat was another. The second burden was one she had carried so long that her shoulders were humped from it. Why must she compare herself with the skeletons most girls tried to starve themselves into being?

It's true, Sarah is several pounds over that kind of skin and bone weight, maybe by twenty-five or thirty pounds, or even a little more, but to me she has the face of an angel. She's a beautiful woman with curves; a woman who is warm and soft to the touch; a woman who should be loved. She's the one I want. I wouldn't want her skinny.

No, Sarah is not the rag, the bone and the hank of hair that Kipling wrote about long ago, but I can tell you, I'm the fool who would be honored to call her my lady fair.

All I want is the chance.

luke pendley

I've been in the bed since I got home from old man Hensley's farm. Seeing Jim Bob in that broken car with a broken neck tore me up so much that I just couldn't think of work or anything else. I didn't call in sick or nothing. I don't give a damn what they do down at Robert's Ford.

I'm not ashamed of it. I cry. I sleep some, and when I wake up, the tears just come back. You cry more when you know the weight of someone's death is yoked around your shoulders. When you kill a stranger, you know the guilt of killing a man, but when you kill a friend—a friend like Jim Bob—and when you know you're the sole cause of it, the weight of that guilt gets so heavy that no amount of tears can lighten the load. And I know, without a whisper of a doubt, I know that I did it; I'm the cause of it.

I know I killed Jim Bob. No, I didn't run the car off the

road. In one way or another Buck did that, but Jim Bob's wreck is burned in my mind the same as if I had been driving that old car of his.

Mama knocked at the door. "Luke? Time to go."

"I'm dressing, Mama. Just another minute."

I'd just stayed in my room, laying in the bed, since Jim Bob's accident. Mama came to the room, of course, but I wasn't ready for her Bible lesson, and I told her so. She went away crying, but she went away.

That was on Monday. Since then she's sent them all to the door, one by one, but I'm not ready for talking. The only thing I'm ready for is dying, and I'd be ready to go this very minute if it would bring Jim Bob back. He's all his folks have got—at least he was—and now... Well, I just don't know, I don't know...

"Luke." It was John at the door. "We've got to load up. Time to go to the church. Come on, boy."

I put on my jacket. The shirt collar was stiff at my neck where the tie felt like a hangman's rope. Damned if Sarah hadn't starched the shirt. She knows I don't like starch.

Jim Bob was Methodist and a mighty good thing: their church is a lot bigger than ours. When we got there—and we were among the early ones, Mama always was—the lot was full of cars and there was that milling knot of back-slapping men in front of the church exchanging jokes they'd saved since the last funeral. There was no laughing out loud of course, but I'd stood there with them time and again, and I knew beyond a few sympathetic clucks, what the conversation was always about.

There was space in a pew up front reserved for us. Our families had always been good neighbors, even after they moved away, out to the farm, but I'm sure a part of the courtesy to the Pendleys was because his parents knew how close I'd always been to Jim Bob.

So, thank the Lord, the Williamses didn't blame me for his death, but that didn't make my own feelings any easier to bear. They didn't know what I knew.

I didn't mean to look, but I saw his mother and father, and the rest of his kin, over in the little alcove of the church where the choir stands, and the sight of them caused the tears to burn my eyes again. I was grateful to finally sit and look at the floor.

There was the Methodist minister, Mr. Garrett Mottley, in his robes, and it looked like there was a preacher up front from every church in the county. I don't think Jim Bob would have liked all this carrying-on, but a burial service is for the family, not the for the body that lies in the coffin, so I'm sure Mama, by her grunt of approval, felt the right thing was being done.

I had to stop listening to the words that were being said from the pulpit. They were talking about a stranger. None of what I heard said up there was the Jim Bob I knew. One day soon I'd have to say goodbye to him, but I'd do it alone. I'd do it high up on the hill behind Granny's cabin, up where we gathered nuts in the fall, where the air is sweet and pure and the sounds of the everyday world are muffled into silence. That's Jim Bob land, not this.

Finally it was over. The Williams family was herded to another room, out of sight, while the casket and the flowers were moved to the graveside.

We waited in little clusters, with very few words to each other, until Mr. Dellinger from the funeral home nodded. Then the people moved from the church to the cemetery where the other part of the ritual followed such a set pattern that everyone knew the lines and the action. It was like a high school play that had been rehearsed until it was letter perfect, and then the whole thing was played in slow motion.

The sameness of what Mama considers a proper Christian burial was here, even to the odor of the soon-to-wilt flowers mixed with the smell of the raw earth from the gaping hole under the casket—the smell of earth not quite hidden under fake green grass.

But it was wrong—it was all wrong. It wasn't right for Jim

Bob, free spirit that he always was. This is not what Jim Bob would ever ask for, but it's what he got.

I couldn't wait for the ride back home so I could get away to myself and think of how I could avenge two deaths.

Chapter 13

sarah pendley

We went to Jim Bob's funeral in John's station wagon, and we'd no more than got back and unloaded when he was ready to go.

"I've still got to drive down to Charlotte today," John said, "don't hold supper because of me."

Well, maybe he did have to go to Charlotte, or maybe he was just trying to get away from the gloom that had settled over our house, even heavier today because of Jim Bob.

John's escape was followed quickly by Luke and Matt. They both had places they had to go. Matt seldom ate the noon meal at home, even on Sunday, so that was no surprise, but since Jim Bob's accident, Luke had been laying up in the bed, not talking, not eating and sometimes crying. I know he cried. I could see it even though he'd dried his eyes before he let me in his room, and he always refused the food I brought, even the fresh buttermilk and the corn bread I made especially for him.

I didn't blame my brothers, not any one of the three of them. If I'd had a place to run, I'd have been gone, too.

As we opened the back door, Mama and me, you could almost reach out and touch the beefy smell of the brown stew I'd left on simmer. When I lifted the lid of that old black iron pot, the aroma in that whiff of steam made me realize how hungry I was. I gave it a quick stir to see that it wasn't sticking, checked the carrots, potatoes and onions, and went to my room to get out of the blue dress Mama had pushed me into wearing.

That dress is going to the Dumpster. I've worn it my last

time. I never had liked it, and now with the recent memories of Jim Bob's funeral, I know I'll never wear it again. It's still a good dress, but I can't take it to the church to give away. If I do, there'd be more lip from Mama. What I decided to do was just find a clean place to put it and leave it at the Dumpster. It'd find a home.

By the time I'd changed and come back down, Mama was at the table with a cup of coffee. "Beautiful service," she said. "I don't much care for the robes that Preacher Mottley has taken to wearing, but what he said about Jim Bob was pure poetry. I know it meant a lot to Annie Williams. God knows I know what it means to lose a child."

I held back my words, but they were in my head: Yes, Mama, and you're about to lose even more. Already you've lost one, Bekka's gone; you still have one more to spoil, and Luke won't take to it like Bekka did. I believe you've almost decided to ignore the other two boys, Mama, just blot them out. And the last one, your only remaining daughter? You're pushing her adrift.

Even as those wild, weeping thoughts were burning in my brain, I knew they weren't fair. I knew I was bathing my own conscience with a heavy coating of the self-pity, but that's how I felt right then. I'm human; I have a right to hurt, too.

All I said was, "Are you starving, Mama, or do I have time to fix a salad?"

"Don't bother, Sarah. The stew will be just fine."

I stirred in a little corn starch to thicken it, and then I dipped two brimming bowls. That, and a thick piece of homemade bread with real butter from old Mrs. Weatherman, was all we had.

Mama ate in silence, but even her silence was warmer than she'd been toward me for a long, long time—since right after the last trial.

Along with the other things, I'd baked two coconut cakes yesterday, one for the Williams family. Matt took it over. I cut each of us a piece and I refilled her coffee cup.

When I sat back down she said, "Sarah, I'm worried about Lukey; I'm terribly worried."

So that was it, that's why she was a little warmer toward me. It was Luke. I said, "So am I, Mama. When he refused the hot corn bread I took up and the bowl of buttermilk I'd just brought up from Mrs. Weatherman, I knew he was feeling mighty low."

I watched her put cream and too much sugar in her coffee. There were tears in her eyes. All this while I'd been thinking mostly about me—about me—and how I felt. Those eyes, wet with unshed tears, plain tore all the self-pity right out of me. I don't have children, and I know you can't love them all exactly the same, but maybe if you're a mother, your heart just naturally goes to the one who needs it the most.

The tears rolled down her cheeks. "He won't let me in, Sarah. He won't let me comfort him. He's all I have."

When she said that, it near killed me, but I told myself I didn't know her pain, I didn't know what I'd do or say if I had a child as near the edge as Luke was.

I said, "He won't let none of us close, Mama. We've all tried."

"But you're closer in age, Sarah. He'll talk to you. You've got to reach him. Bekka could have."

There. She did it again. Wonderful Bekka. But this time I was ready for her. I was steeled for it. I heard it, and, yes, it did bore into me, but I didn't show it.

"I promise you, Mama, I'll talk to him. I'll do what I can." As I spoke, I touched her hand, and she moved it away just a little, or she seemed to. It made me nervous, so I said, "I really don't know what's got into Luke. I know him and Jim Bob were friends all these years, but this is worse than when Bekka—"

I hadn't meant to say that. I try to avoid all mention of Bekka to Mama. I try to keep her from being reminded of what I know is painful to her—painful to all of us.

"That poor, sad Lukey," Mama said. "It's still Bekka, Sarah, that's what it is." I could see the tears well up again. "It's been on

his mind and in his heart all this while. Lukey might never get
over this. God knows he ain't been the same since Bekka went
away. He's more sensitive than his brothers. They were so
close, Lukey and Bekka. Only eleven months separated them.
And then this, this accident that took Jim Bob."

"I'll do what I can, Mama. I'll talk to Luke. I'll just try
harder next time."

"I know you will, Sarah. You're so level-headed and steady;
you're so dependable."

Level-headed and dependable. Well, it's better than nothing, and nothing is all I'd been getting from her.

She said, "Thank you, Sarah," and then she picked up her
fork and started on the coconut cake. The change in Mama was
remarkable. It was good cake; I know now I'd better find that
recipe and put it in with my best ones. It was a cake that could
do miracles. The tears were gone and the cake on her plate was
nearly gone.

"Do you need more coffee, Mama?" She waved me off.

Mama took another bite and then she said, "I didn't see
any of the Moffetts there." With the fork in her hand, the subject had been changed completely. "I know they've been cool
because of that brother of hers and what he did to that niece of
Miz Williams, but, at a time like this, you'd think little problems could be put aside."

"They're out of town, Mama, the Moffetts are out of town.
They've gone to Myrtle."

"They could have come back."

"They might not have known."

"Oh, pooh. There was time for the Gilleys and the Yeltons
to get here from Washington, way out there in Washington State.
Birdie told me they had to fly all night. When there's a death,
you just put the rest of it on hold, that's what you do."

Mama had been beside me in the church. I didn't see her
looking around all that much, but she must have, because she
ran down the list. She mentioned just about everybody who

could possibly have managed to come to Jim Bob's funeral—at least she mentioned enough people to more than fill the church, even the Methodist church.

I must have been just a rehearsal for Mama. When she stopped talking to me, she went to the phone, and, from where she sat in the family room, I could hear nothing but Jim Bob's funeral all the way to the kitchen.

The dishes were there. I rinsed them, and then washed them, and while my hands were busy, my mind tried to find an answer to what I was going to talk to Luke about.

But I said I would, and I will.

wilfred huskins

When the last bit of excess traffic had been siphoned away from the churchyard, we went back to the office. Russ was in uniform, and couldn't change, but he sat in my chair and loosened his tie.

For my part, I couldn't wait to get out of my blue suit and dress shirt. Just taking off that tie was the best part of it. I put on a pair of uniform trousers, and a gray uniform shirt, short sleeves and open at the neck. It had been a warm day for early spring. Funerals seem to call out the worst in the weather, but at least, this time, it wasn't rain. But it was humid. It was one of those days when Florida seems to funnel some of their weather right up to the mountains along with the summer people.

"Well, Sherlock," I said to Russ, "what did you find out?"

I may have offended him with my smart tongue, I'm not sure, but he ignored the question. He just said, "Bigger than old Miz Peterson's funeral, I swear it was."

I didn't want to go into how big is big, so I just waited on him. Russ doesn't like long silences, so I knew that he'd find a way to answer my question without looking like he was answering my question.

He's like the rest of us in Asa Gray County. Sometimes a direct question can just put us off. It sounds too pushy, it crowds us, so we just let on like we didn't hear it. But later on, if it's something we do want to make a point about, we can bring it in from left field like it was a new subject.

He chewed on that match stick for the longest time, and then he shifted it to the other side of his mouth and said, "The Edd Price family was there, back there toward the back of the church—all of them Edd and Essie and Buck and his two brothers."

He shifted his match stick again, so I knew that was all he was going to say right then.

"The act of an innocent man, a good neighbor," I said. I waited a few seconds but there was no reaction, so I said, "Or someone who had his boy there so it would look right to folks around here."

"Which one, Wilfred, which reason?"

Russ did this every once in a while. It was his little game of You-Go-First, so I said, "I'm not sure right now, but after I've had a chance to talk to Buck, I'll tell you."

"He's one cool dude, Wilfred. I've seen him lie when I knew he was lying, and he knew I knew he was lying, but that innocent look never left his face, and he looked you square in the eye, just as nice as you please. You'll have to watch careful."

"Oh, I know, Russ. A lie detector isn't much good except for questioning the honest man. There's a lot of super-good liars and a batch more out there that truly don't know the difference between a lie and the truth, I guess because they've told so many."

"That old Edd Price herded them all together, Wilfred, and he had them there. You can't tell me that don't mean something," Russ said.

And there it was at last, the answer to my question.

As I've said, I trust Russ Silver's instincts as much as I trust something I can see with my own eyes. In working with this man for the past two years, I still can't believe how he can get to the answer with so little to go on. Of course, proving it is another matter, but he knows. He just seems to know.

Even though I was sure Russ was right, I gave him another little nudge, just to see if there was more.

"Maybe," I said, and I could see him bite down harder on the match stick, "maybe Jim Bob's death is a real tragedy, a tragedy for the whole county, so maybe it was just the neighborly thing to do."

"Edd Price has been away too long to know about being a neighbor, all those years in Baltimore. He don't even much talk like one of the Prices anymore. You can count out the neighborly stuff."

"Kin? I'm not sure."

"My wife says they're kin, but it goes so far back it can't be counted, and then only on one side, Essie's. I think you better forget the kin part of it. It's something more than that, and it's sure to swing right back around to Buck. He was up there, Wilfred, right up there on Mace's Knob, sure as I'm sitting here taking your chair and looking like the High Sheriff of the county."

I laughed. "No question about that," I said, "but if you're going to impersonate me, fix that tie."

I went into the next room and got us both a Styrofoam cup of Rachel Woody's strong coffee. When I got back, he had straightened his tie. He was behind the desk with both of those polished shoes on the floor, and damned if he didn't look like the High Sheriff of the county.

"You're looking good with that tie back up where it belongs, Russ. Are you thinking of running against me in the next election?"

"You going to run?"

"I might not."

"Well, then, I might run, but I ain't the sheriff now. You are." He looked at me to be sure I heard him, and then he said, "I'm telling you now, Sheriff, besides sneaky Buck, you've got

one more problem to think about, son. I heard about it from
Marvelle. It's gossip and I didn't pay it no mind until I took a
good look at Luke Pendley in that church this morning. He's
going to be trouble. He's wound up tighter than a coiled cop-
perhead."

"Yes," I said. "I saw him."

"It's all telephone talk, Wilfred, but Marvelle tells me he
ain't eat a bite since he found Jim Bob out there at the foot of
the Mace's Knob."

"He does look bad."

"Not one bite, they say. That boy's always been a plumb
hog about corn bread all broke up in cold buttermilk, but he
even turned that down. Sarah told that to Betty Jean and Betty
Jean told it to my wife's sister, Carlene."

Luke was a worry, no question about that. More than one
in town had heard him say an eye for an eye, a tooth for a tooth,
and even his brother John had told me he was worried about
some rash thing Luke might do.

Up to now, though, there'd been no sign of it. Oh, Luke
was sullen enough, and swaggery enough, and you knew he
had thoughts of revenge, but there was nothing overt—not the
first thing—unless you count the nighttime, drive-by stuff at
Edd Price's house. Still, he is more than a little on the wild
side, and this morning in church, I have to admit, he did look
drawn to the point of breaking.

"You're going to have to watch him, Wilfred. He's about
to flip. He's close to the edge. And, more than that, you're
going to have to find out for sure where Buck was, what he was
doing when Jim Bob went over the Knob." He leaned back
and closed his eyes.

"I know where he was," Russ said. "In my bones, I know
where he was."

"You're a big help."

Russ spit his chewed match stick into my trash can, and he
fished in his pocket until he found a new one.

"It's your problem, buddy-boy; it's your job. It won't be easy, but that's why they pay you better than they do me."

How right he is. It is my job.

Chapter 14

harley phillips

It wouldn't have made me half as mad if he had brought that contract to me—you know, handed it to me, in person—but the fact that it came in the mail was just too damned much to swallow. I thought I knew John Pendley better than that. When it comes to money, I expect him to drive a hard bargain, but here in Asa Gray County, a man's word is all you've ever have to have. Well, that's the way it used to be, before we had so many of the summer people.

I guess too much of the other way of doing business has rubbed off on John Pendley, that's the only excuse I know. We talked this whole thing out right there in Jethro Poteat's office. It was all spelled out—and Jethro is John's lawyer not mine. I watched old man Poteat write it all down on a yellow pad in that fancy script of his. He wrote down just what we said, but that ain't the way this contract that came in the mail is.

The way it was supposed to be, I was to lease 20 acres down there at the end of Pendley Holler, down by the state road, for seven years, with the option to renew for another seven under the same terms. The second lease was to be on the 40-odd acre piece, right there behind old Mrs. Styles' house, under the same terms and conditions. There was no confusion and nothing complicated about it. I understood it, John understood it, and so did Jethro Poteat.

And then John agreed to let me hold a first-refusal option, for one year, on that odd-shaped sixty or so acres that runs from the west side of that second boundary up the hill to the pasture where he keeps a few head of beef cattle and then over to Brushy Creek.

In all, I would be able to farm another hundred and twenty acres more or less, and all of it on terms I could handle, with a portion of the profit, when it started coming in, going back to John. It was a good deal for him. He didn't have to put out a penny, he was getting a little rent money from me, and he was getting a better deal on his taxes.

That's what it was supposed to be. What I got was a contract on the first twenty acres and nothing on the rest of it.

Well, you might know I called Poteat. I figured Margaret had forgot to put some of the papers in that brown envelope, but Poteat said no, no mistake, he just did what John Pendley told him to do, nothing more and nothing less.

I can tell you I was some kind of mad when I made that call to Poteat and got the answer I did.

When I called John—said I wanted to come right over to see him—he put me off, and that made me sizzle all the more. I had a good notion to forget the whole thing. I don't like being jerked around.

"Why don't you come over to the house tomorrow evening," he said, "about eight. I'm not sure what you're talking about, Harley, but if there's something wrong with the papers, we can get Jethro to fix it."

My first thought was to tell him what he could do with his papers, but I do have a grain or two of common sense even, when I'm mad as hell, and that good sense rushed in there to remind me that going over to John's house was a chance to see Sarah, so I said, "Eight? I'll be there."

I was there, scrubbed up and on time. That farmhouse the Pendleys live in has got to be seventy or eighty years old, maybe older. It was built by their granddaddy's youngest brother, the one they all called Uncle Z, because no one was sure how to say his real name, which was Zechariah. Tale is their great, great grandmother took the name out of the Bible and then got to calling the child Baby Z, and it just plain stayed with him all his life. He was always called Z.

The old, white, frame Pendley farmhouse still sits on the last hundred and fifty acres the family owns of Pendley Holler. They tell me that at one time John's great, great granddaddy owned the whole shebang, and part of the next holler.

Back then when we was trying to make our deal, me and John, I accused him of trying to buy back all of the old family holdings—to buy back at least all of Pendley Holler—and he just grinned, so I think that, or something pretty close to it, is his plan.

I could understand John better if I knew for sure that was truly what he's got in his head. A man ought to have a plan of some kind, some kind of near-impossible dream for his life. If he don't have, then, at least to me, life—the pure old tedium of living—can get to be too much of a chore.

But with his idea of buying back all that holler, I think I've got him pegged now. It explains a lot. He don't date, he don't waste his money, but when I think of him as a loner with a plan—a big plan—then I begin to understand that what looks so queer about John is just that he has his eye on his own faraway dream, and that dream has to be first—first above all other things.

I know my own plan—and it may sound silly to you—but my plan is to earn money, lots of it, and to sock it away in government securities, so that if I never turned another lick, I can live like a king.

Now understand, I don't plan to put every dime I earn into bonds. I want a wife like Sarah and I want kids, three or four of them. I want something to earn the money for, something that makes it all worthwhile and that would be Sarah and some kids. And you've got to know, too, that I don't want money just so I can loafer around all the time. Truth is, I can't imagine life without working.

What I do for a living may look like back-breaking labor to you—and sometimes it is—but I can't imagine myself not going out to the fields to tend my shrubs and trees every day. I like watching them grow. I like planting and mowing and trimming; and I especially like the time when we can begin what we call B & B. You can believe me, that's some of the heaviest of the work there is with tree farming, when we root-prune the shrubs, dig them up and tie that rootball in burlap. That's what we call balling and burlapping, and it's deep-down satisfying, but it is hard work.

For me, it's balm for the soul because I can see the results of my years of labor, and it takes years to produce a salable tree. And the balling and burlapping part of it is the sure proof that I'm getting close to market time.

I like the fall, the big market time for a tree farmer. That's when I can add a little bit to my dream; it's the time when I can start getting a little money in to replenish the money I've been paying my crews all the year long.

Oh sure, some dribs and drabs comes in every month of the year. That's because I sell all kinds of shrubs, wholesale and retail, during all the seasons, but the big time for B & B is when the sap's down, when the cold begins to set in.

If what I think about John's land-buying dream is true — and I'm pretty sure it is — then I can understand him better than most of the folks around here, I vow.

But he'd better have some kind of a good explanation for what I got in the mail today from Jethro Poteat, or I'll look for land somewhere else. It's good land he owns in the holler, but it ain't the only land around here. I don't like being made a fool of, not by John Pendley or by anybody else.

Later on, when I got there at the Pendley house, I parked my little pickup beside John's big-tired monster and went to the back door. Sarah met me with a frown on her face and a dish rag in her hand.

"I come to see John," I said. It wiped the frown away, and that's what I meant to do.

What a pretty girl Sarah is. Each time I see her it's like a slow replay of the first time, the first day of school. Today her face is moist with the heat of the kitchen, a strand of her hair swings loose, but those warm brown eyes, the pink of her cheeks and the fullness of her mouth brings back my first memory of her: I can see again the pretty, freckled little girl and the smile she gave me on that scary day when I went to school for the first time.

Sarah started walking back through the kitchen to the hall that led to the front of the house and I followed. She was in control all those years ago on our first day of school, just as she is now. She pushed the hair back and said, "You can go on in the living room, Harley. I'll tell John you're here."

The living room. It was a gesture that wasn't lost on me. It was meant to put me in my place. The living room in the Pendley house is rarely used, and it looks it. Understand that everything is neat and clean, almost too neat and clean, so I was being made into company. I knew they also called it the company room.

Across the hallway, on the other side of the wide front door is what was once old Uncle Z's library. It's now the family room, with a VCR and a TV. There are books there, some new and some old; some, from the look of the worn-leather, must have once belonged to Uncle Z. But it's not really a library these days; it's the family meeting place. It's a large room, with a fireplace, a big oval hooked rug on the hardwood floor and with chairs that were meant to hold a human body in comfort.

I had no more than settled into one of those "company" chairs in the living room when John walked in.

"Sarah put you in here, Harley? Did she think you're a preacher or something?"

I started to get up to shake his hand, but he said, "Stay right where you are, boy. I'll be right back. There's something I've got to do before we get to talking."

He was gone only a minute or so, and when he came back

he sat on the sofa, a matching piece to the uncomfortable chair I was in. "Now," he said, "what's the big problem?"

I started back at the beginning, back when we first had our talk down at Hardee's over coffee and a sausage biscuit. I was afraid it might be boring, rehashing all the things we'd said down there and at Poteat's office, but I had to make John see how impossible the twenty-acre deal that came from Poteat's office was for me.

Maybe the rehashing wasn't really needed, and I know how easily I can drone on if I don't have something or someone to stop me from it. I didn't have to wait long for the reminder from John Pendley. His eyes didn't glaze over like you read about in books, but it was plain that he had something else on his mind. He seemed to be listening for something, and in short order I knew what it was.

Sarah came in with a tray. There were two cups, a glass pot full of coffee, some cream and sugar and two slices of her famous pecan pie.

We don't have pecan trees here in the mountains, but Sarah has a friend, Susan—she used to be a Buchanan—who married a man from down in South Carolina. Susan ships pecans up to Sarah every year. For a mountain girl, with what might be called an imported nut, Sarah makes a pecan pie that won't wait. Nobody at church even tries to make them anymore. Sarah is the official pecan pie maker.

She didn't say a word. She just put the tray down on that little spindly coffee table and started to leave.

"Close them doors as you go, please, Sarah. Harley and me have some private talking to do."

As the double doors to the living room were quietly closed, John poured coffee into both cups and said, "Now, what was it that was bugging you, Harley?"

So I started again, but this time I kept it to the barest essentials. I didn't want to put him asleep again, but I reminded him what our agreement was and I told him what Poteat sent.

"Nothing more than a misunderstanding," John said. "I'll take care of it with Jethro, but I can see how you got yourself all riled up when that letter came." He had himself a little laugh over that. And then he dug into the pie as though he hadn't already had a piece of it with his supper.

To be sure there was no mistake in his mind I said, "It's the 20 acres, John, and the 40 acres, and an option on that bigger piece that goes up to where you keep your cattle."

He nodded.

When I finished my coffee and pie, I went back through the kitchen, said good night to Sarah, and headed toward my truck.

What in the hell was it all about? That's the thought that kept nagging at my confused mind, and then it came to me. John didn't look like Cupid—far from it—and he already said he wouldn't talk to Sarah for me, but, as I walked toward my truck, the whole thing was as clear to me as anything is ever likely to be.

Poteat hadn't made a mistake. John had told him exactly what to do, and then he'd told him to mail the contract, because he knew it would fire up my boiler, and that I'd come raging to him for an explanation.

Good old John. He didn't want a woman for himself, but he had plain old set this one up for me. He figured Sarah might soften a little if I just happened to be there. I couldn't mention it to him, of course, because that would put a stop to it quick, but when I got his plan through my thick head, I was purely grateful to John Pendley. He had made a good reason why I had to be at the Pendley house. If I had it figured right, he'd be making other reasons why I had to be there until Sarah's ice started to melt.

If I was lucky, and if I didn't manage to foul my own nest, I just might have a brother-in-law named John, and he just might turn out to be my favorite in the family—after Sarah, of course.

I didn't look back, but as I pulled myself into the truck, I had a clear view of the kitchen window. Sarah was there. She ducked back, but I saw her.

Maybe. Just maybe...

sarah pendley

I was playing the game of "if" again, and it started with Harley's knock on the back door.

In the early spring, the beauty of the trillium is not questioned anywhere in our part of the mountains, but while that flower is always a treat for the eye, its delicate beauty is getting harder and harder to find. Worse yet, it's around for such a short time. Like most wild flowers, it's almost impossible to transplant. It lives in the woods, and it wants to stay there.

Buck, I have to admit, is the trillium in my life.

There's no question about what he did to Bekka, and God knows it shames me to say it, but most of our time together is a memory I'll cherish for all my days.

I can't say this, not to anyone, because of Bekka—because I know he killed her. If I ever said how I feel about the secret hours with Buck, who could understand it? No one. Not a soul on the face of the earth. I can't even square it in my head, but, whether I say it or not, in my own mind I know. Buck is my trillium, my wild flower, my spring awakening.

And yet I must remember: a trillium is a trillium. It's not meant to last. For a time I couldn't face up to this plain fact, but that's the way it is. The trillium has a kind of special beauty that's here for now. Enjoy it while you can.

But when you want a flower to border your garden, you would do well to think of the dahlia. It's perennial; it's substantial, dependable, and it has a beauty of its own. In something other than a wild and wayward way, the very sturdiness of its stalk and deep green leaves say permanence and strength.

If Buck is the trillium of my life, is Harley meant to be the dahlia? And what's so bad about these thoughts that pound through my brain, all so high flown and noble, all about trillium and dahlias, is that they're too often crowded out of my mind by what our preacher calls carnal.

When Preacher Thomas has the fire and brimstone rolling, when his preaching can make the rafters rumble, the word carnal has a special effect on me, because I know what he means. And when he talks to the men about lusting—shouting the word till he's almost hoarse—he doesn't know he's also talking to me.

My thoughts about the perfect beauty of the trillium just won't stay with that purity, the way a girl is supposed to. My thoughts, and maybe one day Heaven will forgive me for them, my thoughts go to the flesh. And, Lord, how Preacher Thomas can make that word sound.

The shame of it is that it's more than Buck. You could say I was a sinner and that Buck was a slide from Grace, something I might be able to atone for, but, dear God, it doesn't stop there.

I try to make the thoughts go away, but even now—as I watch Harley walk toward his truck—I see the movement of his hips and the massive back and shoulders, and in my mind I see him playing in a forest pool, stripped naked, and I just want to die for the thoughts that come to me, but they keep coming and coming.

What kind of a woman am I?

Chapter 15

wilfred huskins

The day after Jim Bob's funeral I rolled out of my single-use double bed and headed for the shower. I didn't intend to go to the office. If I did, it would be two or three cups of coffee and then some kind of rambling talk with Russ while he double-shined his shoes, and the next thing you knew it would be time for lunch.

No, I wasn't going in. I'd call Rachel Woody, so she'd know where I was, and then I'd just mosey over to see Buck before he got away from the house.

Edd doesn't want me around there because of how it might look to the neighbors, so there was nothing for me to do but to try to ease up that drive without upsetting anyone too much. Maybe Essie wouldn't even see me. It was still early morning and the kitchen is at the back of that old house.

Edd saw me. Before I could get the car stopped, he was at the window signaling for me to roll it down. He didn't want me to come in, that's for sure.

"What's on your mind, Sheriff," he asked in a tone just three shades above a whisper. I knew what the whispering was. It was more of the Essie and "what will the neighbors think with a cop's car in the drive?" but Essie be-damned, I had to talk to Buck.

"I need to have a talk with Buck, Edd. I won't—"

"Well, you won't be doing it here."

"I don't want to have him brought in."

"No, no, Sheriff, he ain't afraid to talk to you none, not one bit. It's just that Essie, she don't—"

"It's got to be this morning, Edd. Do you know of a better place than here? We could do it at the office, but there's damned little privacy there."

"My oldest son ain't home. You know where my boy Harold lives, don't you, Wilfred? Me and Buck, we could meet you there. We ain't even had breakfast yet."

"Nor have I. Tell you what, you tell Buck to meet me there at Harold's house at ten. I'll be waiting."

"We'll be there—"

"I want to talk to Buck alone, Edd."

The old man drew back out of my window for about a foot, fixed those little black raisin eyes on me, squinted them into slits, rammed out that determined Price chin and then he said, "You get two for the price of one, Wilfred. I'll be there and so will Buck."

matthew pendley

I'd been stewing over doing something to Buck Price since I met that scrungy, pigtailed guy from Baltimore and his three friends. They'd been on Buck's trail for a long time they said, and finally got a steer to Asa Gray County.

When the guy who did the talking told me what Buck had done to his sister, it went all over me. It was too much like Bekka, except it didn't go that far. Buck didn't kill his sister. She's still living, if you can call it that.

I tell you, I couldn't talk to him right then, not that day. I just had to walk away.

But since then, since that day we talked, he's been on my mind—the four of them have. We have a grudge in common. It might be a way to lay it on Buck Price without me being involved in any way. All I have to do is point Buck out, help set him up, and they'll do the rest, just like they said. Maybe kill him. I didn't know what or how, and I didn't have to know.

I meant to get with them before now, but too damned much has been happening, and since Jim Bob's funeral yesterday, with two to be avenged instead of one, there's no putting it off any longer. It's time for me to get off my duff. Bekka was my sister, too, but it sure as hell don't look like Luke is going to do a damned thing.

I started looking for the Baltimore dudes at the pool hall, but no one could rightly recall who I was hunting for, though some of the guys did remember some young punks looking for Buck.

The motels were no help either. They don't pay too much attention to who stays there, or how long the room is in use. Mostly they have two simple concerns: rent the room and get the money. So, for me, the motels were zilch.

Still, it was worth checking out, so I went to all of them, every motel within 30 miles of here. I needed to find the guys who wanted Buck. I fumbled my chance once and now I had to give it a try.

It's just plain logical to me. If I owned a motel, I know I'd keep an eye on four guys renting a room. More than that, it's one time I'd be sure to have the license plate numbers. Hell-raisers can do a lot of damage in short order. But I learned nothing at the motels—I mean nothing.

The town police and the sheriff's office weren't a lot of help either, at least not until I ran into Russ Silver at the Mountaineer Cafe. Wilfred wasn't with him so I didn't mind asking about those four guys.

Sure, I knew Russ would tell the sheriff about it, especially if I found them and if something came of it. He'd remember to tell Wilfred then, for sure, but it was a chance I had to take.

I got a cup of coffee at the counter and sidled back toward the booth where Russ sat alone. I tried to make it easy for him. I wanted him to ask me to sit down, and he did.

After we had been there for maybe five minutes, after I could see Russ was about to pay up and go back to the office, I said, "Someone told me they heard that Buck Price was going to leave town, Russ. Too many eyebrows being raised after Jim Bob's accident."

He gave me a funny look. Maybe I didn't pull it off the way I planned. After the look, he used his fork to chase the leftover egg around on his plate and then he said, "Who was that someone who said that, Matt?"

"I just left the pool hall," I said, "no more than five minutes ago. Buck wasn't there like he usually is this time of day."

"Who'd you say it was, Matt? Who told you that?"

I lied and I'm sure he knew it. "Well, I don't rightly know," I said. "I talked to a lot of people at Jim Bob's funeral—more than half the town was there. I wouldn't have thought of it again, about Buck going out of town, except he wasn't at the pool hall this morning. I just got to wondering."

Russ didn't ask again. He just looked at me without blinking. He has a way of boring right into your head, like he can see what you're not ready to tell. I tried to change the subject to what I wanted to know anyway.

"Did you know some guys—guys from out of town—was looking for Buck, Russ? They said they come from Baltimore, back there where he used to live."

The penetrating look didn't falter. He just kept his eyes locked on my face. After a long, long delay he said, "Someone tell you that, too, Matt, someone you don't remember?"

He was making me mad with that staring routine, so maybe I said more than I meant to say. Maybe not, but I'd like to have the words back.

I said, "No, dammit, it wasn't someone I don't remember. It was someone who took up with me at the pool hall, a guy from Baltimore and three buddies. One of them had a real grudge. I only talked to the one, but the others were right there all right."

"Hunting for Buck?"

"One of them was. Did you know about them?"

Russ is a good bit older than I am, he was a cop when I was just a kid, and he can make that age difference seem like a million years when he wants you to know—when he wants you to remember—he's a cop.

"Yes, son, I know about them four, had my eyes on them from the start. The Four Horsemen of the Apocalypse, that's what I called them. Up to no good. But they did nothing I could nab them for—and, like the Chamber of Commerce says, be nice to our summer people or our winters might get a little lean. They weren't staying here anyway, not in our county. They would just come in and knock around for an hour or so. Staying in Bakersville I think—over that way. But they kept their noses clean here, and that's all I cared about."

"Looking for Buck."

"Well, yes, maybe."

"No maybe, Russ. The one with the pigtail, he's the one I talked to, and he wanted to know where Buck lived, wanted to know if I'd point him out."

"And you didn't."

"Hell, no, I didn't."

A minute ago it was Russ who was ready to go, but now it was me. I wanted to head out for Bakersville. I wanted to find those guys. Maybe we could work something out.

wilfred huskins

I was parked in front of Harold Pendley's house at ten minutes of ten. Within two minutes, Edd and his son arrived. Buck was driving. That told me something right there. It was not only the fact that he was driving his daddy's car, but the look on his face made it clear he didn't want Edd along, but when you live at home, when you aren't working, or even trying to find work, you take a certain amount of shit for the privilege. You could see that much written across his face, and you could almost hear him saying, "Now, you stay out of it, Daddy. I can handle this yokel sheriff."

Keeping Edd out of it—out of anything that concerned his boy—was not going to be easy. Not for Buck; not for anyone. Edd was like an old Dominecker hen when the hawk was circling.

125

Jack R. Pyle

Whatever discussion Buck and Edd had had before they got to Harold's house didn't sink into Edd's marble dome. There wasn't a hair on that head, and it reflected the sunlight as we all three walked up the flagstones to the front porch. It was Edd who had the key in his hand and it was Edd who swung the door open and asked me in. Clearly, there was a conflict here. It could work to my advantage or to my disadvantage, so I had to be careful how I steered the conversation.

We were barely in the living room when Edd cleared his throat, but before he could say a word, Buck said, "Why don't you go make three cups of instant coffee, Daddy. It might make us all three more alert."

Buck was taking charge, and he wanted Edd to know it. The "make us all three more alert" had a meaning, too. It meant remember what we agreed to on the way over here, Daddy. Stay out of it.

As soon as Edd was out of the room, Buck turned back to me. "OK, Wilfred," he said, "whatever it is that's bugging you, let's lay it out and get to the bottom of it. I don't have all day."

He called me Wilfred. That was meant to undermine my official position, but I let it pass. I intended to stay just as alert as he was.

"Right. I don't have all day, Buck, and neither do you, so let me say it plain out: You were up there on Mace's Knob when Jim Bob went over the bank."

His blue eyes were cold, but they were dead on mine. There wasn't a blink, not a tic, not a single change of expression. "You were up there, boy." It was a flat statement. I called him "boy" on purpose. Two can play that game. "You were up there; you were the car Jim Bob was trying to pass."

"No, I wasn't, Perry Mason, but if I was, what would that prove?"

There was more of the eye combat between us and he hadn't blinked yet. I kept at it. "Are you willing to swear on the Bible that you were not up there on the Knob?"

126

"Hell, no," he said. "I was up there, going over to Granny Ballew's, but I came home by Burgins Creek. I went the long way. I wanted to see a man about a dog." Another smart-assed answer.

Edd came back with the coffee. "That's right, Wilfred. He come back that way to see a man about a bird dog. He come back from Granny's in the direction of the Knob, but he turned off there toward Ivy Gap. You know that road, and then he turned back to that little community at Burgins Creek."

"How do you know that, Edd? Were you there?"

"Buck told me, that's how. My boy don't lie."

"You don't have to talk for me, Daddy." He said it quiet, but there was steel hidden down there in the low tones. He spoke to Edd, but he still kept his eyes on me. It was almost like some kind of juvenile contest.

I decided to stop playing. It wasn't doing any good. I took my cup of coffee and went over to a pair of high-backed chairs on one side of the fireplace. "Did you see anyone, Buck? Did anyone see you out there at Ivy or at Burgins Creek?"

"That road ain't used much, Wilfred."

"Are you saying you didn't meet a single car, didn't wave at a single person, didn't stop to ask about that dog you might want to buy?"

"Now back off, Wilfred," Edd said. "You ain't got no call to badger Buck. He ain't no criminal. You ain't got no call at all."

"I just asked a simple question, Edd."

"It ain't a question, Wilfred. You're just plain calling my boy a liar, that's what you're doing. You're trying to make him say something that just ain't true."

Buck said one word. "Daddy."

"Now, son, if you ain't going to stick up for yourself, your daddy's got to do it. You told him that's the way you come home from Granny's, over there by Burgins Creek, and now your word ain't good enough. You're a Price, son. Our word is our bond. Always has been."

"Butt out, Daddy. The sheriff here, he's only trying to do his job. I know which way I came home. He won't find out no different. Just stay out of it, Daddy. Let him ask his questions."

You could see Edd was mad as hell at Buck, but it was me he glared at. I let it pass. I've been on the job for a year or two now, so I know that getting dirty looks are a part of my job description. I turned back to Buck.

"All right then," I said, "let's try the question again. You say you never met a car, never saw a person—not one—and that you went over that way looking to buy a dog and yet you never spoke to a soul about the dog or the man who owned the dog?"

"That's right, Wilfred," Buck said. "Didn't even find the place where the man had the dogs for sale. Bad directions, I guess." He was cool; he was in control.

"And you drove all the way over there—miles out of your way, because Mace's Knob is a lot closer way to come home— and you couldn't even find the house where the dogs were supposed to be, and you never asked anybody for directions? If you were in my place, Buck, wouldn't that story sound fishy?"

Buck laughed, took a sip of his coffee and then he said, "Sure it would, Wilfred. Fishy as hell. Sometimes facts are like that. Hell, man, sometimes a guy gets sent up for something he didn't do, just because his story sounds fishy. I can see why you have a hard time believing it, but that's the way it happened."

There wasn't a shred of proof, but I knew then Buck was up there on Mace's Knob that Sunday when Jim Bob went over the bank to his death. I might have distrusted my own feelings on this point, but there was Russ. He's been a cop for what seems like forever, and he has the instincts of a bloodhound, and he felt the same way. His gut feeling was that Buck was up there not only at the same time, but somehow tied into the accident.

And then there was this part about Buck going home by

way of Ivy Gap and Burgins Creek. The story really sounded like a cooked up alibi; it had the ring of a lead slug. We were onto something, but we didn't know exactly how it fitted in.

That was enough to have my antenna vibrating, but when I factored in Edd's behavior ever since I talked to him earlier in the morning, I had another important piece to the puzzle. It was more than the fact that he was nervous and fidgety; he was afraid of what Buck might say. All too often, a parent can't believe that a child has grown up, that he's an adult, that he can think like and act like an adult. Edd couldn't believe it about Buck. He had that parent syndrome that said some part of a child is always a child, and a child is apt to do dumb things.

Edd knew something about that accident—something I didn't know—and he hadn't enough confidence in his son to feel certain Little Boy Buck could keep it from me.

And then there was Buck himself. He hadn't said a word that told me Russ and I were right in believing he was a part of the accident on Mace's Knob. As was the case with his father, he didn't tell me in words, but he told me in actions. Clearly, Buck knew the story of how he came home. He knew it backwards and forwards. More than that, he had himself fully under control. He wasn't going to be rattled by anything I asked, so, except for what I gleaned from my instincts, my morning was a real bust. Even so, I tried it one more time.

"Now think about this, Buck—before you answer, remember back to that time. You drove from your Granny's back to that Ivy Gap road, whatever county road it is, and then you turned off toward Burgins Creek. You were looking for a man who had dogs for sale somewhere in that little Burgins Creek settlement. That's a long haul through there, Buck, and now you tell me that not one time did you see someone mowing the grass, working a field, driving a car—not one soul?"

"That's right, Wilfred."

"And you couldn't find the man who had the dogs for sale, and yet you didn't knock on a door, you didn't ask anyone about that man or for directions—even though you had gone out of your way to go there to see about a dog? Is that what you're saying?"

"Couldn't have said it better myself."

I ignored the smart answer. "Are you willing to take a lie detector test, Buck?"

"Volunteer? Hell no. Get a court order if you want anything more out of me, Sheriff." I heard the sarcasm. This time he said "sheriff," but it had a nasty sound to it.

"Come on, Daddy. I've said all I intend to say."

Chapter 16

sarah pendley

Unfortunately for all of us, there are times when we rush down stupidity's narrow hallway so fast that we don't see the door in front of us. That's the kind of simpleton I'd been. For a long time, I'd been taking a bath in self-pity. I'd been lolling there, neck deep, in that warm comforting tub, soaking in a bubble bath of my own personal misery.

I'm not sure when the first drops of good sense started seeping through to the dried cells of my brain, but today, for the first time, I know how silly I've been.

I guess this kind of painful truth had been pushing in on me for days, niggling at the back of my mind. I wouldn't let it through; the bubble bath was too comforting. I'd shove the thought back and hope it'd go away, but this morning I knew I was losing the battle. They say, "...truth will out." It looks like they're right.

Pretending just doesn't work, not anymore, not for me. All day, almost from first-light, I could feel the truth pouring over me like one of Preacher Thomas' soul-shaking sermons. It's a plain old takeover feeling. It grabs you. There's nothing you can do about it. You don't even know it's happening at first, like the time when I was a little girl and I tried to help Mama when we lost the battle mopping up water.

It got started at that sharp turn of the creek, right there below the house. Who knows what all had washed down from up on the hill that winter. The backup wasn't much at first, but when all that water got caught behind daddy's brand new stone wall, it pooled. In a short time, the creek made a boiling, muddy pond and then it just backed up so much we couldn't get in or out of the house. The brown water finally started seeping under the back door and staining the kitchen floor.

Daddy and the boys rolled up the rugs and tried to sweep the water out the front door, and I stayed with Mama in the kitchen. I'm sure at that age I couldn't have done much, but I helped Mama with the bucket and rags until we both knew we couldn't stop it. The water got deeper and deeper. We just sat down and cried.

Outside the window that day, those swirling eddies kept rising until finally the force of the dammed-up water tore loose a part of Daddy's stonework, and then a wall of water went rushing on down the creek sweeping out all the driveways and bridges in its path.

Our crying didn't help none then, nor has my tears helped this time. Even if you know you're a big, dumb cow, standing around letting your doleful eyes fill with tears, you never want to admit that you're the stupid one.

But, deep down, you know what you might not admit out loud: You know the water was rising.

That morning as I did the dishes, the picture of me as I had been since the last trial come in to overpower any resistance I had. The truth of the matter is that none of my excuses counted because there was nothing I could do to change what was here and now. It was misery, but most of it of my own making.

It was time for me to gather together all the broken pieces and make something of the rest of my life.

As I dried the dishes, I knew those pieces of my life—each one by itself—didn't look like much, but scraps for a quilt don't look like much either, until you take the time and do the work to make a pattern and stitch it together. No one would do it for me. The responsibility for tomorrow belonged to Sarah Ellen Pendley and to no one else.

By the time I got to washing the skillet—yes, this time Mama ate breakfast with me: grits, two eggs, two biscuits and a piece of liver mush—I had it all sorted out in my head. You kind of live your life on two levels, and they don't often match as you go along. The good parts, the parts you remember, are when the levels happen to meet, even if it's only for a short time.

One part of my life was here on the everyday level, and I'd managed to keep that part going along, before and after the last trial. I cooked, cleaned, and made a home for my brothers and my mother. I don't think this is work to be ashamed of, but sometimes it does get all lumped together and pushed off into a corner. When that happens, when you let that happen, it just don't feel like much.

The other part of my life, the part I'd been pulling all out of shape, is where your dreams are. My dreams had collapsed below a layer of self-pity.

I'm not the brightest girl in Asa Gray County, but there's a part of me that can be bone-honest, and this morning I guess I was ready to face the bare truth of it, even if some of it was ugly.

Morning light flooded the east windows in my kitchen, and in that light I knew that the dream part of me had been drowned in my poor-pitiful-Pearl routine—I'd felt so sorry for my lot in life that there wasn't a dream to be seen under the blue funk I had allowed to cover the pretty butterflies in my mind.

You have to have your dreams, but it's the living on the first level that puts together a life. It was the life I had on the first level that made me see how much I had killed the dreams that I needed if I were to survive.

As I put the dishes away, dry the iron skillet so it won't rust, and wipe up the spills on the linoleum floor, I suddenly remember how close Decoration Day is.

I had forgotten Decoration Day—or I had buried the thought of it—and yet it was almost upon us. Is it important? In this house, it certainly is; and, more than that, it's important to me. Since I was a real small girl, Decoration Day was always a time when I felt renewed. As I helped to attend to the graves down there at the churchyard, memories of the past somehow or other made me see a new way to look at the future.

Decoration Day is as important as Christmas or Thanksgiving—always has been, at least to the Pendleys. Maybe it's more important. It's the time when we all get together to repair the ravages of winter on our cemetery, but it's a whole lot more than that. It's a homecoming, a reunion—not just of family, although that is a part of it—but it's a reunion of everyone who has ever attended our church and who could make it back for that one day.

Decoration Day is almost here. In our church, it's always the Saturday before the second Sunday in June. Other churches have different days, but that's ours. We have it on Saturday so people who have moved off can come home for the weekend, and maybe stay over for the Sunday service.

It's a day I always looked forward to, but this year I had never even given it a thought—not the first thought.

Yes, it means extra cleaning, because we always have someone who doesn't have kin around anymore—someone who needs a place to stay—and it means extra cooking because we don't expect people who come from miles away to bring a covered dish.

I expect we do more cooking than most anybody else, because we're close to the church. Most of the time, it's our oven where some of the casseroles get reheated and the yeast rolls baked. And that's only right, not only because we're close by, but because we have been members since way, way before the new church was built. The old one was hit by lightning and burned back in 1934.

In years gone by, before Bekka died, we spent weeks before that special Saturday just planning on what all we would be making. Most times, days in advance, we'd be preparing and freezing all those things that could be done ahead of time.

And now, on this bright early morning in June, what had

been done? Nothing. I'd completely forgotten Decoration Day. Mama hadn't been speaking to me much, so maybe she had forgotten it, too. That special Saturday hadn't been mentioned at church, not that I could recall. Everyone knew when it was — when it had always been — so announcements just didn't seem necessary, I guess. But it's almost here. Something has reminded me of it.

I don't think Jesus watches over us every minute, taking in every detail, but I'm sure He is there when you truly need Him. If He's not with me this morning, what is it that makes me able to see so clearly — and what was it that reminded me of Decoration Day?

It's getting close to the Saturday before the second Sunday in June, time for me to find the renewal that I always felt when I cleared grass and weeds from around Daddy's headstone.

If He didn't tell me, who did? Who told me it's way past time for me to make a life for Sarah Pendley?

luke pendley

I guess I don't have a job no more. That's what Mark Slocum told me. He works in the bay next to me down at Robert's. He said the old man came in checking on the time cards, and he was madder than hell. The old man just said, "If you know someone that needs a job, Mark, that bay next to you is empty now."

Well, it wasn't the world's highest paying job anyway, and once this Buck thing gets cleared up, I won't be hanging around here anyway. I think I'll go to Charlotte. I can make more in Charlotte, and it will get me away from here.

Every time I turn around in this place, there's something to remind me of Jim Bob and Bekka, and ever time I think of them, I want to kick my own ass for not doing the job on Buck right after he walked out of there a free man.

Back then, before everybody started watching every move I made like I was some kind of nut or a bomb about to go off, I could have done it. I can see that now. But, oh, no, I wanted to make a big deal of it; I wanted to haul Buck up in Granny's cabin and I wanted to pour it to him; I wanted to see him squirm; I wanted to hear him beg and cry—I wanted crybaby tears to match those long curls of his.

And then, while he was begging and crying, I'd have done it, nice and slow, and I wouldn't have walked away from there till I knew he was beyond what any First Responder or the EMT could do to help him, even if he was found. There's an advantage to knowing how to save people—you also know something about putting them away, too.

But that's all in the past now and there ain't no callin' it back. I've been laying here in this bed most of the time since Jim Bob's funeral, telling Mama to go away and ignoring the rest. I've been thinking—or trying to think. When I get my head working right, I know that I'm going to have to eat crow with Dylan; I'm going to have to ask him to get that angel dust for me; I'm going to have to ask him to help me avenge Jim Bob and my sister Bekka.

That's the answer. There's nothing to do but do it.

I don't really remember taking a shower and dressing. I tried to move out of the house without making a fuss, but it didn't work. I remember hearing Mama say, "Where you going, Lukey?" but I just kept walking.

All of that is one of those almost memories—not worth remembering. What counts is that I'm at Dylan's house. He walks out to the car. I say, "Get in." He looks at me, hesitates for what seems too long, and then he gets in.

He's waiting for me to talk and I'm not sure how to say it. Quiet is hard to live with, and we both had a lot of it on that ride. When I turn off the main road onto that windy back road to Little Switzerland, he says, "You can take me back home, Luke, if you ain't got nothing to say. I figured you did."

"I do," I said.

"Well then, damn it, spit it out."

It was like vomit and just as bitter. It just spewed out of me. "Get the angel dust," I said, "soon as you can, and, Dylan, I mean now, right now, as soon as you can. It's my fault, I know that, but I can't take it back, I can't change it. You treat me like shit, but I know you know I didn't mean for what happened to Jim Bob to happen."

"Slow it down," he said. "You're driving too damned fast. You're going to kill us both."

I eased off the pedal, but my mouth wouldn't slow down.

"I was wrong in not killing that Buck bastard right after he killed Bekka. I knew then, Dylan, that's the worst part, I knew he did it. She told me some about her and Buck. It didn't mean nothing, just Bekka being Bekka, but when it happened, I knew right then he killed her. I knew it."

"Damn it, Luke. Slow down. You're going to kill us. Pull off at the trout ponds. Park the damned car. Then you can do your talking."

I did what he said. The ponds are just ahead on the right. I slow it down and ease in over the culvert. I shut the motor off and turn out the lights, but I can't stop talking, not even for a second.

All the things that had been running through my mind since Bekka died came to a head when Jim Bob went off that road, and they damned near drove me crazy.

I'm all right. I know what I have to do, but I do need Dylan's help. My mind's OK, it's under control, but somehow I just keep talking.

"I was dee-double wrong when I didn't kill him after the second trial, Dylan. You have to know that, buddy. I was wrong. You guys told me, but I had to plan it all out, I had to make a big deal."

And then I start to cry. The tears came on me so fast there's no way I could hide them. I'm making a blubbering fool of myself and I just can't stop.

Dylan is a good guy, a real friend. He pretended not to

notice, but his silence didn't help me none. I've never cried like that before—not when Daddy died, or not for Bekka, but Jim Bob just broke the dam. Maybe I was crying for all of them—or crying because I know what a shithead I am—but it didn't matter.

I try to hold back and quiet down. I almost get it done, and then the pain comes back in a rush and I just can't stop making a complete ass of myself.

To his everlasting credit, I'll have to say this for Dylan: He never said a word, he didn't touch me and he acted like he didn't see me. It was as though he wasn't even there.

Finally, just as the moon is coming up, I get the crazy crying stopped. Then it gets so quiet I can hear the night sounds and the muffled roar of the rapids farther down the creek. I'm weak and slumped over the wheel like an empty tow sack, with no more tears, no sounds and no strength.

Then I hear Dylan say, "I'll help you, buddy. We'll do what has to be done."

Chapter 17

wilfred huskins

I'd had a few calls in the past four or five days that made me stop and think. They were always when I was at home, and they always ended abruptly whenever I said hello. At first, I just thought, wrong number. Then I thought, kids—a kid's idea of fun. But lately, after maybe six or seven of the funny calls, they began to bug me.

I have a job that offends a few people from time to time. It's one of the drawbacks of being sheriff in this end of the state. I grew up in Asa Gray County. I know the folks here in the mountains don't like the law interfering in their lives—or even what they think of as interfering—so a prank call or two has not been that unusual since I took office, but these calls were different. There were no threats, no words—not even heavy breathing. I didn't know what to make of them.

And then I had another call, one left at home on the machine. I wondered if that message just might be the answer to my questions about the many calls I'd been having for several days. Maybe yes and maybe no. Anyway, this call was from Marylou. The taped message was short. I heard no anger in her voice, but somehow I had the feeling she was talking to me the way she'd talk to a stranger.

She said: "Wilfred, this is Marylou." As if I wouldn't know the voice. "We need to talk." I thought, boy, do we, and then I listened to the rest of the taped message. "Can you meet me at the Cafe in Malaprop's Bookstore in Asheville at seven on Thursday? It's on Haywood, near the Civic Center."

Nice and neat, where and when. Efficiency is ordinarily one of Marylou's good points, but this time it seemed different. "If you can't be there, call my mother. She'll take the message for me." Then I heard the click. "...my mother?" That's what she said.

At that moment, I had a sharp picture of my own Granny Ledford. Granny had a way of saying things that got to the heart of the matter. In times of crisis, her instincts were unerring. I could almost hear her say these words, "This bodes no good."

The tone of Marylou's voice was enough to make me a little leery, but the fact that she asked me to meet her in a public place seemed even more a jarring note, and then when she said, "...call my mother," I had to agree with Granny Ledford, "This bodes no good."

The Marylou I knew would have said "call Mama," or "leave a message with Mama." I never had heard her call Mrs. Carlyle "my mother," even on our first dates.

Something was really different between Marylou and me. "My mother" was about as formal as when I got stopped at the front door by Mrs. Carlyle—by Emily—when I drove to Sylva to talk to Marylou shortly after she left our house for the last time.

Oh, yes, like Granny Ledford used to say, "This bodes no good..." Sometimes that old lady's sayings hearkened back to another day, often with words you don't hear much anymore, but it was best to listen to her.

Granny's been gone a good many years now, so I picked up the dictionary and looked up the word "bode," just to see what her message truly was. I found it there, of course. The word is now considered archaic, but it was there. It said, "bodes ill (or well) to be a bad (or good) omen."

No, Granny didn't say "ill" or "well," but bodes no good was clear enough.

As I drove over to Asheville Thursday evening to meet

Marylou, it was with anything but a light heart. That word "bode" still stayed in my brain. No problem about where I was going. I knew where Malaprop's was, and I knew about the Cafe downstairs.

I hadn't stopped to think of it, but there was a message there, too. We weren't meeting for dinner at my kind of meat-and-potatoes place. This was a Marylou kind of setting. It was a place where you'd be more likely to get sprouts, tofu, and cappuccino. I remembered it. I'd taken her there to buy books while I did other errands, and for all its old-fashioned bookstore atmosphere, it was hardly the place for the great reconciliation. It was not a place I'd choose for "make-up time," with candlelight to set the stage.

As I walked to the back of the store and down the steps, I realized how the word "bode" was back in the center of my mind. It was not Granny's word now; it was my own. The actual word the squeaking stairs said to me as I walked down was "foreboding," a premonition, a forewarning.

Then I saw Marylou, way to the back of the room at one of those little tables. She looked pale. As I walked toward her, she stood and extended her hand, and that gesture was clear, too. No kiss. Not even on the cheek, not even one of those miss-kisses you see all the time. It was a businesslike handshake.

Sure, the message was clear, but I was there; I'd hear what she had to say, although I wasn't there to beg her to come home when I didn't really feel I had done anything all that wrong. Would I like her to come on home? Of course. Of course I would, but I've been stubborn to a fault many times before, and this, beyond question, was one of those times. Pride? Sure. I admit it.

"Thank you for coming, Wilfred," she said. "I know I owe you some kind of an explanation, but I'm not sure I can do it — not in a way you'll understand."

"Try me."

She was drinking a frothy looking cappuccino. I signaled the counterman for two more.

At first she just sat there—not looking at me; not looking at anything, really. I picked up the two drinks, paid the guy and went back to the table.

"Don't push it, Marylou," I said. "When you're ready, the words will come, and if they don't, I think I know."

There were tears in her eyes. It's a hell of a thing to say, but I was grateful for the tears. I just didn't want to think there had never been anything between us. I thought we loved each other—I know we both thought that when we got married, but something had happened.

When at last she spoke, I could hardly hear her. "As I drove over here, Wilfred," she said. "I tried to find words you'd understand for something that is truly my problem, not yours."

I knew this was painful for her. The eyes were still teary and the voice far from strong. I reached for her hand. I wanted to let her know I understood. As I reached, she withdrew. Was it to take another sip of her drink? I don't know.

She said, "I can't explain our situation in any kind of simple way. It's not a simple thing. Just let me say what I have to say to you the only way I know how, in words that I've had in my mind all these weeks, no matter how silly those words may seem. Just listen, please, Wilfred, and try to let my words make sense, in a way that you'll understand. I do want you to understand."

I didn't say anything, but my heart ached for her, and I'm sure she could see it on my face. This time she reached for my hand and I didn't withdraw.

"This much you must believe, Wilfred, when we were married, not that long ago—but it seems so long ago—I loved you. I know that in my own way I still do, but it has changed, it all has changed, in ways that I just can't put into words."

There was nothing for me to say, nothing that would not ring hollow the moment the words were out of my mouth. She squeezed my hand, but I knew it was out of the pain she felt, not out of passion. I didn't return it.

"When I went to Mama's this last time, I knew things were not right—not right in my own mind—but I didn't know how far apart we were—how far from you I was."

I heard Granny Ledford's soft voice again, "It bodes no good..."

"We're at an end, Wilfred. This may sound silly, but for me it's like I'd been spending a quiet evening at home, warm and comfortable, curled up on the sofa, with a cup of coffee, listening to a wonderfully recorded Brahms Symphony. And then the door bell rings. I go to answer it. I take care of whatever it is. But when I return, the spell has been broken— it has been, somehow, irretrievably altered. The symphony, at least for me, is over. Something subtle in my world has shifted. Something has changed, indefinably changed, and then it's reshaped."

Marylou was talking to me, looking at me, but the words were meant for her more than for me. It was as though she were sorting her thoughts and just letting them spill out. I just sat there, listening.

"Right then it was all clear to me," she said. "That moment, that perfect moment, is in the past. The wonderful music, the comforts, the contentment and the aura of the symphony are all gone. And, strangely, all the moments before are gone, too. I don't know where those moments have flown, but I know they are in some distant place—someplace where recovery is not possible, not for me."

Her eyes were brimming with tears and pain. I gave her my handkerchief.

"Am I—" She stopped, wiped her eyes and then looked deeply into mine. "I'm so sorry." She dabbed at her eyes again, and returned my handkerchief. I could see the stain of mascara on the cloth. "Does any of this make sense?"

I said what she wanted to hear. I said yes. I said it made sense. I said it because I think I did understand. I'm not great for Brahms, but somehow her words—how she said them and how I understood them—took some of the pain out of losing her.

Right then I knew it was over. I'm not sure why it's over, but I know it is. We were both there, sitting at that little table, but in that moment, the present was suddenly the past, irretrievably the past. What had been—whatever it was—was no more.

It's not a case of fault—not hers or mine. Who can be blamed for what may have been a natural chain of events that affected the lives of two people—two people who, I sometimes believe, should never have been together in the first place?

So I told her what she had to hear. I told her I understood.

She looked into my eyes; she wanted to be sure. She wanted to be sure that I did understand, and then the tears really began to fall. I gave her my handkerchief again. This time she eagerly reached for it.

As I drove home shortly after that, it was almost without feeling. There was no anger, no hurt, no tears. It was an empty feeling, a coldness in the pit of my stomach, a kind of echoing sadness. And I thought of another stray line, a quote from Dorothy Parker: "Scarlet red for a love that is dead."

Not always, but sometimes my instinct tells me the right thing to do or not do. While I was with Marylou, it told me not to ask about the funny phone calls I had been receiving for about a week. Maybe they were hers; maybe she called and lost her nerve.

For my sanity's sake, I had to ignore the cold lump in my stomach. I forced my mind to move on. I didn't want to replay any part of it. I had to put Marylou out of my mind but when I did, I remembered the phone calls.

Since I didn't ask her about them, I had to wonder as I drove home: what about those calls. Were they hers, or is there something going on I ought to know about? Did I have a new worry to go with all the older relics I couldn't shuck?

sarah pendley

Let me tell you right now, my heart was not in the unpleasant job Mama had given me, but I went upstairs to knock on Luke's door because I promised her I would. When we give our word, we keep it. That's one of the things a Pendley learns real early.

I almost got a whipping once a long time ago when I wouldn't give my word, I wouldn't make Mama a promise. I don't even remember what it was about now, but it was something I just couldn't do, so I point blank refused to say the words.

Mama's face got red, she grabbed me by the shoulder and pulled me around, and I knew I was going to get it for sure, but I didn't. Papa walked in the door just at that minute.

Papa hated a fuss of any kind. "What's going on?" That was all he said, but Mama let go of my shoulder.

"This child is disobedient, unruly and disrespectful, and I won't have it. You whip her or I will."

Papa asked what I had done, and she told him. She told him how sassy I looked at her, and she told him that I wouldn't promise not to do whatever it was again.

Papa turned to me. "All right, young lady..." He just let his voice trail off. It was the way he treated all of us, but we'd better have a reason.

"I can't promise, Papa," I said. "If I promise, I'd be giving my sacred word, and if I did promise and couldn't keep my promise, I'd be lying and sinning, wouldn't I?"

"You can't argue with that, Ora Lee. When a Pendley makes a promise, he means to keep it."

And that was the end of it.

As I say, a promise is a promise—I'd made one to Mama. If a Pendley says she will, she will, so I went up the stairs and knocked on Luke's door.

We went through all the go-away and no-I-won't arguments that you could expect from a brother and sister, but when he saw I meant to stay, rousing the whole house if I had to, he opened the door and let me in.

He sat on the edge of his rumpled bed. I stood. I wanted to be sure I said what I had come there to say, and I was afraid that sitting down might lower my determination.

Luke has a way of saying "dumb girl" to me without even using the words—he'd done it for years—and I just wasn't going to let that happen this time.

Oh, yes, I know this was a time when I should have said no to Mama, but she seemed a little warmer toward me than she had been and I welcomed that, and she seemed so pitiful when she was crying over "Lukey." It may have been weak of me, but I'd given my word, so I kept it.

"Everyone is worried about you, Luke."

"Everyone? Is that what you beat my door down to say?"

"Yes, we all are. You're not eating right. You're turning into skin and bones. We're worried, but that's not why I'm here, and you know it."

"Mama sent you."

"Mama made me promise I'd talk to you. She thought you might listen to me, since we're closer in age."

"Big joke."

"I thought so, too."

"But, Sarah, just to take you off the hook, you tell Mama that I'll be at supper tonight, providing she stays off my back. You tell her if she says one whiny word, I'll get up and leave. You tell her everything is going to straighten out before long and that Lukey—God how I hate that name—Lukey will gain his weight back in time."

"Thanks, Luke. I'll tell her."

I was grateful to him for some kind of message I could give Mama, because I knew I was on a fool's errand as I came up the stairs, and if he was really ready to be a part of the family again, that would be good news for all of us, especially for Mama.

There was only one thing, though, just those few words, but they jarred at my mind. Maybe the words meant nothing; I hope so. But, I think he said, "...everything is going to straighten out before long."

Oh, Luke.

Chapter 18

wilfred huskins

The stark truth of yesterday didn't hit me until I woke up this morning.

Yes, in the hollows and the coves of my mind, I knew it was over between Marylou and me. I knew it; I simply didn't want to admit it.

It was more than the ride home last night and the empty feeling I had then. As I lay there in a cold bed, I forced myself to look at the present, and I had to admit that the realities were plain to see.

I'd been dumped. Was there someone else, or was I just a dud as a husband? I didn't like the answer to either question.

Early morning thinking is harsh enough, but when you use such a time for honest thinking, you get honest answers. Lying there that chilly morning, when I thought about my life since Marylou went to her mother's the last time, I had to admit that all along I'd known.

When I stop trying to put another face on our problems, I had to admit, I knew. There's a part of me that doesn't want to accept the failure of our marriage. But, in truth, I knew it was over when I got home that first night and found the empty little note she left for me; I knew it even better when I went to her mother's house and had to stand on the porch like a door-to-door salesman.

Knowing it is one thing; facing it is another. As we talked in Malaprop's, as we drank our cappuccinos and kept wearing our we're-adult-and-terribly-civilized faces, I overlooked—or maybe ignored—everything I knew was fact.

I couldn't do that this morning. I awoke with the empty spot on the bed beside me and with the unshakable realization that whatever today turned out to be, it would never be yesterday. That was past and gone. I wouldn't lie to myself any longer. The stark fact that my marriage was over was a jolt I couldn't shake off. That realization latched onto the air I drew into my lungs and it was like the icy air you swallow with the final awareness of any other death, when that cold fact finally seeps into your belly and then into your brain.

The coldness I inhaled was more than the unseasonable briskness of the mountain air we can sometimes get, even in June. It was the bone-chilling realization that a part of me had withered with that little bit of civilized talk about a Brahms symphony and a lost mood. Easy talk. But today I knew that no matter how I tried to ignore it, my life had changed and changed radically. I now lived in a bachelor's house.

The shower and all the bathroom steam didn't help, nor did the cold cereal and coffee. We are all guilty of griping about work, but, in truth, it should be lauded. It's natural pain killer, it's the opiate of the poor, it's the healer of the mind and body. Feeling as I did, work was the only way I had to turn.

I called Rachel, told her I wouldn't be in, and that I was heading over beyond Mace's Knob to talk to the folks at Dillingham's store, and to all the people I could find along the road there.

I planned to start with Buck's Granny Ballew and his Uncle Arly. As I parked the car at the old, square-looking, white Ballew house, I saw the curtain on the kitchen window drop back into place. I knew she saw me; I figured she had been told I'd be out there, and I was sure I was expected when no one came to the door to greet me. I had to knock.

The back door was standing open and I could see through

149

the screen as I rounded the corner of the house. The smell of fried bacon clung to the morning glories she had trellised by the back stoop.

She's slightly built, Granny Ballew is, and crippled with arthritis. I could see her trying to get old puss-and-guts Arly to eat a little breakfast, but with his beet-red face and the lost look in his watery-blue eyes, she wasn't going to have a lot of success.

He might drink the coffee, but it was more than likely that he'd rather have a little of the hair of the dog. And sometimes that cure works; sometimes a nip or two of what brought you the misery will help you choose to stay in the world a little longer.

It was quickly over with Granny Ballew. She didn't hedge or lie to me, but there just wasn't much she added to what I already knew. She told me what a sweet and wonderful boy Buck was and how he came every Sunday, that he chopped firewood for her, and how he did all the things Arly wasn't able to do because of his sickness.

And then I tried Arly. He was sick all right, with a virus he got from John Barleycorn. It was hard to miss the symptoms. I wondered how she couldn't know what was wrong with Arly, but maybe she was like I'd been with Marylou, maybe she just didn't want to know.

As I looked at Arly, slumped in a ladderback chair like a half-filled burlap bag of potatoes, lumpy and spreading out over the caned seat, I just could not understand how old Mrs. Ballew could see less than I did. And if she couldn't see it, how could she miss the smell of stale liquor and vomit? Maybe she could still see the Arly that used to be inside that hulk. Mothers seem to be able to do that.

"Do you remember that Sunday when Jim Bob Williams had the accident up on the Knob, Arly?" He rolled those blood-shot eyes in my direction but didn't say a word. "Do you recall what time Buck started back home?"

He blinked at me a few times, pushed a fist at one teary eye and then he said, "I ain't much on memory, not no more. Seems like it must have been like he always done, come in and stay an hour or two. Buck would cut a little wood and do a chore or two and then go on home."

"About what time did he leave that day?"

"I don't know, Wilfred. I just don't know a time, if that's what you want. I don't pay much attention to clock time, anyways. Buck, he's a good boy, though, I tell you. He's not afraid of a little work, you can bet that. I ain't neither, not when I'm feeling good, but I've been pretty sick for a spell."

I left them and went on down the road to where Carlton Laws lives. It's across the road and within sight of the Ballew house. The Laws might be able to give me some kind of time reference. It was worth a try.

Nothing. I got the treatment that lawmen can get out on the backroads. The door was opened only a crack and my questions got answered with a minimum of words.

At Dillingham's store, I found the checkerboard set up, but no one was playing. There were two men there on the porch with chairs tilted back against the front of the store.

As I got out of the car one of them said, "What you doing way out here, Sheriff? You got a desperado on the loose out this way?"

I ignored the humor and tried to find out something about Buck. The gist of my big-time investigation was: No, no one had seen Buck that day, the day of the accident; yes, he did help out his granny right smart; no, he didn't usually come out this way to go back to town—too fur to go out to the highway and then go back thataway. The road ain't so good, but the Knob's a better way.

I asked who had bird dogs for sale.

"Out this way?"

"Well," I said, "here or over in the Burgins Creek Community—anywhere out on this side of the Knob?"

Jack R. Pyle

"Bird dogs? Ain't no one I know. You know someone, Shelby?"

"No, not bird dogs. They's a man over there toward Brushy, he's got some dogs for sale. One of them Shufords. Right about where you turn off for Burgins Creek. Second house below the bridge. They ain't bird dogs, though. Red Bones, ain't they, Wilbur?"

"Billy Shuford? He's got dogs for sale?"

"Shore has. Red Bones."

"Can't be Billy Shuford, Shelby. He likes them Blue Tick hounds."

"No, I tell you, it is Billy, Billy Shuford."

I left them arguing, and I drove out to see Billy Shuford. He was home, messing around in his tobacco plot. He liked to talk, Billy did, but he didn't know anybody with bird dogs.

"Not out this way," he said. "Dilbo Hoskins has some, but he lives way over yonder, almost to Marshall. If you're lookin' for a good bird dog, Sheriff, you might go see old Dilbo. He's got good'uns."

It wasn't until I started driving back to town that I thought about Marylou again. It's going to take some time before I get her out of my mind. One thing I better get in my mind though: It's over. It's past and gone. I know it. I could tell by the set of her jaw.

And about Buck: Well, I found out nothing about Buck, except for one thing. He was lying about the man with the bird dogs. There was something here to find out. I decided to let Russ give it a try. I may be from Asa Gray County, but I'd been away to school and stayed away a year or two beyond that, so, somehow, I just didn't get trusted as much as old Russ.

I'd let Russ see what he could do out here in this end of the county.

sarah pendley
I can tell you I was some kind of glad when Mama brought

her sewing into the kitchen to sit with me while I baked for the big homecoming that Decoration Day always is.

Spending time with me is another crack in the ice; it's a good sign. It's the first time me and Mama had any kind of pleasant talk since Buck got off scot-free. Oh, it's true she took a little time with me after Jim Bob's funeral, but that was for a reason, that was so I'd promise to talk to Luke. Whatever her reason, I was glad to talk to her then, and I'm glad to do it now.

"You making that dress for Decoration, Mama?"

She held it up for me to see. "Do you like it? I've still got a lot of hand sewing to do, and I'm going to make the collar and cuffs out of this old tatting of Granny Hall's. It's from that trunk upstairs. It must have been around forever, and it's going to be just right for this dress."

"Kind of old-fashioned."

"It's meant to be, Sarah. Everything about a homecoming says old or old-fashioned. It's a day for those that have gone to their reward. I don't know why I never made a dress like this one before. Look at this, Sarah, you talk about old-fashioned, I even made covered buttons to go all the way down the front, sixteen of them."

"Lot of work to get in and out of that dress, Mama."

"No, Sarah. I'm putting a zipper in the back. The buttons are just for show."

"Long sleeves—"

"To cover my crepe arms. I declare, the skin on my arms looks like rhinoceros hide. Long sleeves are a good thing for me. It's one of the reasons I chose this old-fashioned pattern."

"Where'd you find that at, Mama? What store had that?"

"No store. It was in Granny Hall's things—the trunk I brought from the old house, the trunk where I found this tatting. It's up in the attic. You remember."

She twisted the hanger and hung the dress from the top of the door to the pantry.

"It's an old pattern, turning yellow. I had to be careful using it; you talk about brittle. I don't remember Granny wearing a dress exactly like it, but it's a lot like the one in her picture, isn't it, the one in the family room?"

The dress was fitted at the top, with a high neck and long sleeves, and it had a full skirt that would go down to Mama's ankles.

"Where'd you ever find that green, gingham-looking print? That cloth looks like it might have belonged to Granny Hall, too. Tiny little flowers and leaves all over the place. Why, Mama, wearing that dress, you'll fade right into the background over there at the cemetery."

"Oh, no, I won't. I'll be noticed you can bet on that. I'll be the only one there in a period dress."

"Yes, Mama, I expect you will."

"You see how long it is? And with long sleeves and those covered buttons. It'll be noticed, you wait and see."

Mama's new dress wasn't something I'd want to wear. I'll probably be in slacks or jeans, anyway. A lot of work has to be done at every Decoration Day, so I know I'd better dress for comfort. But, Mama— Well, Mama never did all that much at a Homecoming, not since Papa died and she went to work at the mill.

Then Mama began the tedious work of attaching the old tatted lace to the collar and cuffs. She paid no attention to what I was doing. She had to be careful to hide her stitches.

I got us both a cup of coffee, and in a few minutes, with the smell of my sheet cake filling the room, and with Mama sewing and rocking in that creaking rocker, it was almost like old times.

The kitchen was quiet for a while, and then, almost in time with the creaking sounds the rocker made, she began to tell me about the little problems she'd been having down at the thread mill. Oh, they were nothing major, just little personality spats and gossip of what all went on down there at the mill—things she always told me before Bekka died. It was truly like old times.

Bekka had always been Mama's favorite, I knew that, but when it was time to talk to someone about her own little problems, it wasn't Bekka. It was me Mama talked to, maybe because I was older, and maybe because I listened better than Bekka.

Whatever the reason, on that cold and wet morning in June, she just sewed, rocked, and talked, and the next thing I knew, I was talking, too. I'd been wanting to tell Mama about laying-up there at Granny's cabin with Buck. It had really been on my mind for such a long time. I told the sheriff, of course, but it's not the same as talking to another woman, even if she is your own Mama.

We've got a few Catholics living here in Asa Gray County, and there's a priest that comes in for mass every other Sunday. I can't say I understand their religion, because I don't, but there has always been one thing that didn't make a lot of sense to me before. I couldn't understand why Catholics went to confession. If you sinned, why tell someone—a man, a priest—about it? I think I understand that better now.

I've never really had anything big that bore in on my mind before, anything that really hung back there making me feel bad every day of my life. I heard about sin at church, of course, but I truly didn't know what it was. Children seldom do. But that was before, that was when I was younger. That was before Buck.

Maybe that's why I couldn't see the reason for telling someone what you'd done. I always felt, if you'd done it, and you were sorry, you could ask for forgiveness all by yourself. But something made me tell Mama all about Buck, all the parts that made me want to cry at how bad I'd been, and how—however terrible I felt—I couldn't help going to meet him if he sent me the signal or if I sent it to him.

I'm truly grateful to Mama. She didn't so much as raise an eyebrow—not even one time. She seemed to know how I felt, honest she did. It was just two girls talking about the problems that one of them had. No fingers were pointed; no judgments were made.

And, as I spoke, I knew how much the confessions must have meant to Mary Agnes McBride, one of my best friends in High School. When she began to talk about going to confession in those years, she lost me. But that was back then.

Now, as I talked to Mama, it didn't change what I had done, but somehow a burden was lifted from my shoulders.

For the first time, I knew what Mary Agnes meant about going to confession, and while Mama can't forgive sins like God can, her quiet listening was something I'll always be grateful for.

I know I'll never be able to explain how just talking to Mama helped me so much, but it did.

Mama had stopped her sewing. She was listening to every word I said, and I know she loved me. I could see the pain on her face and the tears in her eyes.

Talking, just talking—my kind of confession—seemed to relieve a boxed-up part of my mind, and, somehow, my talking was more than just words to both of us: It was a way of letting Mama know how sorry I was for all the shame I brought on the family. It was my way of trying to make her understand.

Somehow, right then, I felt I was a daughter again.

So you see, our talk was more than just getting all the wickedness of Buck out into the open, and more than letting Mama know how sorry I was for all of it. Our time together was something else—something I can't explain.

It was much more than either of the things I've told you about; but, honestly, I can't explain the rest of it.

Whatever it is, it was there for me and it still is. I don't know how to say it any better. It's something that just is—it just is.

Chapter 19

harley phillips

I have to admit that the idea was John's, and at first I was almost too dumb to know what was going on. Sure, I wanted to see Sarah, I wanted to ask her to be my wife, but I just kept charging in there, trying to let her know how much I loved her, and she just kept pushing me away.

It wasn't until John showed me the way with his trumped-up misunderstanding of our real estate deal that I realized the only way I was ever going to get anywhere with Sarah was if I come at it in some indirect way.

When I finally got that through my wooden head, it was carved there for keeps. I had no trouble at all finding reasons why I had to go by the Pendley house to see John. Of course, it had to look real, and part of it was. You never go into a complicated deal like John and me had without some things, some little problems, that just have to be worked out, or you blow the whole thing right out of the water.

You know John is tight as the bark on a sapling, so when a couple of big old trees out there on that leased land had to be cut down because shrubs don't do good in too much shade, John put up a kick. He told me I was leasing the land, but I damned sure couldn't go in there and destroy timber that was old when his daddy was young. Now a tree or two ain't what I call timber, but John, he got so wound up on that one that I thought our deal was going to fall through.

When I think on it, I still don't know if he meant every word he said or whether his loud hell-raising was meant to show

Sarah that there was good reason why I should be over there as much as I was. Maybe it was some of both.

Anyways, John the great protector of the environment, Mr. Greenpeace himself, finally come around when I agreed to take the trees down, send them off to Gilley's sawmill down at Brush Creek and have them made into lumber he could use for the old-fashioned, handmade, pegged-together furniture John liked to make in that little shop of his.

I tell you true, he made that difference of opinion last long enough for me to make three visits to the Pendley house before we come to an agreement.

The last time, Ora Lee, Mrs. Pendley came in and told us to behave. That's just how she said it, like we were both spoiled kids instead of grown men, and I guess maybe that's what we were, because after she said her piece and closed that door, we managed to work out the deal that we now have.

Talking about the same thing, the tree deal, there was another time when I was to meet John there at the Pendley place late in the afternoon. He was late. For a time, I sat in the parlor—or the company room or whatever you might to call it—but when he didn't show up for so long, I went on back to the kitchen.

Sarah was there, of course. That June day was chilly and gray and getting worse. She was baking. I tell you when she opened that oven door and took out two pans of fresh-baked rolls and put them on the stove top, the smells in that kitchen made your knees plumb weak. I just shut my eyes and breathed it in. Fresh yeast rolls. Man, you know your nose is just plain never going to get any closer to paradise than that.

And you also have to know that things have been more than touchy with me and Sarah since all the courtroom confessions come out. I try to pick and choose my words with her so that I won't say something to get her mad at me all over again. But this time I wasn't thinking, I wasn't choosing my words, and they just come out as bold as if I was in my own mama's house.

"Sarah, darling," I said, "unless you want me to die right here, you'll give me a cup of coffee, a couple of them hot rolls and some of that good butter you ain't supposed to be buying from old Mrs. Weatherman."

Well, I tell you, there was a time there I thought I had tore it wide open, and then I saw a softer look on her face. She didn't say a word, but she poured a cup of coffee, put two rolls on a little plate and pushed a bowl of fresh-churned butter across the table to me.

"John's late," I said. I can say the stupidest things when I manage to embarrass myself, which is pretty often anymore when I'm around Sarah. I could feel the blood pumping into my neck and ears. She didn't seem to notice.

"He is, or you got the time wrong." There was no smile on her face, but I thought I saw one, just for an instant, in her eyes.

"Sit down, Harley. You can't enjoy my rolls standing up." She poured another cup of coffee and sat down across from me.

When you're at bat, and when you stupidly swing at every wild pitch, when you go way past three and you're still striking at every sucker ball thrown, and then here comes a slow ball just high enough for you to send it clear out of the ballpark, you know somehow your luck has changed. That's how it seemed to be right then. By doing nothing, somehow I had connected with that ball, and it was sailing off into tomorrow.

She didn't seem wary of me. Her talk was easy, about Decoration Day down at the church, and about the peas just coming in in the garden, and about how much we needed the rain that was fast becoming more than a mist outside.

At that moment, with the heat and smells of the room, with the taste of country butter and hot bread, with no tension in the air, and with Sarah, pretty Sarah, right there across the table from me, I knew how it could be for us, and the thought of it gave me that deep-down feeling you get when you round a curve in springtime and see the fresh green look of a valley spreading out before you. It's a gut feeling. It's a personal rush of plea-sure that can't be touched or tinkered with or it will go away.

And then John came on the porch, stomping his boots on the mat and pulling off a slicker to hang on a peg outside.

"I'm late."

Sarah seemed to be able to anticipate her brother's every move. Before John got fully inside the door, she had taken a towel from the cupboard. As she handed it to him, she said, "Wipe your feet again, John, and get the wet out of your hair and beard before you drip that mess all over the floor."

You might think that the moment was over with John's ar-rival, but that's not the way it was. Oh, it had changed. It was no longer like I had her all to myself in a house of our own, in a kitchen filled with our very own bread smells, but it wasn't over. There was a lingering difference.

As she shuttled us both back to the company room with more coffee and rolls, it was with a kind of acceptance I hadn't felt be-fore. Without seeming to do anything that was different, she lumped me in with her brother in a kind of intimate family way that gave me with the feeling that somehow we, Sarah and me, had passed a milestone or turned a corner, or something like that. Right then I knew I'd have to do something really stupid to get back the sharp-tongued Sarah that I had known in recent times.

That was the best time, but it wasn't the only time. Some-times I'd have to drive away from the Pendley house before I knew it had happened for sure, but once I could think clearly, once I was away from her, I knew there was more of a warm feeling between us, a feeling like the one that had been there way back when Sarah was friendly and kind to a scared boy on his first day at school.

As usual, I would be at the Decoration Day at our church to help with the work on the graves and the mowing and trim-ming, but this time I was like a kid waiting for Christmas be-cause I knew I'd be around Sarah all day. This was going to be a day John didn't have to arrange.

sarah pendley

He called me "Sarah, darling." My mind said those words over and over again, and I heard, as if for the first time, the way he spoke them. "Sarah, darling..., Sarah, darling..., Sarah, darling..."

All along, ever since right after Buck's last trial, I wanted to think there was no taint to the way Harley felt about me, that he wasn't coming on to me just because I was that kind of girl, but when he tried to get me to go for a ride with him, I just couldn't think anything else.

Go for a ride with him! What else could it mean? Out away from town, out where nobody would see us together. I couldn't do it—no, I wouldn't do that secret date thing, not ever again, not with Harley or anyone.

However much I remembered those secret times with Buck, no matter how much they stirred the blood in my veins, that kind of soul-killing thing will not happen again.

There comes a time when the shame of what you've done outweighs all else, and it took more than Buck's sometimes cutting and degrading remarks to make me see my own folly. On that last day, it took the violence that exploded all over Granny's cabin.

I'm not saying that the feel of Buck's hands, the smell of him, the warmth of his body, never entered my mind again. If I said that, I'd be lying. And, yes, in other ways, I'd seen the wild side of Buck before that last day, but when I saw the craziness on that day, when it sunk in my passion-addled head how close I'd come to the hereafter, I knew what I must never do, not ever again. I must never lose the love of myself.

No, I was most assuredly not going for a ride with Harley, or with any of the others. Yes, there has been others with their half-disguised invitations.

Life hasn't been easy for me since I testified at the trial, and when I stop to think of how little good all my blabbing did, it galls me that I ever believed I could bring justice to bear. I know Wilfred believed that what I told in court might convict Buck, but Wilfred was wrong. There's proof of the pudding right in front of my face every day: Bekka is dead; Buck walks the streets; and I'm shamed all over the county, and even with my own family. There have been many times when I'd just like to drive to a quiet place on Lake James and walk out into the deep water and keep on walking, but I don't have the courage for that either.

But now, now that I've heard those words, heard the way Harley said them, there's real hope. And then I let my mind replay the tape. I listen again to those words. I hear him say, "Sarah, darling," and then I let my mind echo and re-echo them. That's when the light from my heart seems to turn off the gloom outside.

From the faraway place of my dreams, I hear the sound of a car. It's Mama. Time to make a fresh pot of coffee. As I make my measurements, I hear her slam the car door and then her feet on the porch.

Like John, Mama takes off her wet things outside, but why women can do this simple act so much better than men just baffles me. When Mama comes in, she doesn't need to wipe her feet again, although she always does, and she's not dripping puddles all over the floor.

"Fresh coffee is on," I say, and then I put a couple rolls on her plate, get out the butter, the raspberry jam and the powdered sugar. I keep it in a bowl. Mama likes to sprinkle powdered sugar over her jam or jelly. She always has. I tried it and it spoils the taste of the fruit, at least to me.

"I hate that job more every day," she said. "I think I'll put my application in at Baxter's again. Oh, the stupidities I have to put up with down there."

Same story. I'd heard it from about the second year after Papa died, but you let her go on. It's her steam valve. It seems to do her good to talk about what goes on down there.

After I poured her a steaming cup of sweet-smelling coffee, she dropped all talk about the conditions at the thread mill and before I knew it we were talking about Buck and me, and about how it all got started way back then. She asked a lot of questions, and I answered, but my mind wasn't really on those days, or Buck.

My mind was on my own life, and I had started to truly believe I might have one once again. The whole world had taken a new turn. My thoughts were on Harley, that big, sweet, lumpy-looking hulk of a guy.

He reminded me more and more of Lucky, the mixed breed Collie that took up at our house one day four or five years ago, and who offered me and all the Pendleys more love than we ever deserved.

We named that dog Lucky because he took up here instead of at some other house where he wouldn't have had a welcome.

It's just no wonder that in my own mind I was beginning to think Lucky might be a good name for me, too.

In my heart I knew how lucky I was. Things were changing, even with Mama. And every time Harley came by the house, I had such a nice warm feeling about the world.

Maybe "Sarah darlin'" had a second chance at life after all.

Chapter 20

wilfred huskins

I had to talk to Buck, and I had to talk to him without his daddy muddying up the waters. I wanted to see Buck's reactions, not Edd's. Sometimes you can get more out of a tic, a shuffle or an eye squint than you can out of an elaborate answer. When Buck is around his daddy, he's always putting on a kind of macho show. He also knows that if he hesitates, Edd will charge in there to protect him.

I've never made any secret of the fact that I hate these kinds of jobs. I just don't like to press in on anyone with questions about their lives.

Mountain pride and mountain privacy are twin layers that run through the rock the folks around here are made out of. My people are, at best, wary of the law or anything that even hints at curbing their right to freedom, whatever its direction.

We don't have much in the way of zoning in Asa Gray County and that's why.

"Hell, man, you tell me I can't do what I want to with my own land? No way."

I'd heard this, and other versions of it, all my life. It's an attitude that prevails.

But it's more than property rights. You don't butt in on a conversation in the checkout line at the hardware store, either. Whatever is being said may be loud enough for you to hear, but it's personal, private and between the people involved. Many a Florida person, a tourist, has been stung by the silence that follows such an intrusion.

I feel safe in saying that around here a lawman is thought of about as poorly as a Florida person—or maybe worse. That feeling of being an outsider in my own county is the biggest thing I don't like about my job, but I was elected to maintain the peace, and I will.

When my time runs out— Well, who knows about that, but right now I can tell you, I wouldn't think of running again.

But, my feelings aside, I had to talk to Buck, and I knew it, and there he was, on a bench outside the poolroom, all by himself. There was nothing for me to do but walk on over there and do the job I was being paid to do.

We had no more than got through the barest of the preliminary polite remarks when Buck said, "OK, Wilfred, as my daddy would say, 'this ain't a social call.' What's on your mind."

Nothing subtle about Buck, so why should I try?

"I've been over there below Mace's Knob, Buck, and your story doesn't check out. Do you want to ride over there with me and talk to those folks?"

We were sitting side-by-side on that green bench facing the street in front of the poolroom. He slid a foot or more toward the end of the bench and twisted so he could look directly at me. I could see the mean side to that pretty face, the side he kept mostly hidden. The look was black and the meaning was clear. But when he spoke, the words were as soft as can be.

"No, Wilfred," he said. "I won't be riding over there with you, unless you're prepared to make an arrest, and you better be damned sure of what you're doing if you do. I said it before and I say it again, you ain't dealing with a yokel now."

"I couldn't find the man selling bird dogs, Buck. I don't think there is one."

"Don't hurt you none to think, Sheriff."

I was on a fool's errand and I knew it, but I went on. "Not many cars out that way on a late Sunday afternoon, Buck. I talked to a lot of people. No one saw you."

"As I said, don't hurt you none to think, Sheriff."

"You were up there on the Knob, Buck. You know something about Jim Bob's accident."

"Don't hurt you none to—"

It was more than I could take from this smart-ass. The smirk, the words, and even the inflection, were insolent. The way he kept repeating the same thing and the way he stressed the word "sheriff" raised the whole thing right up to my boiling point in a quick hurry.

"OK, Buck. Have it your way, at least for now. But don't you forget for one minute that the Pendley girl's murder is still an open case. I haven't given up. When I find the evidence, you'll be back in court so fast you won't know what hit you."

My anger didn't help; it might have made it worse. Buck was as insolent as ever.

"You had your time at bat, Wilfred, and you struck out."

"Well, let me tell you something, boy," I said, "I'm going to find out what went on up there on Mace's Knob, and if I find you're mixed up in it, you can bet your damned life on it, there will be an arrest."

The scowl was gone and a smile replaced it. "Oh, now, the lawman's mad at me. I guess the word will be out. Get Buck. That's what the word's going to be. Get Buck. I don't care what he does, if he spits on the street, get Buck. Let me tell you something, Hick-Town Sheriff, you might run again, but you're going to have to reckon with a lot of Price votes or you sure as hell won't be back in your cushy job. Think about that."

He got up, stretched his arms over his head, just to show how relaxed he was, and he walked into the poolroom.

I hadn't found out a thing, or made a ripple in his arrogance, and he had me so damned mad I wasn't even thinking straight. I walked back to the car, seething.

Still angry and on impulse, I drove out to Edd's, but I parked down the street and walked to the house. Edd was there, hulling peas on the front porch. I walked up to him before he even knew I was there.

"I didn't hear you, Wilfred. You know what Essie thinks about—"

Very quietly I said, "I didn't drive in, Edd. The car is down the street. Essie's got no problem with the neighbors. I came to see you, and if you don't get loud, she'll never even know I was here."

"You ain't here on no social call."

Almost the same words. Like father, like son. But unlike son, this time I meant to keep my wits about me.

"No, Edd, I guess it's not a social call, and believe me, it's a call I didn't really want to make either, because I know how close you are to Buck." I waited a little, and then I said, "Edd, I know about Mace's Knob, I know all about it."

I stopped to let that sink in. Edd is bright as can be, but he's slow. Whatever you say just trickles in. The pea hulling slowed down. "I know all about what happened up there, Edd, but before I make any arrests, I felt I'd better come out here and talk to you."

He stopped hulling peas. "What do you know, Wilfred?"

"Buck was up there when Jim Bob went over, Edd. There was trouble."

"Who told you that?"

"Look, Edd. I want to help. Buck's got a smart mouth. That, by itself, won't help him any. I want you to talk to him, to settle him down."

"Who told you that, Wilfred?"

"Buck," I said.

It was a lie, but there had been lots of lies, ever since we found the body of Bekka Pendley, and most of them came right back to this house.

You could almost see his mind slowly clicking, and then those little black raisin eyes rolled right up at me.

"There's been some lyin', Wilfred, and you're doing it. Buck never told you that. I believed you right up to when you said Buck told you, but I know Buck. If you caught him red-handed,

167

he'd never admit to it. Not Buck. Buck didn't tell you nothin, Wilfred."

"Buck told me, Edd. He had to, because there was a witness. Buck was seen up there."

"Then, let me give you some free advice, Wilfred. You just call in on your radio, tell them deputies to pick Buck up and arrest him. You know all about it, do you?"

He picked up three more peas.

"Now you listen to me, Wilfred," he said, "there's no reason for you to stand out here on my porch, holding up my pea hulling, getting me in trouble with Essie, while you try to pump me. Praise the Lord, son, if you know it all, why pump me? I ain't telling you nothing, Wilfred, that's because there ain't nothing to tell."

Chapter 21

sarah pendley

On Decoration Day, I was up at five. There was so much that still had to be done, even with all the preparations I'd been making for the past few days, but I didn't care. I wasn't sleepy, I wasn't tired, and I was ready for the world. I hadn't felt like this in so long that I'd almost forgotten what it was to be truly happy.

I'm smart enough to know that this kind of feeling is to be soaked up and stashed away for other days that will never quite measure up. It's a glorious feeling while it lasts, and I intend to store it, to hug it to my soul, reveling in every minute of it. And then I'll dip into this little bank account of happiness; I'll bring it out to give me comfort, just a little at a time, whenever I need it most.

And what is that feeling I can neither describe nor duplicate ever again? I can only tell you that in the last few days, Mama has been more like herself. I don't expect, even for a minute, that I can ever take Bekka's place in her heart, but I wouldn't know what to do with that kind of treatment anyway.

What I want is for Mama to be Mama again, to talk to me like I'm a human being, to enjoy the meals I cook, and the house I keep clean, and to let me be a part of our family, just like I was before Buck ever came back to the mountains to live, before Bekka died.

I don't mean that Mama ever said anything against me to the boys, but she has a way of laying her will on you; you come under the influence of her feelings whether you want to or not.

She could never do that to Bekka, but it was always easy for her to do with the boys, and I guess I've been about as bad as they are. I've always gone along with it.

If Mama didn't like something or someone, there was a kind of veil that she seemed to throw over it or over them, and you knew it—we all knew it. She didn't have to say a word; you knew what she thought, and you just kind of went along with it. You just kind of let Mama have her way, and you buried your own feelings.

No, you can't see or touch the kind of veil I'm talking about, but since Bekka died, and especially since the last trial, I've been under that veil. I know it from her treatment of me and I know it from the boys. I can see it more in Luke than the others. He just plain reflects Mama, so there are times when, as far as Luke was concerned, I'm simply not here or not considered.

It's less obvious in Matt, maybe because he tries not to be around the house too much. He'll stay out late or go down to Myrtle on the weekends—anything to be away. John is the only one who even tries to fight the power of Mama's will, and, poor, kind soul that he is, even he can't throw it off completely, not if Mama is in the house.

In recent days, since we started talking again—sitting at the same table and having coffee—I know the veil is lifting and I can feel the heaviness in my heart beginning to lift with it. In a day or two, she'll have zapped her wand all around the house and they'll all know that it's gone, and I'll be their sister once again.

And how am I so sure of this at five in the morning? I just know it, that's all. No, Mama wasn't even up, nor would she be up for hours, but I could feel the difference in the morning air, and I knew we were heading back to better times, all of us.

That alone would have been enough to make my spirits so light I didn't seem to touch the steps as I came downstairs to finish the preparations for Decoration Day, but there was more than Mama that made my spirits high: There was Harley.

It's always been a mystery to me why the things that do you the most good inside, the things that grab at your stomach in the strongest way, are not things that you can truly explain, at least, not to anyone else.

Sometimes I can look out the front upstairs window in winter, down over the valley that borders Pendley Creek, with soft snow covering everything, with only a bunny trail to mar it, and it's so pretty I almost want to cry—I get that knot in my stomach and I almost want to cry.

It was that way early this morning. It wasn't anything I could see, but that didn't make it any less real.

I knew about Harley. For the first time, I truly knew. I knew for sure that he loved me, and that he loved me with a pure heart. He's not like the lip-licking louts down by the poolroom, sniggering and punching each other in the ribs when I walk by, and all because of what I said in court.

They repeated it—I know they did—and some of it with the retelling probably got so bent out of shape that I might not recognize it. But I tell you true, what I had to say there in court—straight out—is enough to make my cheeks burn, even today, with just the thought of it.

Yes, thank you, Lord, there's Harley. Since daylight I knew deep down in my own heart about Harley and his love for me, even though he has never really said a word. Before dawn, with the very first traces of light, I knew for absolute certain what I had been unable to see before. Harley loved me.

The thought of it gave me a feeling that I might just puff up and explode. I don't know that I trust those feelings; I don't know that it's wise to trust them. I'd once felt this same way about Buck. They're feelings that are capable of overpowering you; they can rage out of control like a brush fire in the wind. I know. I know what feelings like that can do to me, and I don't ever want that to happen again.

Yes, crazy as it sounds, right then I knew I loved Harley,

but it scared me. I didn't really trust myself enough to throw the rest of my life into the flames such feelings can kindle. I'd done that with Buck and lost. But I trusted my feelings enough this time to let my heart sing a wild, lilting song that only I can hear. I wasn't ready to say it out loud, and yet I knew I loved Harley. But still, there is a memory, a memory of my own shame, that keeps me in control.

As I put the boiled icing on the chocolate cake, I was heartened by my thoughts of Harley. Even so, like I tell you, I am frightened by them, too.

I have to admit that in my own head I've made myself a problem; I've been so mean to him, so bitchy, that it will take some doing on my part to lead him back on a path that will even permit him to fully trust me, though I can see how much he wants to.

My thoughts right then gave me a private little smile, because I couldn't help thinking of Harley as a frightened colt, one that wanted to walk over to the fence for the apple. He couldn't because he was still nervous, still a little wild-eyed and frightened. Calming him, getting his confidence, was going to take patience on my part.

The next weeks are sure to be a mending time for both of us. It will be a process that will take patience, but I just know Harley is a skittish colt, maybe rangy looking and awkward, but a colt that can be haltered. Still, I also know full well, I don't dare rush it. One thing is clear to me: Whatever I do, I'll have to go slow to win his confidence.

I stopped daydreaming right then. It's Decoration Day and there's still a lot of work to be done. I took the first load of things down to the church at half past six. John had done a lot of the shopping for me, and those boxes were already in his truck: the plastic flatware, and the plates, the napkins and the cold drinks.

I wasn't the only one up and stirring. Arabella Geouge was there, with a fire in the stove to take the chill off the morning air while she put up the tables that would hold all the food as it began to arrive later in the morning.

By eight, we were joined by three or four more ladies, and by nine, we had the situation in hand. The food wouldn't come in until about eleven or later. There was already a lot of the heavier work going on out in the graveyard. I could hear the chain saws. Mama arrived in her new dress around ten.

Well, now, when Mama got there, that stopped things I can tell you. She got all the attention she wanted with that new dress. There was all the talk about the amount of handwork that was needed for a dress like that, and talk about the old-fashioned pattern and where it came from.

The hit, of course, as Mama knew it would be, was the old tatting, that beautiful, delicate and intricate tatting that Mama had taken from a dusty trunk in the attic, tatting done by my Granny Hall years and years ago.

By the time we used the church bell to call everyone in to eat, the results of what both the men and women were doing in the churchyard were really beginning to show. Dead branches blown off by winter winds had been removed and cut into firewood for some of the older members of our church. The other trees had been trimmed, the shrubs were cut back, and all the individual plots were beginning to take on the look of a churchyard where there was a lot of love and a lot of pride.

And Mama—Mama was everywhere showing off that dress and the hand-made tatting. She hadn't done any work on the Pendley graves, but she was having the time of her life with the attention she got in that old-fashioned, ankle-length dress.

I didn't mind that she didn't turn a hand to the graves. She worked out. It wasn't easy what she did down at the thread mill, and there was no need for her to do more work on Decoration Day, not with me and the boys there. I'd get to my own work on the plots after everyone had eaten. I'd have the boys to help with anything heavy.

As I always did, I would weed and trim Papa's plot by myself.

Right now, I knew, that job could wait until all the serving had been done.

Our church has been around for a long, long time, so our cemetery is big, it just kept on going back—all the way to the woods at the foot of Pendley Knob. To this day, not all of that land has been used for burying. There's land enough there, I vow, for another twenty years. The back part has no graves at all, but my brother John keeps it bush-hogged down all summer.

My family gave all the land for the church and cemetery way, way back, years ago. The land wasn't worth much then, and we had plenty of it in those days, before so much of it got sold off, so the cemetery behind the church is big, maybe the biggest in the county. It takes a lot of work every spring just to clean it up. The cleanup is the biggest reason for Decoration Day. But we get the work done, with a lot of prayer and fellowship. We do it all on that one day. "Many hands make light work." That's an old expression you hear over and over again on Decoration Day.

When dinner was over and the last of the dirty paper plates had been bagged up in black plastic, I went on back to the Pendley plot. I took care of Bekka's grave first. John and Matt had done some work on it, but they're neither one very neat, so I made it look real pretty.

I'm glad there was no one there to help me with Bekka's grave, because I couldn't keep back the tears that filled my eyes. The pictures of Bekka that ran through my mind had to be the work of the Lord. He was making me see what I had done to my sister.

Through the tears, I saw the happy times when Bekka was a bright-faced little girl when we were still in grammar school, and I saw the two of us with Easter egg baskets and with school books. I saw Bekka with freckles, before she found out about cover-up makeup. Mostly, I could see the pretty girl who smiled all the time and at everyone. I saw the Bekka that the whole county loved, the Bekka who was always good to her sister, an overgrown, fat girl who might have been from another family. I couldn't help thinking of the crow and the swan.

I blinked back the tears, and I saw my sister in the days before she started pulling out most of her eyebrows and painting her face.

I could see Bekka back in the days when we were friends, friends like I hope we will be again some day, somewhere, when we meet again, when I know she has forgiven me. Heaven? Yes, that's where it will be, I know that I'll be in Heaven when I'm sure she forgives me for not warning her about Buck.

At the foot of Bekka's grave I carefully replanted the forget-me-nots I had dug up from over at the old cabin. I know they're called bluets, but we always called them forget-me-nots, and that's what I wanted her to do.

Forget-me-nots or bluets, whatever the name, they're one of the first things I ever tried to embroider on a pillow case. They're easy to do.

As I transplanted the flowers, I prayed they'd live, but you never know about moving a wild flower.

After my cry at Bekka's grave, after the tears had dried enough to look another human in the face, I saw to the final work on the rest of the plots, the older plots, the Pendleys from years gone by.

My brothers know I always do Papa's grave by myself, so they left it alone. It's my job. I've worked on it by myself ever since the first year after Papa was buried.

As I knelt there, with my forked weed digger, cutting down into the roots of the knotweed and purslane and nutgrass that had made an early spring start on Papa's grave, I sensed Harley rather than actually saw him. He was standing behind me, and when I turned, he had his own forked weed cutter in one hand and a little rake in the other.

"Could you use some help?"

"I always take care of Papa's grave —

"I know," he said. "John told me, but, Sarah, you haven't stopped. What harm could there be in accepting a little help? I have our family plots all done."

Papa's stone is not marble; it's some kind of sandstone, and it does attract mildew. I always bleach it, and it's a job I hate. Harley wanted to help. He truly did. I could see it in his earnest, serious face, so I said, "I always brush bleach on Papa's stone to kill the mildew. It's a job I don't like. Would that be putting too much on you?"

"Of course not," he said. "Some of our headstones had to be bleached, too. I know how. I'll be careful, Sarah. You've got experienced help, not some amateur."

He was careful. Not one drop of bleach touched the wild violets, pennyroyal, bluets and the dwarf iris I allowed to grow on Papa's grave—Papa liked wild flowers best, so I never disturbed them. When Harley was through with that smelly job, he helped me dig out the roots of the weeds that threatened to choke my carefully saved wild flowers.

When the task was complete, we both stood back and looked at our work. "I truly thank you, Harley. Whether I knew it or not, I guess I was beginning to get a little bushed. I was up early and Mama was just no help with all the cooking this year. She was busy. It was all that work with the dress and Granny's lace, but she did look nice in it, didn't she?"

He didn't say anything. He just stood there grinning. I didn't mean to touch him, I didn't want to make a fool of myself again, but, without thinking of what I was doing, I reached out and touched his hand, the hand with the rake in it, and he just grinned all the more.

I knew my face would be beet red if I stayed, so I thanked him again and turned and walked back to the church to start gathering all our serving dishes and pots and pans together.

It truly was a good day—all of it.

harley phillips
Decoration Day is not one of my things; it is not something
I stay at every year—not the whole day. If there's heavy work,
especially on our family plots, I'll go to the cemetery early and
get that done before Mama and Daddy get there, but I never
have been one to hang around out there at the church.

This time it's different. This Decoration Day is an opportu-
nity that's too good to miss. If I have a chance with Sarah, I
know I have to stay alert, I have to use every excuse I can find
to be around her, to let her know I'm not what she thinks I am.

By now, the idea is finally lodged into my thick head. I
know that if ever I have a chance with Sarah, I'll have to make
it happen mostly by myself; I'll have to be around her so much
that she'll get used to me being there.

It might not be the best way to think of yourself, but that's
how the thought came to me. I know that's how a smart, old,
lost dog can find himself a home. He just takes up there at your
house, and after a while he seems to belong, and that's just
what I'm going to be doing in Sarah's life. I mean to take up
with her and make a place for myself.

Good old John, he showed me the way with his trumped up
reasons for having me to his mama's house. I saw it pretty
quick, but it takes more than once or twice. You've got to find
your own ways to do it, you've got to use every excuse to be
near. This one, Decoration Day, is made in heaven for me. It's
a perfect reason to have to be around Sarah all day long.

There was work to be done there at the cemetery after a
long winter, so my being there wouldn't look unusual, and I'd
brought a pickup full of new shrubs to be planted later on.

I planned all that because I wanted to make being there
look natural, and if I still had planting to do, hanging around
would look OK. Yes indeed, Decoration Day was a perfect
time for me to be near her. I knew Sarah was always a big part
of Decoration Day and she'd be there from early morning.

That's why, this year, I'm taking a bigger part in the general clean-up, more than I ever did before. I mean to stay here all day long. I felt sure she wouldn't cut me up, not in front of a lot of other people, so I was sure I'd be able to make a day of it.

By the time my folks arrived, most of the work had been done on our plots—we have three of them, not all together. One is up front and the other two farther back. I'd dug out all the weeds, but Mama did the prettying-up and put out the flowers.

Just as I had it figured out, there were times when I had to go to the church for water or to wash up, and I had a chance to speak to all the ladies who were working there, and, of course, I spoke to Sarah.

There's something different about her today. The smile she has for everyone just lights up her face, and when she speaks to me, some of that same warmth is still there.

She can cut you, Sarah can, sometimes without even saying a word, but I didn't feel any of that today, so I went back out to my work with a light heart. I knew it could just be the polite face she was showing to the other women working there in the church basement, but I couldn't help feeling it was more than that. I hoped it was something she meant for me to have.

John came by to talk to me as I worked on the three plots that are Phillipses or close kin, and even Mrs. Pendley come by showing off that new dress she had made for Decoration Day.

Somehow or other that old-timey dress seemed to go with the reason for all of us being out there on that warm spring day. We take great stock in kin here in Asa Gray County, and that includes all that have gone before, so the dress fit in with old times. It looked just right.

The long dress and the lace, the look of yesterday on Ora Lee Pendley, and the smell of the fresh earth mingling with the mellow smell of the weeds and twigs being burned at the side of the cemetery, took me back in time.

For a minute there, looking at Mrs. Pendley in that long dress, standing way over by the old beech tree near the Pendley plot, made me think of my granny's mother. I didn't know her well; my memories of her are blurred, and the only real ones are photographs, but for just a minute there, my granny's mother, Adelphia Canipe, seemed to be standing over near the beech tree, and she waved to me. But when I blinked my eyes, she was gone. All I saw was Mrs. Pendley, and she walked over my way, speaking to everyone, right and left, as she made her way over.

It was John who told me that Sarah always took care of her Papa's grave, and after we all had dinner on the sawhorse tables and the cleanup was over, I waited for her to come out to work on the plot where Zebulon Pendley is buried.

I tried to remember how the old dog, looking to take up with you, handled it. The dog's approach was never direct, so I did it the same way. I stood off there for a while, and then I moved closer, but it was still at a distance where I could run in the woods if she threw a rock at me. Like the homeless dog, it worked. She paid me no mind at first, but when she first seemed to see me, I knew she wasn't going to chase me away, unless I tried too hard.

I tell you true, I don't even know what was said. I can only tell you that the warm feeling I had from her earlier in the day was still there, and she did give me a job to do, even though John told me she never allowed any of the boys to do a thing with their daddy's grave.

And when we were through, when we stood back to look at what had been done on Zeb's grave, she seemed so pleased that she forgot any kind of shyness she had. She just smiled at me in the way only Sarah can, and she put her fingers on my hand, and then she turned a little pink and walked away, but I can tell you, there was something there; there was something between us, a feeling that I've had, it seems to me like, forever, and for just a second—just for a fleeting second—I was sure she felt it, too.

The rest of that day I had enough good feeling for the whole world. It's a Decoration Day I'll never forget.

john pendley

I was at the church early to run errands for Sarah, just in case she needed help, but the other two boys didn't come until later.

I knew they'd both be coming though, because on Decoration Day, Mama has the whole clan there. If Matt and Luke hadn't rolled out of bed by the time Mama was up, she'd rout them out. It wasn't the Pendley Cemetery—it wasn't called that—but that's the way Mama looked at it.

I noticed that Harley Phillips was there pretty early, too, with a load of his shrubs. Smart thinking. That boy is slowly catching on.

Maybe he don't know it yet, but he's beginning to make time with Sarah. I can see it, especially since her and Mama are back to talking again. I can see Sarah take a quick look at him when he's passing through the room, or when he's busy talking to me, but I don't let on. If I did, she'd backpedal for sure.

Mama got there just before ten, and, as I figured, she had the other two boys in tow. Poor Matt didn't look ready for it. I saw him when he got in last night and I could tell he'd been drinking. From the look of him, I knew right about now he'd want nothing more than the bed and maybe a BC Headache Powder.

After we got the heavier work done on the Pendley graves, the three of us lent a hand to the other people who didn't have the tools or the strength to clean up their plots. Decoration is a sharing day Mama always said, and if we shirked with helping, she'd be on us like a scalded hen.

I saw old man Rodney Miller just standing over there where most of the Millers are buried, looking like he didn't know where to start, so I left the boys and walked over. I knowed he was too proud to accept help, but that thin, old feller needed aplenty of it. His wife had died over the winter, and he was plain old drying up to nothing.

I said, "Mr. Miller, if you'll get on that far end of that limb, we can drag it over there so it can be burned later."

That's how it started, and before long we were working there together, cropping the grass and digging out weeds. There were Millers, and his family's married-in kin, all over the place there to the left of the church, with everything from marble markers to them old hand-made stones that have worn away so bad you can't even read the names no more.

By the time we were through, we made it all look real good, and the old man had color in his cheeks and he was talking like I had never heard him talk before. How lonely he must have been since his wife died, and where were his kids? None of them showed up for Decoration. I know they're mostly in Charlotte, but Charlotte ain't that far.

He told me he just wasn't making it on his Social Security. He said his savings, all of it, had been spent at State on his youngest son's schooling. I offered to buy his land.

He said, "No, sir, I can't do that. There ain't no way I'm going to leave my land. Lived most of my life on that land and I'm going to die on it, too."

I didn't push it. I know a little something about how a man feels about his own land, but as we talked, we just worked out a deal that gave him the money he needed and gave me another 175 acres of Pendley Holler.

Right then, we made up to meet at Jethro's office on the Tuesday after Decoration Day. I'd buy the land from him outright for cash, and he'd put the money in bonds so he'd have income. I'd have Jethro draw up some papers that gave the old man the right to live there—with no taxes and no upkeep—right in his own house, for the rest of his life.

When the church bell was rung for dinner, he turned to me and said, "I'm mighty proud of what you done for me today, John. I'm sure your pappy would be proud of you, too. There ain't many like you."

Well, sir, I tell you, what he said just ran all over me. I

could feel my face getting flushed and red, and I didn't know what to say.

"Now, come on, boy," he said, "don't get all shame-faced just because you done a good thing for an old feller. You know I couldn't have cleaned these plots without your help. Now, hand me my cane from over there by my Pap's stone, and let's go get some of that good grub."

As we got in line, I remembered that picture in the company room. Mama was showing off her new dress again. It was a lot like the one Granny Hall wore in that picture that hung over the mantel. Mama looked mighty pretty in it, and she was looking happy, too, so that was a welcome change.

As we passed by her, she caught hold of my hand and said, "I saw what you done for Mr. Miller, John, and I thank you. He doesn't have enough strength for a plot as big as his. That's the kind of thing we all need to do for each other, not just on Decoration. He's a poor, dear, lost soul since Fanny Miller died. I'm proud of you, John, and I know your Daddy was looking down, watching what you did."

wilfred huskins

The church out in Pendley Holler is not the one my family attends, but around here we pretty much know which Saturday is Decoration for each of the churches. I really wanted to go out to the cemetery on their Decoration Day, because you can get the feel of a place when you have a big group together like that, and I needed to know how the winds were blowing.

The one thing I didn't want to do was to barge out there uninvited, but when Russ asked me to go with him—and Russ is a member of that church—I jumped at the chance.

There was a downright impossible thought gnawing away at my brain that morning, and it was almost scary. The town seemed to be settling down—for the first time since the Pendley girl got killed. I didn't discuss my feeling with Russ because of a childish superstition that has always been with me: if you talk about it, it's sure not to happen. So I hadn't said a word to the one guy I trusted most.

I was scared to talk about my feeling because for the first time I could see a little normalcy settling over the valleys and the coves of Asa Gray County, or at least I thought I could. If it was getting back to normal, I didn't want to hex it.

If you remember, that murder and Buck's two trials kept the whole county riled up, and it's been that way since shortly after my election. Nearly two years of strife in the county, because there wasn't a soul for miles around who didn't have an opinion about that cruel and bloody murder.

"Come on and ride out there with me," Russ said. "I've paid a couple guys from out at the tech school to take care of my family's plot, but I need to go out there and see that it's done right."

At the cemetery, there was a lot of banter because I was there, but it was good natured. "Hey, Russ, who's that with you?" "Did you need protection or are we all under arrest?" "Hide the bottle. It's the cops." There was a lot of that kind of thing, and old Russ entered into the spirit of it by giving them several different versions of, "The only way I could get time off work today was to bring the boss along."

I saw everyone who was closely involved in the tragedy except for the Prices. They go to another Baptist church, over closer to his mama.

Other than the fact that Luke seemed to be avoiding me, I saw nothing that would indicate anything but just what I had been seeing and feeling, so maybe normalcy was not that far away. And I'm not even sure I can say that Luke avoided me, but he did go off to help with another plot just after I arrived. Matt stopped his work to talk. From the look of his bloodshot eyes, I know he was glad to stop for any reason.

Even Mrs. Pendley came by for a few words. She'd been more than a little cool to me since I tried to talk to her about her target practice, so I welcomed the change. Now, I don't mean that she was real friendly—like in the old days before I got elected sheriff. Still, there was a thaw, a welcome thaw.

I spoke first. I said, "You're looking mighty fine in that old-fashioned dress, Mrs. Pendley, and your hair is all done up like a cameo brooch." It was plain to see she liked the flattery. It was a better start than I had made the last couple of times I tried to talk to her.

She said, "Thank you, Wilfred. It's a new dress. I made it special for today over a pattern that had belonged to my own Granny. I found it, all brown and torn, in one of her trunks. I thought it would be nice for Decoration."

"It's just right for the occasion," I said. "Mighty pretty dress, and you do it proud."

She said thank you again and walked on back toward a group of people who were repotting some bright yellow flowers into two cement urns on one of the graves.

There's always talk of the departed on occasions like this. Since Jim Bob's death had been so recent, I heard his name mentioned several times even though he's not buried in this cemetery. The good part is that I didn't hear anyone say anything that didn't accept his death as an unfortunate accident. So that wound, too, was beginning to heal.

In the car, as we were driving back toward town, Russ said, "You wanted to go out there, didn't you, Wilfred?" He had a grin on his face like he'd caught me with my hand in the cookie jar.

"Yes, I did. I just wanted— Well, I don't rightly know what I wanted."

"Sure you do," he said. "You're a cop, just like me, and you wanted to put your ear to the ground out there. So did I."

"You didn't go to check on your workers?"

"Now, Wilfred, don't try to spoof me. This is old Russ you're talking to. You know them boys. They go to that church, same as I do. I didn't really have to pay'em, and I didn't need to check on'em."

"You just went because of me—"

"I went because of us. I wanted to go, and I had you figured. I knew damned well you wanted to go."

Time for me to ask the question. "So, Russ, you had your ear to the ground, too. What did you hear?"

He was a long time in answering. Finally he said, "Not a damned thing. Same as you. Maybe we're afraid to think the world might be settling down again, and that one day soon our biggest worry will be a speeder or a drunk or a kid with a little grass in his car."

Then it was my turn to be quiet.

Finally I said, "Somehow, Russ, I wish you hadn't brought all this up; somehow I wish you hadn't mentioned it at all. Somehow or other, we're all more kid than we like to think. One of my childish beliefs was that if I wanted something to happen and talked about it, it wouldn't ever happen, or if I didn't want something to happen, and talked about it, it was sure to bop me right on the noggin. I had a history test once—"

"Yeah, I know," Russ said. "I know about that one. Childhood superstition. I know about it. I never have been able to shake it, either. Maybe I shouldn't have said a word."

Chapter 22

wilfred huskins

It was Sunday. Decoration Day was over. I had just unwrapped my two sausage biscuits on a paper napkin on my desk, and filled my mug with hot black coffee, when Edd Price stormed into my office. I could hear Rachel protesting in the background, but nothing was going to stop Edd.

"I ain't had a wink of sleep all night, Wilfred," he shouted. "I've been waiting across the street there until you got here. You've got to do something and do it now."

"Now hold on, Edd," I said in the calmest voice I could muster at that hour of the morning without my first cup of coffee, "hold on, hold on. Tell me what's got you so riled up. Is that gang back to driving up and down in front of your house again?"

"It's worse than that, Wilfred, and I expect you to do something about it right now."

"OK, OK, Edd. Settle down. Just tell me what they're up to now?"

"It ain't them—not prankin' anyhow. He didn't come home last night, Buck didn't, and that ain't like him, Wilfred. Buck's a good boy. He didn't come home."

"Well, now, Edd, that's not too unusual for a young man, staying out all night. It's something I did when I was younger and I'll bet you did. too."

"Don't you try putting me off, Wilfred. I ain't one of these damned yokels you can push around. You're the sheriff here and I expect you to do something and do it right now, and if

186

you don't get on this right now, by God, you'll see how much hell I can raise."

His face was red, he hadn't shaved and the lack of sleep and worry had the white part of his pig eyes etched with red veins. I tried the soft approach again.

"Now, Edd, you know we can't even file a missing persons on a young man who failed to come home one night. That happens all the time. There's probably some girl. Give him time."

"Wilfred, if you don't do something and do it now, you're never going to be elected again. I'll see to that, and don't you think I can't do it."

"Knock off the threats, Edd. I'll do what I can, and not because of your pressure, but hell, man, when a boy stays out all night, there's not too much I can do." Then I said, "How long has he been gone?"

"We ain't seen him since yesterday. He just went off somewhere after breakfast."

There was no doubt about one thing, Edd Price was worried about his son. I was afraid he was about to have a stroke right in front of me. His face was a mottled red and purple, and his breath was coming in gasps. I had to calm him down.

"Tell me what I can do. I know you're worried. I'll do anything I can. You can depend on it."

For that moment, he appeared to be a little calmer. "Start with his car," he said. "It's gone, same as he is. Maybe it's stolen. I'll say it was stolen, if that'll get some action. I'll swear it was stolen. You can do that, can't you?"

"Sure, Edd, but we won't call it a stolen car, at least not yet. I'll get hold of the State Patrol and have them keep an eye out for Buck's car, and I'll contact the guys over in Avery, Mitchell and Yancey. They can all look for it."

"What about Madison and Buncombe? Don't you know the police over there? Call everybody. Find his car and you'll find him."

"You just give all the information about his car to Rachel out there at the desk, Edd. We'll be on it, you can be assured of that."

The florid color was beginning to fade a little and his breathing was better. I started to relax a little, too. And then he said, very quietly, "I'm scared, Wilfred, I sure to God am. It's not just being out overnight, although Buck don't do that—he's a good boy, whatever people think."

He slumped back in the chair like a half-filled toy balloon. There were tears in his eyes.

"He's had a couple of calls, Buck has. I listened in on a part of one of them. Someone's trying to get him to take some dope, as best I could figure it out. Angel dust. That's dope, ain't it?"

"Did you recognize the voice? Do you have any idea who it might be?"

"I only heard the last part of it. I don't know who it was. I couldn't talk to Buck about it, Wilfred. I didn't want him to know his old daddy was checking on him, but the other calls—the calls he got before—I watched him, and them calls made Buck so edgy that one time he spoke disrespectful to Essie. I put a quick stop to that, but them calls made Buck nervous, I tell you. Something's just not right. So, don't pass this off as nothing, Wilfred. I've got reason to worry."

I had to feel sorry for Edd Price. All the bluster was gone, all the wind, all the threats, all the steam. What was left was an ugly shell of a man, sagging in a chair across from me. But I had something to be grateful for. He wasn't going to have a stroke. Then he took a deep breath, got to his feet and walked right up to the front of my desk.

"Find him, Wilfred, please find him. We'll move, I promise you. We'll go back to Maryland. I don't want him hurt. Find him for me, Wilfred."

His skin was pale, you could see the veins on his nose and the old acne scars on his cheeks and his black dot eyes were sunk back in his head. But worse than that, there was terror in those eyes.

He turned and walked out of the office. His back was to me as he gave the information to Rachel, but in my mind, as clearly as if he were still in the chair across from me, I could see the look on his face; I could see his fear etched in the lines of his slumped shoulders, the sag of his belt and the droop in the seat of his faded chinos.

Edd had my deep sympathy, but right now, there was something else: There was a great, gaping hole with a question mark in it. The feeling I had had yesterday out at the church Decoration Day—the feeling that peace was coming back to our part of the mountains—was gone.

Poor Edd. He was worried, and I was concerned. I didn't like the new thoughts that crowded in. We didn't need any more trouble.

I had no more than picked up the first of my two cold biscuits when Russ came in. "You're not on duty," I said.

"Forget that, Wilfred. I just passed Edd Price out there on the street and I swear he was crying."

"He may have been, Russ—maybe for a good reason and maybe not." And then I filled him in on what had just happened. When I got to the part about angel dust I had my deputy's full attention. He whistled through his teeth.

"Bad," he said, "sounds real bad."

"Yes."

"Wonder if the guys, the ones from Baltimore, are still around. You remember them, Wilfred, I told you about what I heard at the poolroom. They're the ones that were staying over in Bakersville. Bad bunch. If they're still around, that boy may be in real trouble. They had a big hard-on for Buck. I ought to call over there."

Russ sat there picking his teeth with his match stick and rubbing the toe of one shoe behind the calf of the other leg to bring the shine up. His mind was off somewhere. He had that faraway look.

"I see you've had breakfast, Russ."

"Yeah," he said. "Go ahead and eat yours."

By the time I'd finished my cold sausage biscuits and washed them down with a refilled cup of hot coffee, he was ready to roll.

"Let's go for a ride," he said.

We got in his patrol car and he drove straight out to his house. "Come on, Wilfred, we'll go in my pickup. Less noticeable."

He was right about that. His old red pickup hadn't had a shine in years and there was rust showing through all four fenders, but it was clean inside and the motor hummed with the life of a new truck.

I was not surprised when he headed out toward Pendley Holler. That's where my thoughts kept going. Had the bad blood finally reached the boiling point? If there was a reason why Buck didn't—or couldn't—come home, the Pendleys, even John, would have to be talked to and they'd all better have an alibi.

When we got to the turnoff to Pendley Holler, Russ kept going straight, but not for long.

He turned into that long, dead-end road that goes up the cove there, all the way up to the old Price farmstead, the one Essie thought was too run-down for her new-found city standards. He drove up the driveway, past the house and pulled right up to the barn. There, in a sagging lean-to, sat Buck's sporty little red car.

"He's shacking up with someone," Russ said. "Probably heard us drive in."

We got out of the truck and walked toward the house, calling Buck's name as we went. It's not a good idea to walk up to a mountain house if you don't make yourself known, even in uniform. There was no answer.

Russ kept calling Buck's name as we walked to the locked back door. If Buck was in there, he couldn't have helped hearing us, but there was no sound from inside. Russ kept on calling for Buck as we walked around to the front of the house.

When we found those two doors and the door to the cellar locked, we tried the windows. All locked.

Russ took out the great bundle of keys he always carries with him, took a quick look at the front door, selected an old-fashioned skeleton key, inserted it into a lock that must have been there since the house was built, and the door swung open.

Buck wasn't there and the beds hadn't been used.

"Come on," Russ said, "we've got some rough driving to do," and it was then the whole thing clicked into place in my mind. Russ had been remembering the testimony at the trial, and all the other things Sarah had told us about her meetings with Buck— how they met at her granny's cabin, how Buck walked over the ridge and she met him there.

Russ' old truck, was perfect for the job before us. That's what he had in mind from the beginning, and checking out the house was only the first step along the way. That man was born to be a cop.

Over the winter, the old logging road had washed out in spots, but with low gear, with steering up on the high side of the ruts, we were able to drive most of the way to the ridge.

We walked the rest of the way along that old road. From where we parked, it was little more than a trail.

I thought of the kind of mission we were on. If we went charging down there, interrupting a lover's meeting, I knew Sarah would never forgive me for the embarrassment we'd cause, but I didn't care. The thought of her being dumb enough to listen to Buck's sweet talk again was enough to make me pretty sure that I'd never forgive her either, so it would cancel out.

I tried to keep my mind on what we were about to do, but it wasn't an easy job. It was Sunday, a fine, clear spring day, and the musty odor of walking through the rotted leaves, the bright flowers of the bloodroot and the pinks and the bluets there in the woods fought to take over my senses. Then, when we reached the crest of the ridge and looked down over a meadow filled with daisies to a quaint little cabin, it was like a picture on a feed store calendar.

We walked down, right through the middle of the field, staying in plain sight so there'd be no mistaking who we were, and it was not until we were close to the house that Russ started calling Buck's name, and he kept it up until we were up on the porch, right to the hand-made door with the cord-string latchpull.

Russ rapped hard on the door, but there was no sound from inside and the racket he made had even stopped the sound of birds on the outside. He lifted the latch and pushed the door so hard it banged against the back wall, and still there was no sound. He called Buck's name again, and waited.

We walked in. Nothing seemed amiss in the first room. Russ walked toward the bedroom and I went to the kitchen. I heard him say, "Good God Almighty, I can't believe— Wilfred, come in here fast. I guess our search is over."

It takes a lot to shake Russ up, but something had done it, something in the bedroom, and when I looked for the first time, my disbelief was almost as overwhelming. It was worse than when he found the little Pendley girl right here in this same cabin.

There was Buck, naked and tied spread-eagle on the old iron bed that took up most of the space in that little bedroom. The blue and white ticking of the pad-type mattress was mottled with a maroon field of blood. Buck's long blond hair had been chopped off in uneven shanks. Some of it was still on the mattress, some of it had fallen into the coiled wire springs and some of it, blood-flecked, lay on the floor.

I walked over closer to the body. Russ stayed at the door, leaning against the jamb. There was a network of short, shallow cuts all over Buck's body, some with just a trickle of dried blood and some that had bled more profusely before drying.

Whoever killed him—and I knew he was dead even

before I tried to find a pulse or any sign of life—had made a cut, a rough triangle on his belly, slid the knife under the skin and then tried to pull the skin off with a pair of bloody pliers— pliers that still lay in another pool of dried blood on that sagging mattress.

The skinning job had not worked well, so the flesh was bruised, mangled and purple. On the floor was a ten-cent store variety salt shaker, nearly empty. and I could see grains of wasted salt on the mattress and on the floor. Someone had meant to make Buck hurt and hurt bad.

The way this was done, I had no doubt that Buck had been alive during this whole ordeal. That, of course, would have to be confirmed by the medical people.

Three of Buck's fingernails had been pulled out, probably with the pliers, and there were traces of salt near his outstretched hands with the tightly bound wrists.

The pain that he had endured was obvious from the torn skin where he had fought against the multiple strands of rough sisal cord that secured him to the iron bedstead at all four corners.

By this time, Russ came over where I was standing. "It was the knife that finally ended it," he said. "Right through the heart; like a stake right through the heart."

I must have been aware of that kitchen knife. It was prominent enough, standing erect in the chest, with its wooden handle and wide blade, but I don't remember seeing it. My mind took in only the cuts and the torn skin. I was appalled by the hundreds of shallow cuts, all the signs of the deliberate torture, and the ripped, bruised skin.

It was a horrible sight, and I don't know why, but the whacked off hair that fell where it was dropped bothered me the most. Somehow it's the hair, the long blond hair, that stays in my mind.

Russ had recovered from the first shock. He was back to being a cop again. His eyes were taking in every corner of that little room, and with a stub of a pencil he was making notes in his brown spiral notebook.

"That cord is the kind used for baling hay," he said. "Pretty common around here." He wrote a couple more words in his brown book.

"I'll bet there ain't a decent print to be had—not even on that salt cellar or the handle of the knife. Someone planned this, Wilfred, planned it pretty damned good—someone who meant to kill him, but meant to make him suffer first. I'll bet we'll find few mistakes."

I finally reached down to check for the pulse I knew wasn't there, but I did it anyway.

"You want me to go down to the Pendley's to call for some help, Wilfred? And we ought to call Doc, too. Cause of death looks pretty obvious, but no use screwing up."

"I'll go," I said. "We're not going to do this one alone, Russ. This time, right at the start, I'm going to call the SBI. Let the State boys come in here and give us some help. You stay here until I can get some of our guys out here to keep the place secure, and then we'll just wait on the Bureau to get here."

As I walked down to the Pendley house, I dreaded the other call I'd have to make later on, the call to Edd Price.

Chapter 23

sarah pendley

I'm an early riser, so that next day, Sunday—the day after Decoration—to make it easy for myself after all the cooking and preparation for the day before, I made some sage dressing from some of my own frozen beef stock, spread it on five, thin-cut round steaks, rolled them and tied them, and put them in the slow cooker. I knew they'd be ready when we got back from church. The rest would be easy. While I set the table, the vegetables could be cooking, and by one o'clock I could have dinner ready for all of us, or for whichever of the boys hadn't gone off to play ball or whatever they do on nice, spring, country Sundays.

As was generally the case after church, it was never easy to guess how many would even come home for dinner, but I always prepared for all of them, just in case.

This time all three boys had something to do, so it was only me and Mama. Just inside the kitchen door, she said her head ached and she wanted to take something and lie down.

"Waiting a bit won't spoil your dinner, will it, Sarah? I feel like if I rest for a little, with a damp wash rag over my eyes, it'll pass. My head started aching in Sunday School and that sermon today didn't help it any. He was all wound up about Decoration Day and fellowship, wasn't he?"

She went to the sink for a glass of water. "It's just the two of us. You don't mind waiting do you, Sarah?" It was half a question and half a statement. "You could wake me around 1:30 or 2:00. That wouldn't be too long, would it? It wouldn't spoil what you have planned?"

I told her it wouldn't, and that I'd call her. Actually, the delay suited me just fine. I had meant to have one of those in-the-bag mixed vegetables, with the sauce already there. I don't do that kind of cooking too much. I think of those frozen store-bought things as emergency measures—something convenient when you're rushed. With Mama resting, it gave me time to make a cheese sauce for one of my own frozen packages of beans, and I'd have time to make a sweet potato custard casserole.

As I washed the potatoes and started peeling them, I could see a man coming down the little road from Granny's cabin. I thought the walk looked familiar, but with all the new leaves out along the path, I couldn't be sure. As he came closer, I could see it was Wilfred Huskins and he was in an all-fired hurry over something. Now, what was he doing up there beyond Granny's cabin? He must have come by the house while we were in church, but why hadn't I seen his car?

I wiped my hands on my apron and I was at the door before he got to the steps. "My land, Sheriff, what on earth—"

"Tell you later, Sarah. In a real hurry. Need to use your phone."

"You can use that one," I said, pointing to my kitchen wall phone, "or you can use the one in the company room."

He walked right past me and went into the company room, but if he meant to keep whatever it was quiet, he didn't do a good job of it. He left the door to the hall open and I could hear almost everything he said. He called Rachel Woody first.

"Rachel," he said, "get hold of every man you can find, off duty or on, and send them out to the Pendley place. Tell them to come on up to Granny Pendley's old cabin, and tell them I want them here right now."

I don't know what Rachel said, but I heard him say, "You don't have to tell them why. Just get them here as soon as you can."

There was quiet for a bit and then he said, "Not right now.

I'll explain it later. I want to keep a lid on this for as long as I can, so you just get them here. But all hell's going to break loose. And, Rachel, give me the number for the State Bureau office in Asheville, the SBI office. I never can remember it."

Then I heard him dial another number. The phone in the company room is one of the old dial phones. We've had it in the house forever it seems, and then, years ago, we bought it from the phone company. It's noisy, so I could hear every click of it.

Then he was talking to a man, I think he said Steve, and I heard him say "a killing" and "we need some help from you guys, especially with prints," and then it got quiet, and finally he said, "I'll have Doc here, but bring your guy, too. This one is going to cause one hell of a stink, and I want all the help I can get." There was another long pause and then I heard him say, "It's a local man, old family, and you're right, Steve, I think it ties in with the other one. I think the lid just finally blew off."

That's all I heard. The sheriff must have put the phone down and shut the door, because the company room latch clicked and I heard no more, but my head was already reeling from what he had said on the phone and my mind was racing way ahead of him.

Was it Buck? Who else could it be? If the killing he mentioned tied in with what he called "the other one," it had to be Buck. And then a second worry: How much of this had Mama heard? This old house has paper-thin walls and the company room is right there at the foot of the stairs.

And then I thought of Luke. Could Luke have done it? Oh, say it's not so, Lord, I thought. Mama could take no more of this kind of torment. My mind was full of Luke. I tried to remember where he'd been, when he came in, how he looked when I first saw him last night, but I couldn't get the details straight in my head right then. But I was afraid. I knew it could be Luke.

In no time at all, Wilfred came back to the kitchen. I offered him coffee, but he just shook his head and said, "Not a word of this, Sarah, whatever you heard, and I mean it. No talk at all."

I nodded, and then he said, "Who's here. Who's at home?"

"Just Mama," I said. "She's laying down with a headache."

"Where are the boys?"

I told him I didn't know. That they all went somewhere right after church.

"They were all in church this morning?"

I said they were and in Sunday School, too, and then I told him, because he asked me, that they had all been at home last night, all of them in before midnight. He asked more questions about Luke than the others, but I wasn't really sure of exactly when any of them came home, and I told him that. But I knew they were all in the house before I stopped reading and went to bed, and that was just before midnight. That much I was sure of and I said so.

"When they come home today, Sarah, tell them to stay right here. Whatever their plans are, you tell them I said for them to stay here till I get back. There's a lot of questions to be answered."

Then he ran his hand across the side of his face and down his chin. With a kind of half grin, he said, "Oh, what the hell. By that time, there'll be cars all over the place. You won't have to tell them much, but tell them to stay at home, you hear me? Tell them that much, and don't let any of them come up to the cabin."

He walked to the door, put his hat back on and said, "I gave you a job that's almost impossible to do, didn't I, Sarah?"

His half smile, those beautiful even white teeth, made me think of the number of local girls who were going to be on his trail from this point on. The whole town knew his marriage was headed for the courts. It's the kind of talk that just runs like wildfire, just like the killing of Buck would, if it is Buck, and I'm sure it is—I hope not because of the trouble it'll cause, but I just know in my bones that it is.

He closed the back door and as he did, he opened a flood of bad thoughts for me. For truth certain, all the Bekka memories, and all the strife, would all be riled up again, just when they'd dimmed some and were beginning to be forgotten. How would all this affect whether I have to leave or get married? Another question: Could I marry? Who'd have me? Would Buck's murder—if it was Buck—change Harley? I knew Harley loved me right now, but all that talk would be back—all over the county—talk about me and Buck. Could Harley handle it if the gossip started all over again?

I could feel the warm tears on my cheek, tears I didn't know were there. I didn't even feel them coming on. I was just standing there, looking out the window, watching Wilfred Huskins and Gordon McKinney as they walked toward Granny's.

I'm ashamed to say it. The tears were not for Bekka or Buck. They were for me. Will my problems never end?

And what would another murder do to me? My thoughts were not worries of Luke, as they should have been. They were worries about me. Me. Would my own guilt be back, worse than ever? I know I'll always carry guilt for not warning Bekka about Buck, but, now, was I responsible for Buck, too?

I tell you, there for a while, with all the talk, the bad gossip, with Mama cold to me, and all the rest, I was about ready to find a jumping-off place. I hope I never feel like that again. But here it is, starting all over in my head.

It's never good to dig in the ashes, but now, if somebody has killed Buck, if somebody has poked around in the ashes and started a fire again, it's all going to come back.

wilfred huskins

By the time I got to the end of Sarah's garden, Gordon McKinney came tearing into the drive in his patrol car. He had Sunday duty, so Rachel had no problem reaching him. I waited as he trotted toward me and then I filled him in as we walked back to the cabin.

Within fifteen minutes, four more of my men and two from the SBI arrived. Doc got there before the medical guy from the SBI, but I told him not to disturb anything. I made it clear to everyone that we were going to be working with the State in every way we could, and that we'd do it their way. The yellow plastic ribbons went up. We had the place secured.

Steve Caddis was next to come. He's the only State guy I knew well. I filled him in on Bekka's murder and what I knew of this one, which wasn't much.

"Sounds like family," he said. "Sounds like a debt got settled. That's where we better start, Sheriff. Let's go talk to the Pendleys before they have any more time to compare notes and make up alibis." So we headed back down the path to the old farmhouse.

John Pendley was the first of the brothers to come back, and he was with Harley. John was full of it by the time he hit the door, with all the cars that were parked all over the yard by that time.

"Holy cow," he said. "What is this? Police cars all over the place. What's going on, Wilfred?"

Before we even told him why the cars were there, before any mention of Buck could be made, Steve separated him from Harley and stashed Harley in an upstairs bedroom so we could talk to John. We even sent Sarah out of her own kitchen, and closed the door behind her. And with her sweet potatoes half peeled in the sink, I can tell you she didn't like it.

Of course, we didn't know the exact time of death and we didn't even know for sure what actually was the final cause of Buck's death, but the butcher knife looked like it might be it.

We were pretty sure that the killing must have been done yesterday or even last night, because of the dried blood, so the questioning started with Friday night, ran through Saturday, Decoration Day, and Saturday night and right up to the time the family was in church and in plain sight—way past the time the murder must have actually happened.

John had a storybook alibi for the entire period. I knew Steve had mentally put a little star by John's name, even though he was the only name on the list so far. I knew why. John's story was almost too pat, but Steve didn't know John like I did.

Even in grammar school, John was the kind of guy who took great stock in time. Way back then, his prize possession was a watch he got for Christmas one year. Since that wintry day, the first time I saw his new Timex, John had looked at his watch a thousand times a day it seemed like. The watches changed through the years, but the habit didn't.

Sometimes he looked at his watch when he was trying to answer a hard question, and sometimes he looked at it just to get past a moment of embarrassment, and sometimes there didn't seem to be a reason, but the point is, he was—and still is—a watch-looker.

I don't think John's even aware he's doing it, I'm sure it's not because he wants to know the time. I doubt he even thinks about the hour and minute he sees when he glances at his watch, but somewhere in the back of his mind, that time must have been recorded because, as Steve shot questions at him, John came up with answers, and each of them were fitted into a neat, convenient time slot. I had to admit, it sounded pat; it sounded really phony.

We took John up to the bedroom and brought Harley down. You could see Harley had a question or two he wanted to ask, but with an Asheville lawman there, a guy in plain clothes from the State Bureau, he didn't say a word.

Harley sat down at the kitchen table waiting, but Steve just let it get quiet in there for a couple minutes, and then he said, "Step out here, Sheriff. I want a word with you."

We watched Harley through the window. His discomfort was plain to see. That's what Steve wanted, but I couldn't help feeling sorry for Harley. He's always been more like a great big, bumbling St. Bernard puppy than anything else, and this police thing had him almost cowering, a puppy with his tail between his legs, trying to figure out what it was all about.

When the door to the kitchen was shut, Caddis said, "Who is this guy, Sheriff, and how does he figure in, except as a backup for some of John Pendley's story? Is he a part of the family?"

I filled him in. I told him about the never-quite-got-off-the-ground romance between Harley and Sarah, and how it now seemed to be warming up, with the help of big brother John.

"He could have done it." It was a flat statement.

"Could have," I answered.

"But you don't think so?"

"No, I don't."

"He had reason, at least some might think he did."

"He's just not the type."

"That's often the case. Still waters..."

"Sometimes," I said, "but go ahead, hit him as hard as you want. See what he knows."

"Do you think he'd lie for John? Cover for him?"

"He wants to marry Sarah."

"That's a yes. Let's go back in."

This time there were no precise hours or minutes, and I think Steve missed that part of it—I think he was disappointed that Harley's answers didn't sound so pat.

As Steve Caddis had done with John, he started all the way back to Friday afternoon and worked his way forward.

Friday night, after work on his tree farm, Harley had gone over to his parents' house for supper, and then he went home, watched a little TV and went to bed. No phone calls. No one to say they knew he was there.

The Saturday part of Harley's story began earlier than John's out at the cemetery, but the parallel was there, and he corroborated John's Decoration Day answers in a way that added credence without sounding like he was anybody's backup.

More than that, there were a couple hundred people at the

cemetery. There would be no problem in checking each detail of both stories. I think Steve was disappointed in what he got from Harley, but I could see that Harley was being added to the list—not because of what he said, but because of the fact that one day he might be a brother-in-law. That alone could easily be a good enough reason to be involved somehow, and the fact that he was already a business partner only added to it.

There had been no mention of Buck and no explanation for the questions, nor had Harley asked. When it was over, he was told to go on home.

We meant to talk to Sarah next, but that's not the way it happened. Sarah asked if she could finish making her sweet potato casserole while she answered the questions. She looked scared. I guess she wanted something to do, something familiar, something that might help to steady her. Steve said sure, but she had no more than picked up the paring knife when Ora Lee Pendley came pushing through the door.

"Now, I want to know what's going on here," she said, even before the door had time to swing shut. It was Ora Lee Pendley front and center, and I guess it was just as well that Steve got to know her then as later. Her outburst wasn't really a question and she didn't wait for an answer.

"I take a nap and the next thing I know the house is surrounded by police cars and you two have taken over my kitchen."

I spoke first. "How did you sleep through it?"

"One of my little blue pills, that's how."

I introduced her to Steve.

He said, "There's been a little trouble, Mrs. Pendley. That's why the police are here. We need to ask your daughter a few questions, and when we're through we'll need to ask some of you."

She took a sharp look at me and then at Steve. "Questions of Sarah? What's she got to do with it?"

"Probably nothing, Mrs. Pendley, but the only way we can

get to the bottom of it is to ask questions of anyone who might know something—even if they don't think they know anything. Something your daughter knows, or has seen, might just tie in with what we already know. You just wait in the other room. We'll talk to her, and then we want to talk to you, too."

You could see Ora Lee Pendley bristle. Clearly Steve didn't know her like I did, and it seemed to me he was going to have as much trouble as I had had with the target practice incident.

"If you're going to question Sarah, sir, I intend to stay right here. I don't know that she's up to grilling by the police. She tried to help the sheriff when my other daughter—"

I could see tears in Mrs. Pendley's eyes, but before I could say anything, she glared at me and said, "It was the police that ruined Sarah's reputation back then. So if you don't mind, I'm staying."

Sarah saw the direction this was heading, so she took the onus off both Steve and me.

"It's all right, Mama. I'll just go in the family room and wait. You can talk to this man and Wilfred. When you see they're only trying to clear up this thing, whatever it is, then I can talk to them."

Without waiting for a reply, Sarah left the room. Steve began.

"Mrs. Pendley, tell me where you were on Friday night."

Ora Lee Pendley gave me a look that would wither a tough old dandelion that had weathered the winter. It was as though I had brought all this on her. Then she turned toward Steve, and the lines at the side of her mouth pulled down even farther.

"I was right here, that's where," she said. "In my own home."

Steve waited. He let the silence hang there. As the tension built, Ora Lee looked at me and then back at Steve, then she went on, "After work, I came home and finished the hemming on my new dress, the one I wore to the Decoration at the church."

And then she launched off into the wildest tale I bet Steve

had ever heard. All about the pattern from an old trunk, and how she had to search all over for the right kind of material, and how much trouble it was to make covered buttons, and how it was trimmed with tatting that her granny had made.

I'll give Steve credit. At first he listened, just to get her calmed down and then he politely tried to end the talk of the dressmaking session, but Mrs. Pendley was not to be deterred. She told him about the buckram she used in the collar and cuffs, "to keep them flat so the tatting would lay flat," and she told him about the embroidery she had done all the way down the front of the dress, on either side of the covered buttons.

Steve tried several times to cut the dressmaking lesson off, but it was a losing battle. Each time he tried to bring the subject back to a recitation of events of Friday night, she answered his question briefly, and then launched back into a subject that had become one of the big events in her recent life.

Finally he said, "Mrs. Pendley, I don't want to know how that dress was made. I don't care how the dress was made. I want answers to my questions."

Ora Lee Pendley must have been a real charmer back in the days when Zeb was courting her because even now she had a classic beauty that had withstood two real tragedies that I knew about, not to mention the rearing of five children, and the life of a working woman in a thread mill, but there was no beauty in the cold blue eyes that snapped on Steve's face.

"You're a rude young man, I'll tell you that," she said, "young enough to be one of my own sons, but so full of yourself that you have to put other people down, just so they'll know what a big man you are."

"I'm sorry—"

"No, you're not. You want to lord it over me while you ask a lot of stupid questions; you want to play the big lawman. I've had that bit from Wilfred, too. I am not impressed—not with you or him."

For a moment, I didn't know what Steve was going to do.

You could almost feel his anger, and then after a full minute of silence he said, "So, Mrs. Pendley, you came home from work and did your sewing. Was anyone else here?"

Then it was Ora Lee that had my attention. Her hands were white where she gripped the sides of her chair, the knuckles bulging, but her face was without the anger that I had seen just a few minutes earlier. The rage seemed to have passed. Maybe Steve would get more answers than I had.

"My daughter was here, of course." It was a monotone.

"Anyone else? Your sons? Any visitors?"

"The boys may have been in and out. I don't remember."

"But it was just supper and sewing after you got home from work, is that it?"

"I guess you could say that."

Steve skipped to the next day, and his tone was a little lighter and a little more casual.

"The next day you went to the Decoration at the church. What time was that?"

"About ten, I guess. I like to sleep late when I get the chance, so I slept in, and then got up and showered and put on that dress I told you about. Maybe I shouldn't mention it again, since you don't like old-timey dresses with tatting." She was back to being Ora Lee Pendley again, back to needling him and he knew it.

"I'm trying to follow the sequence of events on that day, Mrs. Pendley. The dress is insignificant."

"The dress, young man, was the hit of the day. They'll be talking about this Decoration for many a year to come."

Steve said, "Yes, ma'am, they might. It just might be a Decoration Day to remember."

That's as close as he had come to telling anyone what had happened, but it seemed to make no impression on Mrs. Pendley. It was as though she were reliving her yesterday's glory as she showed off that dress.

Fortunately for everybody, the rest of the questioning of

Ora Lee Pendley went along without incident or rancor, but Steve did have to listen to a lot more about the dress.

"If you want me to remember where I was all day long, the only way I can do it is tell you who I talked to and what I did, and most of that, young man, whether you believe it or not, had to do with my dress. I wanted to be sure everybody saw it, and you can bet they did by the time the day was over. Why, some even remembered when my Granny wore a dress just like the pattern I used. How can I tell you one thing without telling you the other?"

Steve was able to piece Ora Lee Pendley's day together, but in the end, he did it her way.

It didn't add a lot to what we knew, but parts of her answers made John's account, and Harley's, seem to be a part of the same patchwork.

Matt was next. Actually, Steve spent more time with Matt than with any of the others so far, but he ended up with even less information.

John knew where he was and how long he stayed because of his time compulsion, but brother Matt didn't have the slightest idea of time, and seemed to care even less.

The session with Matt was frustrating to Steve, and I could see why. The questions were clear enough, but the answers just didn't seem to go anywhere.

After Matt had been questioned and was sent on up to his room, Steve said, "Damn. I hate answers like that. It's like washing your hands with rubber gloves on—nothing penetrates."

"We can check it. We have to anyway."

"Sure we can," Steve said, "but it's like starting from zero. Well, not quite. He's one laid-back guy, I'll say that."

"On your list or off?"

"He's still on. That might be a pose."

Before we could call Sarah back in, Luke arrived. We both saw him coming across the back yard from his car. His head was rubbering all around, looking at patrol cars and then at the others, trying to figure out what it was all about, or that's how it seemed.

"He's cool," Steve said. "You think he knows he's being watched?"

"I doubt it."

"I'm not so sure. Hell, man, if it was me out there, I think I'd hike it for the house to find out what it's all about. There's at least three patrol cars out there. There's something suspect about that behavior."

"You may be right, Steve. Look at him, he even checked the license on the blue car, to see if it's out-of-county. Does it belong to one of your guys?"

"Yes. Off duty. Lives out on this end of Buncombe County, not too far from here."

And then we heard Luke on the porch. He stopped at the door and deliberately wiped his feet.

I know Sarah was on those boys all the time about foot-wiping, but this seemed to be almost too slow, almost a ritual foot wiping, considering the cars in the yard out there and the questions that had to be in his mind.

When Luke came in the door, he looked at Steve and then at me and then he said, "What's going on, Wilfred? What is all this?"

Chapter 24

wilfred huskins

As the sheriff of Asa Gray County, I didn't really have to be the one who went out to tell the Prices about Buck's death, but in my own mind I was the only one to do it. What's worse, I knew I had to get out to Edd and Essie's house before all the telephones in the county started carrying the news before I could get there.

I suppose it's the same the world over, but I know how it is here in Asa Gray County: good news might not make it all over the county until nightfall, but bad news will spread like heat lightning.

I told Steve Caddis what I had to go do, and then I walked back to the Pendley place and appropriated Gordon McKinney's patrol car.

The ride into town was one of the longest I've ever made, not because of the distance—it's no more than five miles—but because every time I tried to figure out how I was going to tell the Prices—particularly Edd—I ended up sounding sanctimonious or stupid.

As far as Buck is concerned, I felt the way a lot of people all over the area felt. He was just plain bad news. He was trouble and he would always be.

I know you're supposed to remember that you were young once, and that it takes a little time to grow up, but there are some people that never will became a part of the community they live in. Some people, it seems to me, are just plain old bad seed. I'm not convinced that's not what Buck was. So, in some ways, for the whole town, his death might just be a blessing, but you can't tell that to a parent, can you?

I thought about what I might say, I kicked it around in my mind, but the closer I got to the house, the more I knew there was no way to put a good face on Buck's death.

I never have known Essie that well, they had lived away for so long. And we didn't attend the same church, so I didn't really have a chance to know her. But Edd is one of those old men who never seem to have enough to do, so he spends his time chewing on something that, as he says, "ain't the way it o'rt to be." I knew Edd—everybody knew Edd.

As I pulled into the drive at the old Westall house that the Prices rented, I still didn't have any idea of how I'd begin. I saw Edd and Essie on the porch.

I saw him get to his feet when he saw the patrol car, and I saw her put a hand on his shoulder. He didn't rush out as I knew he wanted to do, because she held his arm.

When I was ten feet from the porch, I knew I didn't have to say a word to Essie. It was clear to me that she knew; she knew in the same kind of strange way that mother's always know. Somehow the umbilical cord between mother and child is never fully severed. When tragedy strikes, mothers never need a cop to arrive at the door. They know, as they have through the ages, so the postman doesn't have to bring the letter edged in black.

Edd was a different story. All the arrogance was gone. I saw those red-rimmed, black eyes still wet with recent tears, in a pallid-looking face. Edd Price's whole manner begged for good news—news I didn't have.

"Edd—Essie," I finally managed to say, "I don't know how to tell you how sorry I am—"

And that's all I managed to get out as I watched the old man sink down into the big, flowered wicker chair behind him. He didn't collapse, he just seemed to hunker down into it in slow motion; he just settled into that chair, and as he did, it

looked to me like he got smaller and smaller. I mean it. Right
before my eyes, all the wind came out of him and he seemed to
fold in on himself, until the man he was, was no more than half
the size he had been only a minute before.

And then he started to cry. It was something I never want
to see again. You could hardly hear the sobs that were jerked
out of his body, but they were worse than if he had screamed
them out. He pulled his legs up in the chair, pulled them up
toward his chin and hugged them close to his chest. The man
was a little ball of quivering flesh, unaware of me and unaware
of Essie.

At that moment you could see the stuff that Essie Price was
made of. Whatever her thoughts of Buck, she did what was
necessary for the living. She was at Edd's side, on her knees,
one hand on his arm, one hand on his brow and she was sooth-
ing him with quiet words I couldn't make out.

It was a private time. There was no need for me here. I
said, "Mrs. Price, is there anything I can do?"

"If you will, Sheriff, call Dr. Bennett. He's my cousin. Tell
him to come out as soon as he can."

She turned back to Edd. I was forgotten.

I made the call and left.

Let me tell you, compared to my investigation of Bekka
Pendley's murder, this one, Buck's murder, looks like the case
of the century. Nothing adds up.

Back then, back when we investigated Bekka's death, I had
all kinds of evidence against Buck, even though it turned out to
be not good enough to get a conviction.

Buck's daddy's lawyers knew that he had an ongoing rela-
tionship with Sarah, and I knew, too, because Sarah told me
about it in detail. So, yes, I knew he had some luck on his side,
but I still thought we could get a conviction.

His prints were there in that cabin, there was all kinds of
evidence that he had been there, but it was all muddied up by

the fact that just about every meeting between Buck and Sarah had happened right there in that old log house. It knocked the props right out from under our case.

The other things, his lost pocket knife, the pack of condoms with his prints on it, and all the other details that pointed right at him, these were all nullified by the admitted evidence of his affair with Bekka's sister Sarah.

All those Asheville lawyers had to do was cast a doubt, and that was easy enough, given the many times Buck had met Sarah there at the cabin. His lawyers were quick to admit Buck was there, but, they said, that only accounted for his many prints at the crime scene. His lawyers pounded that one point home again and again, so the jury, both times, was hung.

My case, and I truly had hopes for it at the beginning, was based on finding Buck's prints—what appeared to be recent prints—all over the place. None of them, however, were bloody prints; none of them established the fact that he was actually there at the time of the murder. Nothing, not one piece of evidence, was strong enough to erase the doubt the jury must have felt.

This killing, however, Buck's own murder, is a lulu, not from a lack of prints—they're there, plenty of them, but they're prints from Sarah and Ora Lee, and even a few from the Pendley boys.

The prints we really want—the damning prints—were just not found. As it turned out, there were no prints on the butcher knife or on the pliers that had been used to try to strip off Buck's skin or to pull out his fingernails; there were no prints on the glass salt shaker or the screw driver, or the match box. And, while there was considerable blood all over that little bedroom, there were no bloody prints and all of the blood was Buck's, tested scientifically. It was all his blood, without question.

It was easy enough to see what had happened to Buck. We could piece it together from the evidence that was there, but it pointed to no one specifically. We were pretty sure someone had tolled old Buck to the cabin in broad daylight, waited for him inside and then bashed his head with a piece of firewood. That piece of wood was still there, with blood on it, probably where it had been thrown when the job was done.

After he was knocked out, he had been stripped naked, dragged to the bed and trussed spread-eagle to the four corners of that old iron bedstead with multiple strands of baling twine.

There was a partial roll of duct tape with uneven rips where it had been torn off to cover his mouth, but it, too, was free of prints. All the tools that had been used on Buck before he died were there—pliers, an ice pick, a long handled screw driver—all clean, all tools that belonged there according to the Pendley boys, even the masking tape and the baling twine were items that were kept in the cabin.

There had been an attempt to burn Buck but the burns were not serious and it looked like that method of torture had been abandoned, but it had happened. The burned match sticks and the open box of big, wooden kitchen matches were there, but there were no prints of any value.

Let me tell you, I'm glad to have the SBI here with me on the case. In spite of their experience and all the technology the State has available that we don't, their experts keep coming up with a goose egg at every turn.

Every lead has been run down and not one of them is worth a tinker. There has been talk of department incompetence in town— my department—so you can see why I would have hated to be the Lone Ranger on this one.

There are no quick answers to Buck's murder.

At the same time the Pendleys were being questioned and requestioned, the hunt was on for the guys who had asked for Buck at the poolroom, the guys who had made threats, the guys who had been staying at a little motel over in Bakersville, That investigation netted nothing—the same as the evidence we found in the cabin. The guys from Baltimore were gone without a trace. The registration at the motel either never existed or didn't exist anymore, and the management and maids were of no help.

The descriptions we got in Bakersville and at the poolroom would have fit half the people in any club in Asheville: long hair, medium build, grungy clothes—the uniform. There was not one feature that really distinguished any of them.

What we got from Russ wasn't much better, and he had talked to them more than once, but his evidence was a disappointment to me. It just wasn't much. Russ usually pays a lot more attention than that.

"They were nothing-punks," he said, "no-good nothings. I might have believed those stories of what they were going to do to Buck when they found him if they had moved in and done something, anything. I think they might have had a reason to want to get him, but it was all talk, hot air."

When I persisted in questioning Russ he said, "Shit, Wilfred, get off my back. You saw them—maybe from a distance—how would you describe them? They all looked alike. They needed to be scrubbed down with lye soap and then dunked into near-boiling water, and then sent over to City Barber for a haircut and then maybe you could describe them."

Russ was no help. But we tried to find the Baltimore gang—our guys and the SBI. Believe me, we ran down every lead, no matter how trivial it looked. We tried to find those punks in every way we could, because it would have been nice—it would have been heaven-sent—to find an outsider to pin this murder on.

Oh, how many problems that would have solved. Everyone around here would have someone to hate, and we wouldn't be turning on ourselves as we did after Bekka's murder.

But there is no trail to follow because there's no motel evidence, no sign of them left behind, no registration, no tag number—nothing.

The sad conclusion has to be that there is no outsider to pin the murder on. The guys from Maryland were just people who had been here and were now gone.

Two weeks have gone by. We're no nearer to having an answer or even a partial answer. We still don't know who Buck's killer is. We don't know if it's one person or more than one. Even if we could find a way to tie the outsiders to it, we have no names and almost no description. So, the guys from Baltimore, wherever they are, seem to be home-free. The SBI boys haven't given up on that angle, but I have.

We have repeatedly and painstakingly gone over the stories of each of the Pendley boys, and even Ora Lee and Sarah, and there is no way that I can see to tie any of them into Buck's murder. None of them expressed any regret that he had come to such an end, and I guess I'd feel the same way if Bekka had been my sister.

There's a hole in Luke's story. He was hard to deal with every time we questioned him. It was almost like he wanted us to think he had killed Buck, but when we ran down every detail of what we dug up, there was only a period of time, something a little over an hour, that we couldn't account for, and it was just not enough time for the amount of torture that had been done.

The medical guys were firm on this point: From the dried blood, to do what had been done to Buck, it would have had to exceed two hours elapsed time—and even up to four. From the evidence and the medical examiner's report, Buck's ordeal would have had to have covered a period of time—several hours.

The closest thing we had to a suspect was Luke. I didn't think we could make a case that would hold up, because we could account for all but a little less than an hour of his time. Unless we could come up with more proof, it just wasn't enough.

Still, Luke was right up there on the SBI's short list, but whether we could keep working at it and ultimately make it stick was questionable, at least in my mind.

After my fiasco with trying to build a case against Buck for Bekka's murder, I was more than willing to let the State guys, the SBI, carry that ball.

The truth is, we had no idea who killed Buck, but we knew a good deal more about the details of his murder.

We knew that his death had been long in coming and that the first blow had probably been struck even before dinner was on the tables over at the church for Decoration Day.

The evidence the medics furnished pretty well confirmed our first guess that Buck had been bashed in the head with one firm blow that put him completely out. Too bad the blow wasn't a little harder. A stronger blow might have killed him before someone—someone who had a strong stomach for blood—tried to burn him, rip skin and flesh from his body, cut him, gouge him, tear out his nails and slash off his hair in great yellow hanks while he lay there trussed up on that old iron bed with his mouth sealed shut with duct tape.

The cause of death was the old wood-handled butcher knife that had been pounded through his rib cage so far that the point of it pierced the blood-soaked mattress he lay on.

Once the knife was driven through Buck's heart, his death was no doubt swift, but it was clear that he had lived, that he had suffered, that he had been long in coming to the point of death.

The torture Buck must have had with the ice pick, the pliers, the screw driver and the cuts had not been done at the time of or after his death. That torture had preceded his last breath. It had all taken time. The condition of the wounds, the clots of blood, the dried crusts of it, all indicated that this kind of painful punishment must have been going on for at least three or even four hours before Buck finally breathed his last.

To me, none of it pointed to Luke.

Maybe it's just another reason I shouldn't run for sheriff again, but my mind doesn't want to stay on this case. We've been over all the ground, we've questioned and requestioned everyone—even Harley—and, damn it, we have no idea who might have done it.

We know people who had reason to kill Buck, but there's no real suspect in any one of them, at least in my mind. I'm more than ready to give up on the case, but the SBI boys are not.

No, I haven't told them how I feel, but when I finally get home at night, I'm whipped down by the futility of it. We're nowhere. When I finally hit the sack, I'm weary of the foolhardiness of this whole stupid investigation—our part and theirs.

To everyone, me included, it looks like a grudge killing—revenge because justice may not have come from the courts.

There's a lot of that kind talk all over the country, brought about by acquitals because of expensive attorneys, or loopholes and technicalities. People are outraged and they talk of what they'd do if it were their kid, but thank God most of the time they don't act on it.

Even as a rookie lawman—and I admit I am—I can hear that kind of talk all over the place. The sound of distant thunder, perhaps, but don't think the danger isn't real.

But, yes, the investigation goes on. I'll stay with them on this case, and I'll give it everything I have, especially since I'm the one who called for help from the SBI, but I can tell you honestly, my heart's not in it—not any more.

Chapter 25

ora lee pendley

Nobody ever asks me how I feel, and maybe it's because they want me to forget, but you don't forget when somebody takes away the light of your whole life. Bekka was that to me. Oh, I know you're not supposed to play favorites—and you try not to—but I think if the truth ever gets out, all mothers have one of their young'uns that has a kind of special place.

Lord, it near killed me when they found Bekka up there at Granny's dead and beat up something terrible before he started on her with that log chain. My Bekka was a good girl, a truly good girl, and you don't find many like that these days.

The first shock of her being taken away was like icy water on my soul, and then came that dull nagging that stayed in my brain whether I was asleep or awake. The misery went on and on and finally every day blurred together. Life wasn't much. Each day was just existing; it was just making do; it was all a painful time when it seemed like I slogged along, making it through one day and then another, all of it knee-deep in a kind of nameless thing I can't explain, not to no one.

Until right after the second trial, all my days was like that, every minute and every hour since Bekka went away to the angels. I know that's where she is; she's with the angels. She's the new one up there in heaven, the pretty little blonde angel with the painted face. I'm right proud of my young'uns, all of them, but Bekka was the good one, the one I'm proudest of.

When they told me Bekka met Buck up there at Granny's cabin, I just couldn't believe it happened, not my Bekka, not knowing the kind of girl she was. But I know for sure about Buck. He was a no-good. Everyone around here knows the kind he was.

But Bekka was there, at least on that day. I don't know how he got her to come, I don't know what kind of lies he told her, but I know, I just know, she wouldn't go up there to meet him unless she'd been tricked into doing it.

After Bekka went away, I still went to work every day. What else was there to do? All of it, every minute, was a painful kind of drudgery, the worst a body can ever live through, but my life changed the day they set Buck free. I'll never forget that day, not if I live to be as old as these old hills.

That day, the last day of the second trial, when the truth of it come through to me, when my mind was sure of what had happened there in court, that Buck Price was truly going to get away with murder, I just sat there unable to even move. I couldn't believe what I heard.

Yes, deep down I knew all along what that second hung jury meant. I guess I must have known the truth of it the night before when I thought of the other kind of justice come into my mind. There is a justice we know here in the hills.

But I guess sometimes your mind ain't ready for what you hear or what you know, and it just goes blank on you. That's the way it was that last day in court.

I could see them all down there in front of the courtroom, rejoicing and carrying on, and when Buck started up the aisle, laughing and smiling at everyone, with his arm around his mama and all, it was just too much for me. Right then I began to feel the steel come back to my body. I shot out of that seat and I pushed Sarah out of the way to get to him.

Right then I was ready to kill him. I wanted to grab him as he came by; I wanted to gouge out his eyes, rip his hair out, and then chew the flesh from his bones with my bare teeth. I wanted to feel him squirm and scream as the pain ate away at his body. I wanted to give him the pain he gave Bekka, and I wanted to do it right there in the courtroom—right in the room where he had escaped the justice that was surely due him.

And he knew. When he looked up to find me there, standing at the end of that row, I saw it in his eyes. I saw fear there. He knew.

Since Bekka went away, I had not been as alive as I was at that minute, standing there on the aisle, waiting for Buck to come closer. Standing there, waiting for him, was a crazy thing to do.

Then, as quick as the crazy feeling came over me, something made the rage drain out of me. Maybe I knew in my bones where I was and that the time wasn't right; maybe something made me know that I really wouldn't be allowed to give him what he truly deserved, that I really couldn't pull out that hair, that I couldn't tear at his flesh, that I couldn't make him suffer and scream with pain, the only way he could even partially atone for what he done to my baby, to my Bekka. Good sense came over me from somewhere. How it got there I'll never know, but in that instant, my idea of what seemed a perfect chance for Buck's repayment passed. Doing such a thing was not right, at least not right for right then.

Some kind of inborn mountain canniness, some kind of country common sense, made me see that I couldn't do what I knew I must do. His people were all there, and the lawyers from Asheville, and I could see Wilfred Huskins splitting it up the aisle to where we stood.

Nothing happened to Buck there in that courtroom—at least nothing to relieve the pain I had, but all the same, something had happened to me and to Buck.

His fear was real, as well it should be, because I knew right then what I had to do. That's the very minute when I stopped being a helpless woman, a grieving mother, a sobbing do-nothing, and Buck knew it, same as I did.

I walked out of that courtroom with my feet back firmly planted on good mountain soil. There was no question about what I had to do—for me and for Bekka.

Buck had to pay, that much was sure, but I didn't know how to do it. Not knowing is what made me such a hellion with all of them, and I know I was, but particularly with Sarah.

I don't feel one bit sorry for what I done to Sarah. She had acted like a strumpet with Buck, which is bad enough, but then she told it all on the witness stand to the everlasting shame of all the Pendleys and the Halls, wherever they live. I'm not sorry, not one bit.

She told enough to dishonor three generations at the first trial and, my Lord, at that second trial, I guess Wilfred persuaded her to get right down to the gory details of what happened because a whole lot more of it come out. Oh, she had the good sense to look shame-faced about it, with her eyes on the floor most of the time, but you can't sugar-coat something like that. Oh, dear Lord, how I hated to listen to all she said. I wanted to just melt down into my seat.

Now understand, I'm not so goody-good that I never knew moments like Sarah must have had with Buck. I'd be lying if I said that. I could forgive her for what she done with Buck; I could even forgive her for telling it to the world like she did, but what I can't forgive is her not warning Bekka. You can't put a good light on that.

Bekka was a flirt—nothing more than that, but she was a flirt. Sarah knew Bekka was playing her flirting game with Buck. Sarah has admitted that much to me, and she knew he was spoiled and had a temper, and she also knew what most of us didn't know, that Buck could go wild when he was doping.

The dope. I blame Wilfred for that. He should have stopped it. Dope here in the mountains and Wilfred let it happen, just let it happen. If I'd been sheriff, you can bet a pusher wouldn't be safe around me. But Wilfred just let it happen.

What have we come to? Dope, here in Asa Gray County. I still can't believe it, and yet I know it's all around me. It's not been cleaned up, even after what happened to Bekka.

Looking back now on my first thought of how I could get

Buck, it was a dumb thing I did with Matt's rifle. Besides, a simple shot to the head would have been too good for him. But using Matt's rifle to kill Buck wasn't the only dumb thing I considered, although none of the others plans were ever known to anyone but me. The rifle practice would have been forgotten like some of my other crazy ideas, but it came out because of Sarah and her mouth.

No, I don't feel sorry for the way I treated Sarah. Not for one minute.

It eat at my mind when the long days went on and on after that second trial without me finding a way to get Buck Price, and it bore in on me like a heavy weight every time I saw him strutting down the street, and it tore my heart out to know — and I surely did know — that my little Lukey was out to get Buck, same as I was.

Paying Buck Price back was always on my mind, every day every hour; it was my first thought every morning. It kept me alive and it scared me too, because I had Lukey to worry about. He's just a boy, with a boy's mind, and killing Buck was a job for a careful person who could think it through. I had to come up with a way to take care of Buck. I had to do it before Lukey did something that would put him in the pen. I knew the lawmen would get Lukey, even if they didn't get Buck. I had to move fast; I had to take care of Buck before Lukey did something foolish.

And then one day it all started to happen, it started to unfold. I could see a part of the way ahead. It was almost like the hand of the Lord was guiding me, because, without me even thinking about it, answers would come to me, ways would be opened, details would just fall in place. And they all fit into the prettiest pattern you ever saw.

The dress I wore to Decoration was just one of the pieces. I don't know why I was rummaging in the attic, but I opened that old trunk I brought over from the Hall place, and there it was. That yellowed old pattern is a lot like the dress that Granny

Hall wore for that picture that hangs downstairs, but that's not why I picked it up.

I had already decided that I'd get Buck on Decoration Day. I knew the activities of that day would take me away from any suspicion because everyone would know I was there, the Pendleys are always at Decoration.

As I sat there in the attic with that pattern in my hands, I knew why the Lord had brought me up there. The dress—one I would make over this pattern—would be the key to everyone remembering me at Decoration Day. No one would be there in an old-timey dress—no one but me. And then, like His hand was guiding me, just under the first till of that trunk, I found Granny's tatting and I knew, with that beautiful handwork on the dress, there wouldn't be a soul, man or woman, who wouldn't remember Ora Lee Pendley at Decoration Day.

The green print I chose for the dress was the color of the new spring leaves in the woods surrounding the cemetery, so all I had to do was talk to everyone, laugh and carry on, and then, when the time was right, just drift into the woods and blend in with the leaves while I made my way to Granny's cabin where I'd have Buck ready for the kill.

I have Sarah to thank for solving the hard part of the job for me. I didn't know how to get Buck to come to the cabin, but Sarah made it easy when she told me about the signals they used, and the words they used, so a date and hour could be set for them to meet.

She needed to talk that day, so I just led her on. I heard it all, and I knew how to use the words she said. All I had to do was set the trap and wait for the rat.

Decoration Day was a tight schedule for me. I didn't go with Sarah—I never did, so it would have looked odd if I got to the church anything other than late, but you can bet I had the boys up and dressed so we could be there a little before ten.

The rest was easy. I showed off my dress, I preened and twisted and told about finding the tatting. I took care to talk to everyone in the church kitchen and then I went out where they were working on cleaning up the graves and I made sure I was seen and seen again. Then, when I knew I could do it, with time to spare before Buck got to his "date," I slipped off into the woods and hurried across the toe-path to the open field where the cabin has been all these years. I stayed in the woods until I got to the spring and the little creek that runs away from it, and then I made a bee-line to the house. I was there early.

I don't know what it is that makes a man whistle on his way to one of his lustful encounters, but it happens often enough that we've all seen it, there ain't a woman alive who hasn't seen it, and it was happening that morning, too. Buck came down over the field from up at the ridge where his daddy's land meets ours. I was watching, but it was the whistle that first alerted me; it was the whistle that had me ready for him when he stepped inside the bedroom door.

I could see him through the crack. He poked his head in the outside door first, with a big smile on his face.

"Sarah girl, where are you? I knew you'd call. I knew you couldn't forget old Buck. Most of the time you want it worse than I do."

His remark about Sarah fired the anger deep in my belly, and then I remembered Bekka—I remembered what he'd done to Bekka. The building, waiting rage in me boiled up so fast it nearly blocked my windpipe with acid vomit, but I didn't make a noise. I waited.

He walked to the kitchen and I heard it again. "Sarah, stop the games." Then he came toward the bedroom where I was hiding behind the door. "Already in there, are you. What a wench—"

And that was the last thing I heard him say. I bashed his skull with a piece of firewood, the biggest piece I could handle without spoiling my aim. He fell. I wondered if I had killed him, but there was no time to worry about that.

If he was dead, I had no worry, but if he was alive, I only

had a short time to get him under control. Buck is a big man. I had to have him tied and tied good. I stripped him first and then dragged him over to the bed. I don't know if I could do it now, Buck's right at two hundred pounds, but at that moment I had the strength of ten. I got him up on that bed and I tied his hands and feet to the four corners of the iron bedstead and I sealed his mouth shut with two pieces of silver tape.

By the time his eyes were open, he couldn't move. Baling twine is stronger than it looks, and it wasn't just one strand of it. I knew I had to have Buck tied good or I'd end up like Bekka. I was sure; he couldn't move.

Oh, he tried. When he saw me standing over him, you could see the terror in his eyes. He strained at the cords that held him, but he only managed to cut the strands into his flesh, but what did that matter when he'd soon learn what pain really is?

I used the knife first. I cut little slits in his skin. I thought about writing the word "Bekka" on his belly, but I tell you the Lord was guiding me all the way, and I didn't do that. It would have had the Pendleys under suspicion forever, however much we could prove that we were all at the Decoration, all day long.

My first visit with Buck was short. It was all I could do to get him trussed up like the pig he was before I had to get back to the cemetery to show off my dress a few more times before dinner would be served out there under the trees. Even though I wasn't with Buck very long the first time, it was long enough to tell him what I intended to do—I didn't want any doubts about that—and I had enough time to make a few cuts just to watch the blood ooze up a little, and to see the pain and the terror in his face.

As for Buck, big man that he was, his eyes bulged out and he strained to get loose, and then he saw his belly and the blood, and he just fainted. Fainted, like some young girl. That part was a surprise to me. I expected the fear in his eyes and I tell you true, it was almost enough to make me stop, but I remembered Bekka, I kept remembering Bekka, and I knew there was more that I had to do.

225

The rest of it was easy—the part about going back and forth from the cabin to the cemetery. It was all a matter of laughing and talking and timing. No, it wasn't easy, going past Bekka's grave like I had to, that part wasn't easy, but I was sure she understood what I was doing, and why I had to do it. Bekka was with me and so was the Lord.

Thinking back on it, there were times in that cabin with Buck when I was using the pliers and the ice pick and the screw driver that were almost more than I could bear, but I always remembered Bekka. I remembered what he had done to her. Yes, Lord, I remembered.

The second time when I went back, I realized I might get blood on my dress, so I took my clothes off before I went in. You should have seen Buck's eyes. He didn't know what my nakedness meant, so I told him. I told him very calmly that my plans had not changed, that there was likely to be more blood, and that I didn't want any of it on my clothes. The hope in his eyes dimmed and the terror returned.

Each time I went back to the cabin, when my time with Buck was over, I went to the spring and washed off, letting the red blood pale to pink as it followed the bed of the stream. I wiped the water off my body with my hands, stood in the breeze of that warm spring day until I was dry, and then I put my old-fashioned dress back on and hurried to the Decoration.

In all, I made five short trips to the cabin, and each one, it seems to me, got harder for me to do, even when I tried to remember how little pity he showed for Bekka. But I didn't stop. I made myself do what I had to do.

The worst time was the one next to the last trip. I saw his belly heave a little. This time it wasn't just fear that I saw in his eyes. It was something more, and then the vomit came gushing up. He was losing his breath. He was going to die; he was going to drown in his own puke. I ripped the tape from his mouth and that mess came spewing out. Before he could get his breath, before he could begin to shout, I tore another piece of sticky silver tape, and when I saw the green bile was at an end, I wiped his mouth and sealed it again.

I was weak by the time I got washed up that time. As I dressed, I knew that the next time I came would have to be the last. Buck had had his punishment and he knew why he was there. I was certain he knew, because I told him over and over again. I felt sure he wouldn't last, not this way, and neither would I.

My last visit was short. I killed Buck. I drove the knife through his chest, I hammered it through with an iron skillet, and when it was done, I put the skillet away.

I've thought about it since. What a strange sight it must have been, a middle-aged woman without a stitch of clothes on, wearing only a pair of Medi-Stroke latex disposable gloves.

There are five pairs of them, five pairs of those gloves, hidden at a spot along the path. One day, when all the investigations are over, I'll be sure those gloves are permanently destroyed, but for now, they're safe where they are, hidden carefully, covered by last year's leaves, and beneath a mound of the thickest green moss you ever did see.

Sorry for what I done to Buck? Not one bit, not for a minute. I'm sickened by it. It was the hardest thing I ever had to do in all my life, but I'm not sorry. No, sir, not one little bit. He deserved that much and maybe more. Bekka has been avenged, and I've saved my son from the pen. Lukey wouldn't last long in a jail.

Don't talk to me about being sorry. Don't even mention that word.

And when the Roll is called up Yonder, I'll be ready for whatever comes my way. I know what I did. I don't expect to get off. I know what the Bible says. I killed Buck. In some way, I expect, I'll have to pay for that, but the good Lord knows the Pendleys got no justice in the courtroom over there in Madison County, so He knows something had to be done.

One day I'll have to stand before the Master. I can't escape that. But I believe I'll get justice in that great courtroom in Heaven. And that's all I ask.

the end